Praise for Emily Diamand

Ways to See a Ghost

'A fresh and original story from a writer who is as unpredictable as she is talented' Mary Hoffman, *Guardian*

'Diamand's plotting is adept, and she excels at the perennial comedy of showing how childish and selfish adults can be compared with children' Amanda Craig, *The Times*

'An exciting story, full of high-speed drama and breathtaking escapes' *Bookbag*

'I was enchanted, gripped and freaked out by this book in a way I haven't been since *The Graveyard Book* by Neil Gaiman' Liz Bankes, *Armadillo Magazine*

Flood Child

'Possesses all the qualities I look for in a novel and then some . . . An amazing, accomplished story' Malorie Blackman, Waterstone's Children's Laureate 2013–15

'Funny, clever and a towering adventure' *The Times*

D1078168

Emily Diamand's debut novel, *Flood Child* (first published as *Reaver's Ransom*), won the inaugural *Times*/Chicken House award for Children's Fiction in 2009, was shortlisted for the Branford Boase Award in the same year and was awarded Best Young Adult Fiction in 2011 by the American Library Association. *Ways to See a Ghost*, the first book featuring Isis and Gray, was published in 2013.

VOICES IN STONE

First published in Great Britain in 2015
by Templar Publishing
Northburgh House, 10 Northburgh Street, London EC1V 0AT
www.templarco.co.uk

A CIP catalogue record for this book is available from the British Library.

ISBN: 978-1-783-70093-6

1 3 5 7 9 10 8 6 4 2

Typeset by Palimpsest Book Production Ltd, Falkirk, Stirlingshire

Printed and bound by Clays Ltd, St Ives plc

Templar Publishing is part of the Bonnier Publishing Group
www.bonnierpublishing.com

EMILY DIAMAND

templar

Chapter One

Isis

Isis spent four days in hospital, afterwards.

After she stopped being dead.

The first night she'd woken suddenly: her eyes wide in the half-dark, her throat gasping and gulping down air, her mind flooded with vicious images of the icy cold wrapping itself around her. Impossible memories overlapped. She knew that she hadn't survived, she remembered dying – the swift up-pull, leaving her body. Yet she was alive again somehow, her chest rising and falling. Somewhere nearby a machine bleeped quietly and other people snuffled in their sleep.

She murmured, and her mum, Cally, was there in an instant, stroking Isis's hair.

"Shush, love, it's all right. It's all right now."

In the daytime Cally hardly left Isis's bedside. She held her daughter's hand, read to her, brought her treats from the hospital shop or watched telly with her. That afternoon, she squeezed Isis's hand and said, "I have tried to get Michael – I mean Daddy – to come and visit. I know you must want him here. But the agency told me he's working on a liner which is cruising in the Antarctic at the moment. They promised to pass on the message, but it won't be possible for him to get off the ship until it returns to South America in three weeks' time."

Isis heard the anger beneath Cally's calming tone. Isis felt it too; he couldn't even be here for *this*.

She smiled a tiny bit, enough to let Cally know she understood.

"I'm used to it," Isis said, even though she wasn't, not really. The hurt nearly matched the pain of her bandaged ice burns and the nagging pull of the drip in her arm. But then Dad never made it home for Christmas, or her birthday, or even a spare week in the summer holidays. Not since Angel.

If Isis had died, would he have come to her funeral, or would there have been an excuse for that too?

"I'll keep trying, I promise," said Cally, squeezing Isis's hand a little tighter. "Why don't you email him when you're feeling a little better?"

What would I tell him? "I froze to death. I flew above the world with a creature millions of years old, and my dead little sister brought me back to life."

"No," said Isis, as loudly as she could – which wasn't much more than a whisper.

Only a few weeks later Isis was back at school.

On her first day back she hurried into the warm September sunshine, scanning the playground. The black tarmac was full of jostle and noise, children wearing their new navy sweatshirts and still-black trousers. Everyone was chattering, meeting friends they hadn't seen all summer, catching up with news. A group of wide-eyed Year Sevens were being herded about by two older girls.

A few pale and silent shapes were drifting between the students: two girls playing hopscotch, wearing white pinafores over their long dark dresses, and a young boy in knee-length shorts and a green blazer, pretending to be an aeroplane. Isis ignored them, her eyes gliding over their misty outlines.

A moment later she spotted Gray. He was coming out of a shabby concrete building which the teachers called North Block and everyone else called The Fridge. He was talking to another boy.

Isis hadn't seen Gray for weeks, not since the hospital. He'd been battered then, and silent with shock, but now he looked back to himself. His hair was cropped so short it wasn't much more than black fuzz on his head, making his ears look bigger than ever, and his mum's efforts also showed in his brand-new, slightly too big uniform and shiny-black shoes. The only hint of what had happened in the summer was a small scar on his forehead, pink and pale against his caramel skin. Gray was listening to the other boy, who was shorter, with a freckly face and mousey hair cut into a boy-band flick.

Isis made her way across the playground.

"Hi," she called, a smile lifting her mouth. Her whole body felt lighter now that she'd seen him.

Gray and the other boy turned around.

"Isis," said Gray, acknowledging her – but there was no answering smile, and his eyes flickered over her face, looking for something. "Are you. . . all right now?"

She nodded. "I'm fine. I asked Cally if we could go over to your dad's, after I got out, but she wouldn't even ring him."

Gray shook his head. "I wouldn't have been there anyway. Mum hasn't let me go to his place since. She says he's irresponsible, and we could've all been. . ." Gray stopped, glancing at his friend.

"It wasn't your *dad's* fault," said Isis.

"I know, but all the same." He hoicked his bag onto his shoulder, getting ready to go. "I haven't said anything about. . ." He looked up, but in a reflex, as if hardly aware of the action.

Isis nodded, grateful he'd not said the word. Devourer. *Monster.*

"I wondered if you wanted to talk?" she asked, the words bursting out in a rush. She couldn't say more, not here, but those days in August and the night that ended them had been filling up her mind, using all her thoughts. Gray was the only one who'd understand.

He didn't answer, and his expression wasn't what she expected. Gray seemed reluctant, even fearful. "Um, I can't now," he said.

"We've got to see Mr Gerard to register our UFO club," said the flick-haired boy.

Isis laughed, not sure if he meant it.

"UFOs *do* exist!" snapped the boy. "Gray's shot a film of them. It's been on telly – he's practically famous!"

"Oh. Yeah," said Isis. She waited for Gray to correct him, but he didn't. He only walked away, throwing a last comment over his shoulder. "I'll see you around, all right?"

"All right," she answered, although it wasn't. She'd been counting the days until school started, waiting for the moment she could finally talk everything through with Gray. It hadn't gone even a tiny bit how she'd imagined.

In the hospital, Isis had waited for Cally to talk to her about Angel, but after two days she still hadn't.

"Mum?" asked Isis.

Cally smiled. "I like it when you call me that."

Isis smiled too, then carried on. "Do you remember what happened down in the mortuary?"

Cally seemed to freeze for a heartbeat.

"I don't think I'll ever forget it," she replied. "Seeing you alive then was the best moment of my life."

Isis nodded, her head against the pillow. "What about when we held hands?"

Next to the bed, a small face peered up at them eagerly beneath a bob of curly blonde hair. It was a little girl, dressed in a pink party dress. Isis's little sister, Angel.

"I holded hands too," she cried. "I do it!" She patted the sheets with her pudgy fingers, but they didn't leave a single wrinkle on the bedding.

Isis took a nervous breath, then continued, "Did you see Angel?"

Cally's face was still, apart from a twitch of her jaw and the tiniest flicker of her eyes. "Angel is dead, Isis. She died five years ago."

"But did you see her?" asked Isis, more urgently.

Cally shook her head, her face still blank.

"Not true!" Angel shouted, her fists thumping onto the bed now, though still without any effect. "Mummy seed me!"

Cally shivered, doing up the buttons of her cardigan. "You were suffering from hypothermia. Maybe you thought you saw Angel because you wanted her to be with us. . ."

"She *was* with us!" cried Isis. "She's with us right now!"

And that was the only time Cally walked away from her in the hospital, standing without a word and leaving through the ward doors. Angel raced after her mother, coming to a stop only as the doors closed, their handles visible beyond the fabric of her dress.

"Mummy!" she shouted, stamping one foot. None of the other patients looked over. "Mum*my*!"

After a moment, Angel turned and ran back to the bed. Isis held out her arms, not caring if anyone was looking, and Angel climbed up onto her lap. Angel's sandals didn't mark the sheets, her body made no impression on the bed covers. Isis wrapped her arms around her little sister.

"You've still got me," Isis whispered, "always and forever."

"Always and forever," answered Angel. But the words sounded mournful the way she said them.

After a few minutes the ward doors re-opened and Cally walked back in. She sat down by Isis's bed, her face serious.

"Please don't say things like that," she said quietly. "Not about Angel." Her voice quavered to a halt, and she took a deep breath. "I know I've talked a lot about the spirits, and made you go to seances, and. . . all the things I've done. But those two hours, when they said you were dead. . . I realised I'd been making you live in the shadow of Angel's death. Everything I did, all the plans I made, I was always looking back to her, even though you were right there with me. It was only when I thought you were gone, that I understood how much. . ." She shut her eyes, and a tear dropped through her lashes, but when she opened her eyes again she was smiling. "It felt like a miracle, getting you back."

"But Angel. . ."

Cally shook her head. "Every day of my life I wish she were still here, but I've got *you*, Isis." She reached out, and put her hand to Isis's cheek. "Oh! You're freezing!"

Cally started fussing with the blankets, pulling them around Isis. Angel pushed up with her arms, fingers splayed, and poked her head and shoulders straight through the covers.

"I here!" Angel shouted, scowling furiously at Cally. "I *here*!"

But the blankets settled without a hint of the little girl's presence. And although Isis desperately wanted to explain to her mum, she didn't know how to, or which words to use. Instead, her five-year habit of silence settled back in.

Angel stood up on Isis's lap, her chubby face level with her older sister's. "I *are* here?"

Isis gave the tiniest of nods. "Yes," she whispered.

"You tell Mummy?"

Isis wanted to say yes, she'd tell Cally and somehow make things right for her sister-ghost. But Cally seemed so sure she hadn't seen anything in the mortuary. Isis had held their hands together and when she'd done that with Gray he'd been able to see what she could, Angel linking their sight. Maybe it just didn't work with Cally.

"I'll try," Isis whispered to Angel.

"I'll try too," answered Cally, fiddling with a pillow. "You'll see. Things will be different now."

And that was that. Isis couldn't talk about Angel, which meant she could hardly talk to her mum about all the other things that had happened out in the fields with Gray and the ghost Devourer. She'd been forced to hold it in, every word, waiting until she could see Gray again. He was the only other person who'd seen what really happened.

And now he was walking away across the playground. Isis stared at his back, the swing of his arms. Suddenly he looked like a stranger.

Isis didn't manage to talk to Gray later that day either. They didn't share any lessons, and at lunchtime he'd been with his other friends. She had worried that the other boys might start asking questions or make fun of her if she approached him then, so she went to another table instead, eating quietly by herself while around her everyone chatted and laughed.

In assembly that afternoon Isis watched Gray file into the main hall with the rest of his form. Isis was with her own class, which meant there was no opportunity to sit together. Isis let her thoughts drift as Mrs Dewson, the head of year, began her start-of-term speech. She welcomed the pupils back to school, and told them to be nice to the new starters. Just behind Mrs Dewson a tall thin man was wearing a navy blue suit and black-rimmed glasses. His hair was combed across his head, slicked down like it had been painted on.

". . . this year you'll be making choices about what subjects to study," said Mrs Dewson.

The tall thin man darted in front of her.

"Every child will be properly dressed at all times!" he shouted, jabbing his finger in the air. "Any boy not wearing a tie will be punished, as will any girl with her hair incorrectly pinned back. I have a fresh cane this year, ready and waiting."

No one paid him the slightest attention, and Isis made no sign of seeing him either. She didn't remember him being around last year, but there were a lot of ghosts about the school today, and not just in the Victorian buildings. Maybe he was one of the ghosts let loose when she and Gray had torn open the ghost Devourer in the summer? Isis shivered, remembering the deathly cold of the monster as it filled the August night, its body swollen with all the thousands of ghosts it had consumed, a blackness blotting out the stars. She and Gray had destroyed it, preventing it from becoming something far more terrible. But they'd released spiralling swirls of ghosts in the process, and the effort had nearly cost Isis her life.

Mrs Dewson carried on, oblivious. "Now I'd like to make a special mention to someone who's shown outstanding qualities over the summer holiday. Gray Elias, would you stand please?"

His name jerked Isis's head up. She stared, along with everyone else in the year, as he stood up. Gray looked as surprised as Isis, and embarrassed too.

"Gray did something very brave this summer, which should be an inspiration to all of us."

Isis squeezed her hands into fists. *No, don't!*

"He risked his own life to help one of his fellow pupils."

Heat rushed to Isis's cheeks, and her stomach seemed to sink into her feet.

Mrs Dewson turned her head, surveying the lines of seated children. "Isis Dunbar, would you stand up please?"

Faces in the rows around her turned to stare. Isis got up slowly, trying to look normal and unremarkable.

"Pupils who don't walk on the correct side of the corridor will be punished!" sneered the ghost, glaring at her.

Mrs Dewson spoke loudly to the whole year.

"Gray and Isis were out with their families this summer,

when very unusual atmospheric conditions led to a storm with intense lightning. I'm sure you'll be as shocked as I was to hear that Isis was caught in it" – there were gasps from all around, now everyone was looking at her – "but with no concern for his own welfare Gray tried to get her to safety. He did this even though everyone else believed she was beyond hope."

All heads turned to look at Gray. Isis looked at him too, trying to read his face. The story Mrs Dewson was telling was one of the versions told by the adults who'd been there. All were slightly different, and none were correct. Apart from Gray and Isis, the only living person who knew what had really happened was Philip Syndal, a man who'd been possessed by the Devourer and who'd wanted the creature to take over Isis's mind instead. He was in a psychiatric hospital now.

Gray still looked embarrassed, but he was standing a little straighter, even smiling.

"Thanks to Gray's bravery," said Mrs Dewson, "and the sterling work of the emergency services, Isis was saved." Everyone shuffled and craned their necks to look at her again.

"*Dead girl.*" The words were said quietly, but loud enough for everyone near Isis to hear. The red-hot blush pouring up Isis's neck was making her even more visible, when all she wanted was to disappear.

"Of course," said Mrs Dewson, "we don't all have the opportunity to be so brave, but I hope this term you will all be inspired by Gray's actions. . ."

The whispers continued, and a couple of girls giggled. *Dead girl.*

Isis sat down, even though Mrs Dewson hadn't said to yet. She fixed her eyes on a safety notice, reading the red-printed words over and over. IN THE EVENT OF FIRE, LEAVE IMMEDIATELY BY THE EMERGENCY EXITS. Desperately, she tried to block out everything else.

Eventually, assembly was over.

"Be safe going home. We'll see you tomorrow," said Mrs Dewson, as everyone began filing from the hall.

"Keep your backs straight!" shrieked the teacher-ghost. "If you bring shame on this school, you shame yourselves as well!"

As Isis's class walked to the cloakroom, Jess's gang muscled their way up the line.

"What's it like being dead?"

"Did you see Jesus?"

Isis blushed even more, looking at the floor to avoid the girls' eyes. *Ignore them and they'll go away*; only adults would think that might work.

At her hook, Isis crammed her arms into her coat, heaved her school bag onto her back and headed for the doors as fast as she dared.

"Hey," shouted Connor, the boy who'd whispered in assembly, "you going home to your coffin?"

"You're not funny!" Isis snapped back.

"I'm not dead either," he said.

Isis would've punched him if she knew how. Instead she spun around and headed out of the door, running for the gates. *Wait until they can't see me*. That's when it would be safe to cry.

On the other side of the fence she could see a little girl peering through the black metal bars. As soon as she saw Isis, Angel shot through the fence, the iron sliding straight through her blonde fluff-curls and pink dress. She hopped from foot to foot, waving at Isis.

"I did waiting!" Angel shouted. "I did waiting all day!"

Isis smiled even as she tried not to cry. She held her arm so it looked as if her hand was just hanging at her side, and small invisible fingers slipped into hers.

Isis walked home alone, holding her sister's hand.

Chapter Two

Isis

When Isis came in through the door of their flat, Cally was waiting for her, rushing out of the kitchen to greet her with a kiss.

"How was your first day back at school?" she asked.

Isis shrugged, dropping her bag by the door. Angel hopped her way to the living room. "I waited, I waited, I waited waited waited," she sang soundlessly, clambering onto the sofa and disappearing inside one of the cushions.

"Did you make any new friends?" Cally asked. "Is there anyone you'd like to invite round for tea?"

Isis stayed motionless, close to tears. But her mum only smiled, looking eager; she didn't know what had happened at school and Isis could see she was trying to make an effort.

Isis shook her head, following Angel towards the living room.

"I just want to watch a bit of TV," she said, trying to keep the tremor out of her voice.

"*Peppa Pig*!" squeaked a voice from inside the cushion.

"You must be tired," said Cally. "Do you want a drink? Apple juice? Orange juice?"

Isis turned back to her mum. "Have we got those?"

Cally nodded. "I bought them when you were out. I know it's a bit extravagant, but first day back and everything!" She headed for the kitchen and Isis followed in surprise. On the kitchen table was a plate piled with biscuits, and an empty glass, waiting for her.

"I told you," said Cally. "Things are going to be different now."

Isis picked up a chocolate digestive, while Cally poured her an orange juice. Isis felt a tiny bit better. She was safe here, and Cally was making good on the promise she'd made in hospital.

"I did something else while you were at school," said Cally.

"What?"

A smile crept onto Cally's lips. "I got a job!"

Isis stopped eating, a biscuit halfway to her mouth.

Cally laughed. "Really! A real job!"

"But what about your psychic readings, your performances?"

Cally's smile became a wince. "I'm not doing any more of them. I've. . . come to my senses about all of that. You probably didn't realise this, but some of the people in the Welkin Society weren't very trustworthy. And I think Philip Syndal was–" she frowned a little–, "well, not a mentally stable person."

Isis almost laughed. Her mum didn't know the half of it.

Cally turned the kettle on. "Like I said in the hospital, I've realised it wasn't healthy for you to be surrounded by talk of ghosts. We need to move on, don't we?"

In the living room, Angel was singing. "I waited, I waited. I did waiting all day."

"What job have you got?" asked Isis, beginning to hope. This might change everything – her mum would be out working, not depressed in their flat, they'd have money at last, and there'd be no more hanging around community centres while her mum tried to make a career as a stage psychic despite not being able to see ghosts.

"Well, it's wonderful," said Cally. "I'm sure a higher power must have guided me there. I only popped into Crystal Healing to get a small rose quartz, but I got talking to Constance and she told me she's just opened a new treatment room at the back. She needs someone to mind the shop when she's doing her healing sessions." Cally beamed. "It's only part-time to start with, but Constance has such a powerful aura, I'm sure she'll be fully booked in no time."

Isis put down her half-eaten biscuit. "You're working at Crystal Healing?"

Cally nodded. "Isn't that great?"

"They sell incense, and packs of tarot cards."

"And crystals, and healing bells, and a wonderful selection of books."

"I thought you meant you'd got a job in a supermarket or something," said Isis.

Cally laughed. "I would hate to work in a supermarket, you know that."

"But why do you have to work at *Crystal Healing*?" Isis didn't mean to wail, but that's how it came out. Maybe she'd be okay if no one from school ever went past the shop or looked in the window. . . But, what if they found out? What if they *went in*?

Cally's smile drifted into a puzzled frown. "You've asked me so many times to get a job."

"Not *there*!" Isis grabbed a handful of biscuits and marched back into the living room. She threw herself on the sofa, switching on the telly.

"I don't understand," Cally called after her. "I thought you'd be *pleased*!"

Isis stared at some programme where children got to redesign their bedrooms. She ought to be pleased, and Cally was trying to change. But why couldn't her mum do something normal, just once?

"Your mother's right," whispered a voice from behind her. She twisted around but there was no one there. As she turned, a biscuit crumb caught in her throat and she began to cough. Or maybe it was the dust that was suddenly filling the room? Every surface seemed to be breathing out particles; motes danced in the sunlit air, fibres floated up from the sofa, dust balls rolled out from beneath the coffee table.

It wasn't a breeze – the windows were all shut.

A straggle of spider's web began to un-weave itself from a ceiling corner, wafting in a single line through the air to a point near Isis's head. Still floating, the spider silk gently coiled in the air, winding itself into a ball, and with each twist it caught the dust and fibres, spinning them in its tiny whirlwind.

Isis got up slowly, moving away.

Now dust was pouring out from underneath the TV stand and rising up from the carpet. Frayed scraps of paper peeled and fell from an old tear in the wallpaper. Above the sofa, the spin of spider silk was transforming into a swirling, mouldy-smelling column. It became a body and a head. Arms formed from the gathering fluff, draping across the back of the sofa. Long, thin legs slithered out, crossing themselves at the knees.

At last, sitting in Isis's living room was the recognisable shape of an elderly man, dressed in an old-fashioned tweed suit, a fez perched on his head. Across the formless shape of his face, the dust and dirt was beginning to crust, like drying mud, bulging into bony features and a long, beaky nose. Holes cracked in his eye sockets and blue light glinted through them.

"Mandeville," whispered Isis.

"The very same," said the ghost, lifting his fez in greeting. With every moment he was becoming less a creation of dirt, but even as his body settled into its final form, his skin remained patched and flaking, his suit tattered and threadbare. He was human-looking, but rotten.

"What are you doing here?" Isis whispered. "I thought you were. . . eaten."

Mandeville smiled, relaxed and amiable. "I must admit, I did think my doom had arrived when Philip Syndal directed the Devourer to consume me, but thanks to your prompt actions only a little of my essence was absorbed before I was freed. When you opened a tear in its monstrous side I was one of the first to escape in the general stampede of spirits. After a period of rest and recuperation, I thought I would come and pay my respects to my saviour." Mandeville bowed his head. "I am most grateful."

"I didn't do it for you."

Mandeville shrugged, sending a puff of dust into the air and making Isis cough. She glanced back at the kitchen, checking that Cally was busy. She turned up the volume on the TV and a boy's voice blared out, complaining to the show's presenter about the way they'd transformed his bedroom.

"I appreciate that the effort was for your sister," said Mandeville. "Nevertheless, I benefited." He peered around. "Where is she, by the way?"

A small voice called out of one of the sofa cushions. "You goway! You horrid!"

Mandeville tutted. "She has the matter backwards. I believe the correct form is for a child to be seen, but not heard."

"You *poopy*!" shouted the cushion.

"Children are no better when dead," muttered Mandeville.

Isis folded her arms.

"What do you want?" she whispered. "And what did you mean before, about my mum being right? Supermarkets weren't even invented when you were alive; how would you know if she could work in one or not?"

Mandeville raised his eyebrows, cracking the papery skin of his forehead. "I was not referring to her employment. I was discussing her decision to retire from the Welkin Society. Probably the first sensible thing she has ever done, leaving that nest of self-deceivers. And speaking of Philip Syndal, as he is now incapacitated. . ." One of his eyebrows slowly dropped, leaving the other raised in question.

Isis only needed a moment to work out what he wanted. Someone to be his link to the living. Someone with whom he could be a star, even though he was dead. When Mandeville had been alive, he'd been obsessed by the Victorian psychics of his day. When he'd died and discovered them to be charlatans, he'd set about finding genuine psychics. Isis knew that Mandeville had put decades of effort into Philip Syndal, but while the man had become a celebrity, performing to huge audiences and making regular appearances on television, he'd never even revealed Mandeville's existence to his fans. Now that his time with Philip Syndal had ended so horribly, the ghost was still searching for fame.

But Isis shook her head. "No."

Mandeville sighed, letting out a plume of green mould spores.

"My dear, would you destroy my hopes when they are all that hold me together?"

"I won't do it!" snapped Isis, louder than she meant to.

"Are you all right?" Cally called from the kitchen.

Isis glared at the elderly ghost. "Yes," she shouted back.

Mandeville smiled, his teeth dangling in his mouth. "Shall I take that as a maybe?"

"It isn't," she hissed, "it's a no. No! *No!*"

But Mandeville was already crumbling. In a blink, he was a falling fountain of dirt, then a stain on the sofa, then nothing.

When she was sure he'd completely gone, Isis turned the TV down and sat back on the sofa. She stared at the television programme, her thoughts a thousand miles away from the boy and his bedroom. She picked up one of the biscuits and put it in her mouth, instantly spitting it back into her hand. The biscuit was now soft and stale, the cream filling fuzzed with bluish mildew.

Chapter Three
Gray

What was it like, Gray?

It was scary, that's what I remember.

Not at first. I mean it was just a boring school trip, even though Mr Watkins, our geography teacher, was trying to make out it was really exciting.

"We're incredibly fortunate to be on this trip today," he said, standing at the front of the coach before we set off. "UK-Earths doesn't normally open up to visitors, but they've made an exception for us because of, well, community relations. I want you all on your best behaviour, giving a good impression of our school."

Jayden called out, "How come we're the ones who have

to do community relations? It's not our fault there's been protests."

I laughed, and other people did too. I mean, on an excited scale of one to a hundred, we were definitely less than ten.

Mr Watkins glared at Jayden. "You are all *extremely* lucky to have this opportunity, so make the most of it."

"So lucky," I muttered to Gav, who was sitting next to me, "getting a trip to a big hole in the ground."

Because that's what it was. An opencast quarry a few miles out of town, and the reason they needed community relations was because of all the stuff about it destroying the countryside and bringing tons of trucks through town. There'd been loads in the paper, even a protest camp nearby somewhere.

Not that I'd been bothered, but Dad was of course. Summer was over, all the crops had been harvested, so he couldn't go out crop-circle hunting. Which meant other things, like conspiracy theories and the quarry. Or conspiracy theories about the quarry.

Mum even got a phone call from him about it, which put her into a right outrage.

"I can't believe your father," she said, storming into the kitchen like it was my fault. "He says I shouldn't let you go on the school trip."

"Why?"

"Because it's against his *principles*! That is so like him."

I wasn't really surprised because Dad has principles about a lot of things, like me not being allowed a mobile phone. That's definitely the worst. Not being allowed on a school trip, well that might've been a good thing.

"If I can't go, can I have the day off?"

Mum glared at me. Normally she might've said that then Dad could take the day off work to look after me, but she wasn't letting me visit him. Not since she found out about him taking me out UFO hunting all those times. I had to tell her because it was the only way to help Isis. Dad had warned me not to and he'd been right; when Mum found out she went mental! She said he was irresponsible, and swore a lot. And later it didn't matter how much I said I actually liked going UFO hunting, because by then she had her killer come-back.

"Look what happened to your friend Isis."

"She did survive," I said, but Mum just gave me one of her looks.

I was amazed that Dad even knew about the school trip, seeing as I hadn't seen him since the summer. I wondered if he was cyber-stalking me – him and his UFO-freak friends are always setting up 'search and alert' programs.

But Mum said, "He read about it in the local paper, and he claims that proves it's just a publicity stunt and that we shouldn't be supporting the 'corporate destroyers of the environment'."

"Well they are destroying the environment," I said.

Mum only rolled her eyes; sometimes I wonder how Dad and Mum even dated, let alone got together and had me.

"I don't mind not going," I said, sort of hopefully.

"It's not about whether you mind!" snapped Mum. "It's about your education. She signed the form with a fast jab of her pen, nearly tearing through the paper. I knew then there was no way I was getting out of the trip. Mum was probably going to escort me onto the coach herself.

Um, are you sure you need to know all this for your. . . therapy? I could tell you just the main things, if you want?

No, tell me in as much detail as you can remember. It's very important that you leave nothing out, even things you think I might not believe. Especially those. You need to get things off your chest, like exactly how you caused so much devastation.

But that wasn't our fault! They said it wasn't.

They may say, but we both know better. You are responsible for millions of pounds worth of damage, and billions in financial loss, so every detail is important.

But I already told the police. . .

I am not from the police, Gray. As far as you are concerned, I am a therapist brought into school to deal with the aftermath of what you did. So you can tell me the truth. Now, look at me, that's right, straight into my eyes. . . you will tell me everything, every detail.

Everything. Every detail. . .

Our coach shunted through the traffic in town, with the

other coaches behind us. Our whole year was on the trip, so we were practically a convoy. It took a while, but eventually we were out past all the roundabouts and heading into the countryside. It isn't far to the quarry, but the coaches went slowly because the road was so bendy. It took at least half an hour of driving, but eventually we turned down this new-looking road, heading for a pair of tall gates with a high, chain-link fence stretching off either side. We passed a sign that said UK-EARTHS: CAUTION HEAVY VEHICLES and the gates were opened by a couple of people in bright yellow jackets and safety helmets.

I don't know what I was expecting, but it wasn't very impressive. A car park and some mobile offices.

"Is this it?" Jayden said as we got off the coach. It's what we were all thinking. You could hear a rumbling clattery noise in the distance, but that was the only sign of it being a quarry. We milled about while the teachers got us into our class groups and checked our names off lists. The staff from the quarry came out to meet us, led by a woman in a smart suit. Mr Watkins rushed over to talk to her, all smiling and hand-shaking.

Jayden nudged me.

"Community relations."

Teachers from the other coaches joined Mr Watkins, and there was more pointing and checking of lists. Then he came bustling back to where my class was standing, followed by the smart-looking woman.

"4B," he announced, "this is Dr Harcourt, who is the um. . ."

"Public Affairs Director," she said.

Mr Watkins smiled in this sucking-up way. "Yes, Public Affairs Director of UK-Earths. She is going to guide us around the quarry today, and you're very lucky to be the first group going onto the site."

None of us said anything.

"Isn't that great?"

A few people nodded. Was he expecting a cheer?

Dr Harcourt stepped past Mr Watkins and smiled at us. Not a genuine smile; like she had to, you know?

"So, class 4B. . ." she said, then she turned her smile at Mr Watkins. "I thought class 4F were going onto site first?"

Mr Watkins shook his head, and his bald patch went bright pink. "I'm afraid 4F are being. . . well, there was a bit of rowdy behaviour before we left school which resulted in the class losing their first place."

Dr Harcourt's smile got even faker. "Oh. I see." She didn't seem very happy, like she wasn't used to things going differently to how she'd planned. She threw an annoyed glance at us, like we were the ones who'd played up, and led our class to one of the Portacabins, where one of the men in hi-vis jackets gave us each a fluorescent tabard and a red safety hat. He did a test of the warning siren, which sounded like a foghorn.

"If you hear that, you need to get out of the quarry, straight away," he said. "We let off three blasts, two minutes apart, before any blasting, and also if there are any safety issues anywhere in the quarry. So if you hear the siren, get back here, and don't mess about, okay?" Most of us nodded. The ones not listening, well I reckoned it was only evolution if they got blown up.

Dr Harcourt led Mr Watkins over to a computer while that was happening, and they starting checking our names again, this time to an on-screen list. She still didn't look happy.

"I think we should get the other class, the ones who were meant to be going first," she said.

"Don't worry, my lot won't mind going out of turn – they're happy about it, just look at their faces."

She didn't.

"That isn't what I meant. We have everything organised and this change of events is not. . ."

But Mr Watkins was shaking his head. "It won't be possible," he said. "We can't go back on discipline in that way. The class have to take their punishment otherwise there'd be. . ."

"Anarchy," whispered Jayden, grinning at me.

"Revolution," I whispered back. "The breakdown of society as we know it."

Mr Watkins didn't go quite that far, but there was no way Dr Harcourt was changing his mind. Teachers can be like that, I guess, because they're so used to bossing everyone about.

We had to wait in the office for ten minutes while she argued at him, but he wouldn't budge, and eventually Dr Harcourt was the one who gave up, saying that she'd be writing to the head teacher about it.

We lined up at the door, and Mr Watkins came along, checking we all had our hard hats and stuff.

"What is her problem?" he muttered to himself. "What does it matter which class goes in when?"

It mattered a great deal. Dr Harcourt should have worked harder to ensure things were kept in order. And she should not have assumed that you would all emerge unscathed.

Chapter Four
Gray

When everything was checked, they led us out through a door on the other side of the Portacabin. Now I could see what was hidden from view when we'd been in the car park.

The hill sloped away from us, and the grass and soil had been cleared off a wide strip of it. There were big mounds of earth piled up at the bottom of the slope, and broken trees stacked into tangly heaps. The rumbling clattery noise was from a couple of massive diggers, busy scraping up more soil and uncovering the grey-white, clay-looking layer beneath. The big teeth on their buckets had left scratch marks, like the hillside was being gnawed on by giant rats.

"Wow," said Jayden, "look at those!" He was pointing at a couple of huge dumper trucks, the biggest you've ever seen, wheels as high as a house. But I didn't care about them; I kept staring at the diggers, chewing away at the hillside.

When I was younger I was really into bird spotting, and Dad used to take me out to places to look for them, wooded valleys like this one. There couldn't be any birds living here now, not even an insect, probably.

"It's such a mess," I said, and I got why Dad hated the quarry.

Mr Watkins heard and glared at me, but Dr Harcourt only smiled her phony smile.

"Yes, I suppose it might look a bit of a mess, if you don't understand what you're seeing. But of course our environmental controls are to the highest standard, and after we finish here, in around 2050, we'll be reseeding the site with grass and planting new trees."

"Isn't that great?" said Mr Watkins, sucking up again. I didn't say anything, only looked at the long grey trunks of the piled-up beech trees. They would've towered over us when they were standing. They would've taken a hundred years to grow to that size.

Dr Harcourt turned to the rest of the group. "So, can anyone tell me what we're mining for here?"

A few people put their hand up. I mean, everyone knew – it'd been on the TV news, and not just the local stuff no one ever watches, it was even on *Newsround*. But still only a few people put their hand up – the rest only ever answer if they're made to.

Dr Harcourt picked Liam.

"Rare earth metals," he said, looking a bit panicked at actually having to answer.

"And what are they?"

"Um, metals that are rare?"

Mr Watkins frowned at us. "We covered this only last week."

"Oh, um. . ." You could practically see the cogs working in Liam's brain. "They're formed in supernova explosions?" Dr Harcourt nodded. "And. . . they're found all over the planet?" Liam trailed off and Mr Watkins sighed.

"Would anyone else like to tell Dr Harcourt what we know about rare earth metals?" he said.

Ruksar had her hand up so high it was amazing she didn't dislocate her arm. Dr Harcourt smiled at her.

"Rare earth metals are seventeen metals, mostly lanthanides," she said, all pleased with herself. "They can change the properties of other metals when they're mixed with them. They are usually only found in low concentrations and they're also really difficult to mine. They're often found together with radioactive materials, so—"

"Not here!" snapped Dr Harcourt. "There are no radioactive elements at this site, I'd like to make that *completely* clear."

"Oh," said Ruksar, going bright red.

Dr Harcourt looked away from her, all smiles again. "And does anyone know what rare earth metals are used for?"

After what happened to Ruksar, there were even fewer hands up this time. Mr Watkins looked around. In lessons he picks on someone who doesn't want to answer, but he probably didn't want Dr Harcourt to think we're thick, so he chose Gav.

"They're used in smartphones, and tablets and things. . ." Gav trailed off. I mean, by then we'd said everything we knew.

Luckily Dr Harcourt was pleased. "That's right," she

said. "Rare earth metals have some unusual properties that make them perfect for use in new technologies. Without them, we wouldn't have touchscreens, and think how boring that would be."

Mr Watkins giggled. Honestly.

"So shall we go and have a closer look?" asked Dr Harcourt.

Mr Watkins nodded enthusiastically, and it didn't really matter what the rest of us wanted.

"The diggers will stop working while we're on-site," she said, "For safety reasons."

A few people made disappointed noises, and she smiled. "But don't worry, we're going to give you a special demonstration."

Now I think about it, there was something about the way she said that. It was about the only time she sounded excited.

We walked out on a gravel track, wide enough for even the biggest of dumper trucks to get along. There was a bit of mud, and I noticed that all the people from the mining company, even smart Dr Harcourt, were wearing boots. Of course, we were all wearing our school shoes, and pretty soon people, well girls, were making a fuss about it.

"My shoes are dirty!"

"I can't walk in this!"

Mr Watkins started getting stressed and snappy, and Dr Harcourt looked like she wished she could just have us hauled away and disposed of. But she still carried on with her lectures.

"The rights to quarry here were allocated more than fifty years ago, but at the time it was thought the only use would be clay for brick making, and there were other more accessible supplies of that. However, about ten years ago UK-Earths bought the rights, for a modest sum, and things got very exciting after tests revealed what an astonishing deposit of rare earth metals we are dealing with here. An extremely unusual mixture, in a very concentrated deposit. We believe this will be an incredible boost for our economy, and open up new applications in a range of hi-tech industries." She stopped and none of us said anything. She looked a bit put out, like we were meant to be clapping.

"What you need to appreciate," Mr Watkins broke in,

stressing again, "is how amazing this quarry is! Rare earth metals shouldn't even be here according to the geology of the surrounding area. . ."

He wittered on about clay and sedimentary rock while we walked, and Dr Harcourt looked as if she wished she could squash us like flies. Mr Watkins listed all the different theories about how the oh-so-special metal had ended up in a hill near our town: ancient volcanoes, prehistoric rivers, the effects of glaciation. Of course they were all completely wrong, as it turned out. But you could tell he wasn't really talking to us – he was trying to impress Dr Harcourt. Maybe he was hoping she'd give him a job.

I wasn't really listening because we were getting close to the most interesting things in the whole boring place, which were the two diggers. From where we'd started out, they'd looked small enough to be toys, but as we got nearer, there were murmurs of excitement at the size of them. The diggers towered over us like mechanical dinosaurs. If you'd stuck three of our coaches on top of each other, those machines would still have been taller. The caterpillar tracks alone were as high as a bus.

When we were about 15 metres away from them, Dr Harcourt held up her hand and we all stopped.

"Can't we go and see them up close, miss?" asked Gav.

"It's doctor, actually, not miss," snapped Dr Harcourt. "And we have to stop here. It wouldn't be safe to get any nearer."

The digger's driver looked like a flea from where we stood.

"Why's the driver wearing a gas mask?" asked Jayden.

"It's not a gas mask," said Dr Harcourt, smiling her weird smile. "It's a dust mask. Just basic health and safety, because he's out here all day."

"Do the children need one?" Mr Watkins asked, sounding a bit worried.

Dr Harcourt shook her head. "Not for one visit! If they got jobs here it would be a different matter." She turned to us, and said in this really patronising way, "So who'd like to work here?"

Liam's hand shot up. "Me! I want to drive one of those!"

"Would you like a demonstration of what it can do?" Dr Harcourt asked him.

Suddenly everyone was enthusiastic. Dr Harcourt waved

at the driver of the closest digger, and I saw him raise his hand in reply. There was a roar and blast of diesel fumes as the engine started up. This close, it wasn't a distant clattery sound, it was like a motorway full of cars; most of us put our hands over our ears because it was so loud.

"Shouldn't we move back a little?" yelled Mr Watkins.

"It's perfectly safe!" Dr Harcourt shouted back.

The digger's arm jerked and lifted, the bucket opening smoothly.

"We have been preparing the site for some time," yelled Dr Harcourt over the noise, "but it's only recently that we've reached the layers of material we are interested in. These two machines aren't clearing topsoil any more, they are mining rare earth metals."

"Do you do all the mining that way?" Ruksar shouted.

Dr Harcourt shook her head, as the digger arm moved through the air and began to lower.

"Impressive as they are, these machines can't extract enough raw material by themselves. Very soon we are going to start blasting. By which I mean explosive charges will be used to dislodge far greater quantities of material from the hillside."

"Can we see *that*?" someone shouted. Now the trip was getting better!

But Dr Harcourt shook her head. "The entire site will be cleared, and the explosives detonated by remote control. No one gets to see the blast go up, I'm afraid."

Behind her, the bucket smashed into the ground with an enormous *thunk*, and everyone in our class jumped. The jaws bit, then closed and lifted. You could see that even though they talked about clay, what the machine was digging was more like soft rock. Chunks fell from the bucket jaws as the arm lifted up again.

"Each scoop of these diggers moves ten tons of material," shouted Dr Harcourt.

The top of the digger spun on its base, and the bucket jaws opened again, dropping ten tons of rocky clay. The sound rumbled like an earthquake. A cloud of grey-white dust rose up and spread into the air above us.

"I think maybe we are too close," called Mr Watkins.

Dr Harcourt looked at him. "There's really nothing to be frightened of."

But Mr Watkins was right, because now the grey-white dust was drifting down, settling on everyone's hair and faces. It was all over me, coating my skin, inside my mouth. People were coughing and wiping their eyes. My eyes started watering, scraping grit every time I blinked, so everything was sparkling and blurred.

You know in *Superman* films, how the kryptonite glows? Well that's got to be wrong, because kryptonite's only a chunk of Superman's planet and you can't have a whole glowing planet. I bet kryptonite just looks like ordinary rock, otherwise Superman would fly off as soon as he saw it. The rock in the quarry looked ordinary too, and we all thought the dust was just dust.

"You'd be amazed at the quantity of ore-bearing mineral we have to mine, to get usable quantities of metal," shouted Dr Harcourt over the noise of the digger. "Wouldanyone-liketoguesshowmuch?"

Her words were really fast and close together, her voice high-pitched like a recording sped up. I stared at her. Was she mucking about?

"Areyouallrightthere'snoneedtomakeafussit'sonlyabitof dust," Mr Watkins said, also at super-high speed.

I stared at them through the dust and tears. What was going on?

Then everything went black.

I read once that black holes have such strong gravity they pull everything towards them, even stars, and if you were in a spaceship you'd just plunge in and nothing you could do would stop it. It was sort of like that. I couldn't see where I was, but I still had this feeling of falling, like I'd dropped off the top of a skyscraper, at night, with no lights on anywhere, not even stars.

It was really quiet.

My dad always complains during sci-fi films when they have sounds of explosions and spaceships whizzing by.

"It's a *vacuum*," he shouts at the TV. "How can you have sound without air?"

Well this was silent, like a vacuum would be. I had my mouth open, screaming, but there wasn't any sound. Only silence and blackness and me falling. On and on, so I thought it would never end. Then – *bang!* – I was back where I'd been standing.

I stumbled forwards and fell over.

"What are you doing, Gray?" shouted Mr Watkins.

I lay on the ground and thought, *Am I having a stroke? Maybe I'm going mad, right here.*

Then I saw everyone else.

Zack had his eyes wide open, and was standing stock-still. Jayden was letting out these squawking noises and Ruksar was sitting with her head on her knees. Three metres – but what felt a thousand miles away – Jared threw up.

The digger engine cut out, and in the sudden quiet I could hear Gav shouting, "Help me! Help me!"

Mr Watkin freaked out, at a super-fast speed.

"What'sgoingon?" he speed-squeaked.

"What'swrongwithallofyou?"

He was shouting at us, shouting at everything, telling us to do one thing, then something else completely. I managed to sit up, my body feeling all strange and stretchy like it wasn't mine, and then I saw the shapes.

Shapes? What do you mean?

At first I thought it was my eyes, or an earthquake. The ground seemed to be shimmering, something drifting out of it like a heat haze, except the haze was piling up into small pillars instead of drifting away, each one as tall as a person. You know how snowmen don't look anything like people, not even the right shape, but if you see them at night they're still spooky, like they might turn their head as you walk by? Well the shapes were like that. I could feel them watching, even though they had nothing to watch with. I was sure they were closing in on me.

"Mr Watkins," I croaked, but he didn't pay any attention because Hayley was screaming. A lot of people were screaming by then, and Mr Watkins was flapping around shouting contradictory instructions.

Only Dr Harcourt seemed calm. Not even a bit worried that we were all going mad and being sick. She was examining us; she looked like she was taking mental notes. It's weird how now I can remember her being like that, really clearly, but at the time I hardly even noticed because the shapes started making this noise, over and over.

Yooooo. . . Yooooo. . . Yooooo. . . Yooooo. . .

Your friend, Isis. I wonder what she would have made of what you saw?

Isis? She was in 4F, the class that was supposed to go in first. . . oh. Is that why Dr Harcourt was so put out about the change in order?

Now don't try to put things together. You only want to talk, and tell me everything.

Well Isis didn't see anything, because no one else got taken into the quarry after us. They couldn't, could they? Not with all the ambulances and angry parents.

As I said, Dr Harcourt was wrong to assume that a single exposure to the rock dust would have no effect on untalented children. She was only thinking of one child, instead of all of you.

'One child'? Are you saying Dr Harcourt arranged a whole school trip just to get Isis into the quarry? But anything could have happened to us! Why did we all have to be involved, if Isis was the one she was interested in?

Calm down, Gray, there is no need to become agitated. Relax, focus on the watch I'm holding, notice the way it glitters as I move it from side to side. Now, that's better, isn't it? And to answer your question, wouldn't it have been extremely difficult to take a single child into the quarry, without drawing attention to the act? But a school trip, what could be more ordinary than that?

How. . . do you. . . know about Isis?

I have met her, and I know of her remarkable abilities. I've met you as well, Gray, although you don't remember. Now please, stop worrying about things that don't concern you. Shut your eyes, that's right, and continue telling me your story. Every detail.

Chapter Five
Gray

Mum and Dad both came to the quarry. It was like a disaster movie – police, ambulances and parents screeching up in their cars.

Mr Watkins started that.

"What have you done? What have you done?" he yelled at Dr Harcourt before pulling out his mobile phone and dialling 999.

"There's no need to panic!" said Dr Harcourt, but it was too late, because Mr Watkins was already shrieking into his phone about an accident at the quarry, and how a class of school children was involved. You can imagine how that went down.

You know, it's weird though. I'd have thought it would've

been on the news or something. But there was nothing, not even in the local paper.

It is easy to divert local press from a news story, Gray. A terrorist alert is sufficient, or a decent-sized power cut. Reporters are easily distracted by anything that causes a lot of fuss and activity, even when it amounts to nothing in the end. Those that cannot be distracted, well there are other means. . .

Are you saying someone covered it up?

I am making observations. Continue telling me what happened to you and your friends.

Well. . . Gav staggered past me and puked again, this time at Mr Watkins's feet.

"There must be something toxic here!" Mr Watkins screamed. "Oh God, what if the deposit *is* radioactive?"

Dr Harcourt stepped calmly away from Gav. "That is not possible. I think the children have become overexcited, so I suggest we get them back to the office."

"*Overexcited?*" shrieked Mr Watkins. "They aren't toddlers!"

Dr Harcourt carried on in this annoyingly calm way. "If rare earth metals were toxic, they wouldn't be allowed in touchscreen devices all over the planet. Perhaps your pupils are playing some kind of prank?"

Mr Watkins gave her the filthiest look ever, then grabbed hold of my arm and started trying to pull me up.

"Come on!" he shouted. "Everyone out of here!"

Those who could, ran, but most of us staggered. The driver climbed down from the digger, pushing up his dust mask. He went over to help Ruksar, but Dr Harcourt snapped at him.

"Get back in the cab. Put your mask on!"

"But look at the state of them," he said. "You shouldn't have brought kids in!"

"I'm dealing with it!" she shouted, and he backed off, pulling his mask down again, below his worried eyes.

Mr Watkins took Jamilia's arm, because she was definitely the worst.

"What did the driver mean?" he asked Dr Harcourt.

"He didn't mean anything." she said angrily. "He's just panicking, like you seem to be."

"I'm not panicking," he yelled. "I'm responsible for their *welfare*!"

We must have looked a sight, stumbling, crying and choking our way back to the Portacabins. The rest of our year was waiting there, watching us with open mouths and wide eyes. A few people laughed, but they stopped when we got closer and it became obvious we weren't mucking about.

The man who'd given us the safety helmets came rushing out of the Portacabin office looking properly upset.

"Are they all right?" he gasped at Mr Watkins.

"Do they *look* all right?" Mr Watkins shouted back. He'd lost it by then, and he turned on the other teachers, who were staring open-mouthed like everyone else. "*Help us!*"

In a few seconds all the adults were rushing about, grabbing kids from our class and trying all sorts of rubbish first aid on us. Head between the knees. Glass of water. Wrap up warm.

Only Dr Harcourt didn't seem bothered; she just disappeared into the Portacabin office, and I didn't see her again that day. It was like she vanished.

It didn't take long for the ambulances to arrive, which was pretty cool. This paramedic lady checked my heart and breathing and stuff. While she was getting on with it, a man walked up and showed her some kind of ID.

"I work for the Health and Safety Executive," he said, "Can I ask your patient a few questions about what happened?"

"You arrived quickly," said the paramedic, a little crossly.

"Accidents have to be investigated," he said.

"Well, he's fine to answer questions."

The paramedic went to help someone else, and the man from Health and Safety asked me about what had happened, and what I'd felt like. As he wrote my answers down, I had this weird feeling I'd seen him before. He looked. . . like you actually, now I think about it.

I'm telling you – there was no one who looked like me. No one.

Oh. No one.

Please continue.

Anyway, it turned out one of the teachers had phoned the school about what was happening, and the school phoned parents. My mum must've driven over at super-speed. I could hear her shouting at people before I saw her.

"Where's my son? Is he all right?"

And then she was grabbing me into this crushing hug. "Gray! Oh my God!"

"Let go!" I said, trying to push her off. "I'm fine."

Mr Watkins came over. "They've all been checked over," he reassured her, "and everything seems normal." Mum let go of me but she still looked really worried. She got a hanky out of her pocket and I could see her hands were shaking.

"It's all right, Mum," I said. And I did feel mostly better by then. "I've got a bit of a headache, that's all."

Mum burst into tears.

"He could have died!" Mum sobbed at Mr Watkins, who I noticed was this weird colour, sort of grey.

"Please. None of the children have been seriously hurt. The paramedics think they possibly had a reaction to the dust, a bit like hay fever. It may even have been psychosomatic."

"My son doesn't make things up!" Mum said, wiping her eyes with the hanky.

Which was when Dad turned up.

"Gray!" he called, walking fast through all the kids and parents and emergency services people. Mum turned, glaring, and whatever she'd been planning for Mr Watkins got hurled at Dad instead.

"What are *you* doing here?"

"The school phoned me," Dad answered, glaring back.

I looked between them and knew what was coming. I felt like running for cover.

"I'm surprised you were bothered," said Mum.

"Of course I'm bothered!" said Dad. "He's my son!"

"Oh, so you're suddenly full of parental care?"

"How can I be if you won't let me see him?"

"You nearly got him killed! You didn't even *try* to keep him safe!"

"Look around you, Jenice!" Dad waved his hand at everything going on. "You agreed to this school trip, not me." He pointed at the paramedics. "Things happen!"

"They do when you're around!"

Dad went this sort of purplish colour then.

"I told Gray to stay at home that night. *You* brought him out to the field!"

"Because *you'd* filled up his head with UFO rubbish."

"Can you stop?" I asked, but I don't think they even heard. People were starting to stare, one girl had even stopped crying and was now listening closely.

"Gray's not a little boy any more," said Dad. "You can't wrap him in cotton wool forever!"

"You lied to me about where you took my son. Not just once, but time after time, for *years.*"

"He was never in any danger."

"He could've died! Your girlfriend's daughter did die!"

Of course Cally had to choose that moment to appear.

She came out of nowhere, through a gap in the crowds of kids, wearing this ankle-length red dress, like a witch or something. Her face was white, her mouth was open and her black hair was trailing out behind her. Mental-looking, I thought.

She didn't even notice us at first, just ran up to the paramedics and started hassling one of them.

"Where is she? Where's my daughter? Is she all right? It was on the radio that something had happened up here, but no one will tell me *anything*!" She didn't even give the paramedic a chance to answer, just spun away and started questioning everyone in our class. "Isis! Where's Isis?" she was calling, high and panicky.

My mum folded her arms. "Your girlfriend's here."

Dad didn't need to be told. His eyes were stuck to crazy-Cally. Lots of other people were staring at her too, and even though I was glad she'd distracted them from us I felt kind of sorry for her as well so I went over.

"Gray?" Her eyes were huge in her face, and she was almost panting. "Where is Isis?"

"She's fine," I said. "Nothing's happened to her." I pointed to everyone milling around the coaches. "She'll be somewhere over there."

"Oh!" Cally let out this weird sighing breath. "I heard there'd been an incident and I thought. . ." A smile broke through the mad look on her face, and tears filled her eyes. "Thank you, Gray!"

Before I knew it, she was hugging me; she even kissed me on the cheek! I managed to push her off, but then I stumbled backwards into Dad.

"Cally," he said from behind me.

That's all it was, but you should've seen Cally. She stared at him, then looked away, then looked back. Bright red spots flashed in her cheeks, and her eyes went bigger than ever.

"Gil," she whispered.

I got out from between them as quickly as I could. It was like nothing else was happening around them, like I wasn't even there.

Mum was watching them too, and frowning a bit.

"They had a big fight over what happened," I explained to her.

Mum nodded. "And now they're making up."

She sounded. . . sad, you know? I looked at her, trying to work out what she was thinking.

"Do *you* want to get back with Dad?" I asked, very quietly.

Mum startled, then laughed.

"No, love, I really don't!"

"You've got Brian though, haven't you?" I said, to make her feel better. He's Mum's boyfriend; they've been going out for years.

"Yeah," said Mum.

"You've got me too."

Then she properly smiled at me, and gave me a hug.

I hugged her back, and I didn't even care that everyone could see. It was the kind of day no one would make fun of you for something like that.

A minute later, I heard kids cheering.

"What's happening?" said Mum.

"We're all going home early!" someone said.

Mr Watkins was in such a panic he'd said that anyone whose parents had turned up could leave.

It wasn't even lunchtime yet!

The cheering and general happiness even broke Cally and Dad out of their little world. They were hand in hand, smiling like idiots.

"I'd better go and find Isis," Cally said to Dad.

"Can I come over later?" he asked. His eyes were glued to her.

"I'll have Isis. . ."

Then Dad did look my way. "Why don't you come, Gray? You haven't seen Isis for ages – you could play computer games or whatever, like you did in the holidays."

"*Gil!*" snapped Mum. "He needs to go home and rest, not help you with your romancing!"

"Oh yeah, of course," said Dad, seeming totally

unbothered by Mum now. "What about another time, Gray, when you're over this?"

"I know Isis would love to see you," said Cally. She looked at Mum. "They really did become great friends over the summer, before. . ." she trailed off.

I thought Mum would go off like a firework, but she only stayed silent for a minute, then said, "Well, it would be good for Gray to see Gil, and I don't want to stop him seeing his friends." Which was the opposite of everything she'd been saying up to then.

Mum pulled me towards her. "Not until he's better though."

"Sounds like a plan," said Dad, and they were all smiling, like they'd solved everything.

I wanted to say something, but how could I explain? The thought of spending time with Isis. . .

You must have been happy. It can't have been easy being kept apart from your friend, after what happened to you both in the summer. A terrifying experience, so nearly losing her.

You know about that?

The ghosts in the sky, which your father still believes were UFOs. Philip Syndal's plans for the Devourer to consume Isis, and how you tried to save her. Everyone thinking she was dead, even you. I know all of it, apart from how she was able to survive.

But no one knows all that except me and Isis! How did you find out? Who told you?

You did, Gray. In your own words. I even have a recording.

But. . .

No more questions. You were telling me about meeting Isis again, after all you'd been through.

All we'd been through. . .

A monster had been inside her. I don't mean when people talk about a bad person and say 'monster'. It was a real monster. Crawling up her, wrapping around her like a snake. A mountain of darkness which poured out of her mouth, squirming and wriggling.

I wanted to be normal with her, honestly, but. . .

Every time I saw Isis I was watching her eyes, waiting for them to blank out the way they had that night. She'd told everyone at school she hadn't really died, but I knew she was lying. Cally had been screaming, and the paramedics had shaken their heads.

Then she'd come back to life, somehow. Down in the mortuary, where they keep the dead bodies.

And whenever I saw her, all I could think was: *Are you still Isis? Or are you just some* thing, *using her body?*

So no, I didn't want to spend time with her. The truth is, she scared me.

Chapter Six

Isis

"Now this is meant to be fun," said Mrs Craven, smiling at everyone. "There are no right or wrong answers. I know you all had a bit of a strange day yesterday, so I thought we'd take it easy today."

On the other side of the table, Jess sat scowling at Isis. This definitely wasn't going to be fun.

It was the day after the disastrous school trip, and the class was full of chatter and gossip. Some students weren't in today and everyone was talking about them, which meant that, for a little while, they weren't talking about Isis.

Within a few days of the assembly, the entire school seemed to know what Mrs Dewson had announced about

Isis getting struck by lightning and Gray saving her. But the story had been exaggerated as it spread and during break one day a group of Year Eleven girls had come up to Isis, looming over her, and flicking their hair.

"Were you really dead for two days?" one of them asked.

Isis shook her head, wishing she were anywhere else. "Just a few hours, and anyway the doctors said they made a mistake. I was alive the whole time, really." They'd been wrong of course, but she kept that to herself.

Despite her denial, the girls followed up with the questions everyone was asking her. *What was it like being dead? Did she see heaven?*

Isis shook her head again, backing away from them.

"I don't remember," she lied. "I don't remember any of it."

"Boring," said one of the girls, and they wandered off. Isis breathed a sigh of relief, but she knew another gang of questioners would be on at her soon enough. Her only defence was sticking to her story, playing it down. Eventually, after a torturous week or so, the interest in her dwindled, leaving only her new nickname: 'dead girl'.

The one person she wouldn't have lied to was Gray. Every break and lunchtime she'd tried to find a way of speaking to him, but she never managed to start the conversation she was so desperate for.

"Do you want to talk now?" she'd asked the next time she saw him, but he shook his head. And the times after.

"I've got computer club," or, "I'm meeting Jayden," or, "I can't right now."

A list of excuses.

Had she done something? She couldn't think what.

Then one lunchtime she'd noticed him spot her and veer away. Gray was avoiding her, and a nasty little voice in her head gave the reason for all his excuses – *He doesn't want to be seen with the dead girl.*

She gave up trying to speak with him after that, even though she still noticed him, wherever he was. Today she had noticed his absence.

Isis looked at Jess. Why had Mrs Craven partnered them together?

"It's not fair!" Jess had wailed, when Mrs Craven pointed to Isis's table. "Why do I have to go with *her*?"

"Isis has no one to work with," said Mrs Craven.

Jess huffed a sigh, grabbing her paper and stamping over to Isis, sitting down opposite her with a thump.

"We all know why you're on your own," hissed Jess. She slapped her paper on the table, lifting her pen. "Let's get this over with."

Isis looked down at her own sheet. It was printed with a series of questions which, according to Mrs Craven, would help them choose their course options later in the year. Most were obvious variations on 'What do you want to do when you grow up?'

"You go first!" snarled Jess. Isis took a breath, about to read the question aloud when she tasted a taint in the air. Dirty and pungent, like damp and peeling wallpaper. Her stomach clenched, her shoulders stiffened.

Why wouldn't he leave her *alone*?

Mandeville was everywhere these days. In classrooms and corridors. Standing in shop windows as she walked home. He'd appeared in a corner of the library during a wet lunch break, leaving an entire shelf of history books dog-eared and yellowing afterwards. During a geography lesson, she'd had to focus desperately on the teacher, because he'd been wafting around the class, sending pupil after pupil into convulsions of sneezing. He was often in the playground, waving a skeletal hand or smiling at her through his snaggle-teeth. The little aeroplane boy had squeaked the first time he saw Mandeville, running straight through a wall and disappearing; Isis hadn't seen him since.

And now Mandeville was materialising right next to her, dustily congealing onto the plastic school chair. He was much too tall for it, and forced to draw his knees up, his green-grey skin showing through the threads of his trousers.

Isis shifted in her seat, facing away from him as much as she could. If only she could run out of the classroom. Run out of school!

She glued her gaze to the paper.

"Who do you think has the better job?" she read, trying not to cough. "A lawyer or a car mechanic?"

"Whatever," answered Jess. "A lawyer, because they earn loads of money." She gave a sudden shiver, rubbing her arms. "Why is it so cold in here?"

"Is this girl one of your friends?" asked Mandeville, surveying Jess with his ice-blue eyes.

Isis ignored him. "A mechanic makes people happy

though," she said to Jess, "when they fix people's cars. My mum thinks her mechanic is great. She says he keeps her on the road."

Jess answered Isis without looking at her. "Your car must be a heap of rubbish, then. A lawyer can just buy a new car, so they don't need mechanics." She wrote 'lawyer' on her sheet of paper, next to the question.

"What a charming girl," said Mandeville.

"Go away!" Isis mouthed at him, not making a sound.

Mandeville tilted his head. "All I want to do is help you."

Jess ran her finger along the next question on the sheet. "What kind of job would you like?" she read. "This is so lame!" Her eyes flicked up to Isis. "Go on then, what job do you want to do? Something that makes people happy?" Mandeville tutted and Jess coughed, scowling a little deeper. "I think you're making me ill."

"Isn't she delightful?" said Mandeville. "She reminds me of my descendants, and why I never visit them."

Go away! Isis wanted to shout, except she couldn't even admit he was there.

"I don't know what I want to do," Isis said to Jess. It was hard to imagine doing any normal job, with Angel and

Mandeville around. "Maybe. . . something where you can be by yourself?"

She instantly regretted her words, because Jess laughed and said, "You've got that already! Is that why you're so creepy, so you can be alone all the time?"

"I'm not creepy," said Isis, but Jess only laughed again.

"*Unique* is the word I would use to describe you," said Mandeville. "No one else here has your talents, my dear."

"*I* know!" said Jess, pointing her pen at Isis. "You could work for the council, emptying dog poo bins! You'd *definitely* be by yourself, and you wouldn't stink much worse than you do now!"

"I'm not doing that!" said Isis, fighting back tears. She wasn't going to cry, not here.

"Dog poo dead girl," said Jess, smiling nastily.

"What do *you* want to do, then?" asked Isis. "You couldn't be a lawyer, you have to be clever for that."

Jess's smile vanished. "Write what you want," she said, "you'll still end up doing something pathetic. *I'm* going to be rich, and live in a big house and have loads of designer clothes."

"But what *job* will you do?"

Jess shrugged. "I'll probably win *The X Factor* or something." She wrote 'earn lots of money' as her answer.

Mandeville reached out a long arm and tapped Jess's pen with a bony finger. The nib seemed to disintegrate, the plastic becoming aged and brittle. Ink smeared across the paper and over Jess's hand.

"Hey!" she cried.

"She used to be such a sweet, caring girl," said Mandeville. "How sad the way she has changed."

Isis turned and glared, trying to show with a flick of her eyes that he should get lost.

"Doubtless you don't believe me," said Mandeville, "but we need only ask her family."

He turned and cupped his hands to his mouth. Isis could see his mouth move, as if he were calling out, but there was no sound. A shape began to form behind him, a new smell filling the air, oddly mixed of wet clay and roses. The ghost of a tall woman was materialising in the classroom, her presence wavering and uncertain. Isis could see her short grey hair, pale eyes, and the long scarf draped around her shoulders. As the woman turned her head, looking at Jess, a warm smile spread over her face. The woman's mouth moved, but Isis couldn't hear what she was saying.

"What are you *doing?*" Isis hissed at Mandeville.

Jess looked up, unaware of the ghosts. "I'm doing this stupid exercise. What are *you* doing?"

"Allow me to introduce Jess's grandmother," said Mandeville. "A lady named Marie. Jess used to call her Gran Marie."

"*Gran Marie?*" said Isis, too surprised to be silent.

"What?" asked Jess.

Mandeville leaned in close to Isis. "She wants to pass on a message to your little friend."

Isis could see the other ghost speaking, but she couldn't hear what the woman was saying. There was a sense of enormous distance between her and Jess's grandmother, very different from the ghosts Isis normally saw. As if the woman was speaking from somewhere else. As if she was thousands of miles away.

Jess glared at Isis. "Why did you say 'Gran Marie'?"

Isis could feel herself blushing. "No reason. . . I mean, the words just popped into my head."

"Gran. . . my grandmother died two years ago," said Jess. "Don't you dare talk about her!"

Mandeville poked Isis, delivering a frost-cold shot into her shoulder. "You should give Jess her grandmother's message," he whispered. "It might help Jessica remember the sweet child she was, instead of the bully she has become. You could steer her in a whole new direction. With just a few words, you could change her life."

Isis looked into his eyes, gleaming only a few centimetres from her own. They were distant blue stars, and he was as cold as space.

"She was an artist," Mandeville whispered.

Isis looked at Jess, and her lips formed the words. "She was an artist."

Jess's mouth opened.

Mandeville whispered in Isis's ear. "Whenever Jessica visited, her grandmother would take her into her studio. Marie would work on her paintings, and young Jessica would play with bits of paint, and do her own childish drawings. They made one particular piece together. A collage of flowers."

"You made a picture of flowers with her," said Isis, following his lead. But this wasn't like the Devourer; Mandeville wasn't making her speak. She simply wanted to wipe away that look of scorn that Jess turned on her every day. "You both signed the picture, you and your grandmother. She had it framed and you were going to hang it on your bedroom wall, but your dad never got around to it. Now it's under your bed."

Jess's pen fell flat on the paper.

"Your grandmother always thought you were very talented," Isis went on. "She said you could be an artist yourself when you grew up."

Jess was staring at her. "How do you know that?" she said, her voice not much more than a squeak. "Who told you?"

"She doesn't want you to waste your talent," said Isis. The words were kind, but there was no kindness to her voice.

"You see?" whispered Mandeville. "It's not so hard, is it?"

Jess's hand was over her mouth; her eyes were round and white-rimmed.

"You *died*!" she said through her fingers. "Something happened to you when you died, didn't it?"

The blood drained from Isis's face and her mind was suddenly clear again.

"Oh my God!" squeaked Jess. "You can speak to the dead, can't you?"

Isis couldn't talk. Shock tingled through her.

What had she done?

Behind Mandeville, the figure of the woman was fading, melting into the air. Her mouth opened and she said something.

"Thank you," said Mandeville, repeating her words.

Jess stood up, her chair scraping back loudly. "I want to move!" she shouted. "I'm not sitting with *her*!"

Chapter Seven

Gray

Of course, Mum took me to the hospital.

"I don't care what the paramedic said, I want you properly checked over."

We had to drive to A & E, and since I didn't even look ill we had to wait for everyone else to get seen first, which took hours.

"It's probably an inner ear infection," said the A & E doctor, after he'd finally checked me over. "Your ears contain your balance system as well as your hearing, so a viral infection can make everything go a bit haywire. It's not very pleasant, but you'll be fine in a few days."

My mum folded her arms, and gave him one of her looks.

"Did his whole class have an inner ear infection?" she said.

"I'm sorry?"

"I told you already, my son was on a field trip when his whole class was affected by rocks or dust or something. All the children were throwing up afterwards. That's why I brought him here, not for you to tell me he's got a virus!"

"Well, I don't have any information about that," said the doctor, "and his symptoms are consistent. . ."

"Has he been poisoned by gas?" snapped Mum.

"It wasn't gas," I reminded her. "It was dust, I told you."

Mum turned to the doctor. "Has he been poisoned by dust?"

The doctor was looking a bit frazzled. "This really seems like a viral infection," he said.

"Then I want a second opinion," said Mum.

"I can't find anything wrong with your son," said the doctor, really patronisingly. "His temperature and blood pressure are normal; he has no lumps, bumps or unusual spots. He said he felt dizzy and sick earlier without any vomiting, which is consistent with an inner ear infection."

They glared at each other and I was worried Mum really would make us wait to see another doctor, which would have meant being here hours longer.

"I'm fine now, Mum," I said. "Can we just go home?"

"I suggest he gets rest and plenty of fluids," said the doctor, "and go to your GP in a week if it hasn't cleared up by itself."

Mum glared at me like it was my fault, and we left. All the way home she muttered stuff about stupid doctors. . .

Doctors.

Hang on, you're the doctor, aren't you? The one from the hospital where Isis died. You asked me loads of questions then as well.

I was expecting this; you are beginning to remember events from your previous hypnotic state. Yes, I was in the hospital.

I forgot all about talking to you in the hospital. Why did I forget?

For the same reason you will forget this conversation when it is ended. You will only remember coming to this office, and having a rather dull session with a rather dull therapist.

Now I'd like you to get back to telling your story. That's right, look at me, don't fight it. . .

I woke up the next day feeling fine. But Mum must have been worried because I got the day off school and she didn't even hassle me to get up. Normally she's on at me from the crack of dawn, but that day I didn't even get dressed until lunchtime. I guess by then she'd held off for as long as she could manage.

"How are you feeling?" she asked, putting her head round the living room door.

"Fine," I said, because I wasn't thinking.

"Well then, maybe you should do something?"

I looked round at her. "I'm watching telly."

"I mean actual activity. Why don't you go outside for a bit?"

Sometimes I think Mum hasn't got over me not being eight any more. She still wants me to rush out into the garden and play football, like that'll solve everything.

"There's nothing to do in the garden."

"There's fresh air," she said, "and moving around."

"The doctor said I should rest."

Mum made a pretty rude comment about doctors, and started on about how fresh air is the best medicine. I don't know where she even gets that from, but she nagged on so much that I couldn't listen to the telly. In the end I got up.

"All right then. But only for ten minutes."

"Half an hour."

"Don't blame me if I have a relapse."

"I'll call an ambulance if you do."

Mum's always that way, you know? It's like she has some internal timer which flips her over from caring to sarcastic.

So I went outside. There really isn't anything to Mum's garden. It's just about big enough for a washing line, a few scraggly plants, an apple tree that's never really grown and a rockery that Brian made her for one birthday. It was quite good when he did it, with big lumps of stone and little plants growing through. I wonder if he was trying to make a point, seeing how Dad's a landscape gardener. Anyway, none of us has ever weeded it, and now it's just a pile of rocks and dandelions.

I went and sat on one of the rocks. If I had even slightly normal parents, I could've been out there for ages – playing games on my phone, texting my mates, stuff like that. But since my dad's a conspiracy-theory nut who freaks out if anyone even mentions me getting a phone, all I could do was, well, nothing. Not even as much as when I was in the living room, because now I wasn't watching telly. Just looking at the air and thinking, you know?

I was so still, after a few minutes the birds forgot I was there and started hopping back out of the undergrowth. There's nothing special in our garden, just blackbirds and sparrows. The blackbirds must've had a late brood, because there was a fledgling hopping around near the fence. It had most of its proper feathers, but still a few tufty ones poking through, and it was sitting in the grass cheeping, while its mum and dad flew in and out of the garden with caterpillars in their beaks. I got into watching, and that's why I didn't notice anyone coming up behind me.

Yooooo. . .

I stopped breathing.

Yooooo. . .

I turned around, my heart beating like mad. On a stone

right behind me was a pale figure, drifting up from the ground. It was the colour of scratched glass and smaller than me by a metre. The things at the quarry hadn't really had a shape, but this one did have something like a face. Two dark smudges and another below: eyes and a mouth.

Yoooo. . . Yoooo. . .

"What do you want?" I whispered, but it didn't answer, only turned a bit of itself into an arm and reached out with it.

I ran as fast as I ever have, flat-out full speed for the house. I lurched at the back door, flinging myself inside and slamming it shut behind me. The Yale lock clicked and I leaned against it, breathing in gasps.

Then I thought, *Don't stay by the door!* I mean, if you've ever seen any films, you know that's the worst place to be. I jumped away, ran into the kitchen and looked for something I could use to defend myself. Except I had no idea what would even work.

I went back to the door, put myself a couple of metres away from it and held up the frying pan.

Nothing.

I waited.

Still nothing.

Mum came out of the living room. "What are you doing?"

I lowered the pan.

"Um, you know."

She raised an eyebrow. "I don't. What are you up to?"

"Honestly, nothing."

Mum narrowed her eyes and looked at the back door. She walked towards it.

"No, don't!"

Mum completely ignored me, which she always does when she thinks she's on to something I've done wrong. She put her hand on the lock, turned it back.

"No! Mum, there's a. . ."

She looked me, properly challenging. "A what, Gray?"

"A rat," I said, desperate. "I saw a rat in the garden."

Mum pulled her lips tight, and for a moment I thought I'd convinced her. Then she flipped the lock and whipped the back door open.

A square of daylight, the straggly greens of our garden. Mum peered out.

I took a careful step towards the door, hardly daring to breathe.

"If I find out you are up to something. . ." said Mum, and then she walked out of the back door, right into the garden.

I stood frozen. Then I realised, in films that's the bit where she gets eaten, and I couldn't just say inside and watch it happen, could I? I rushed out after her, frying pan up and ready.

"I can't see any sign of a rat," said Mum. I ran the length of the garden, looking for the strange ghostly shape. "Mind you, with all the bins out in the alley, I wouldn't be surprised. Mrs Jenkins' dog is always at the bags, breaking them open, no matter what she says about it being foxes. . ."

I even clambered onto the rockery and looked in the nettley gap behind it. Nothing, just our wobbly fence and the apple tree. And a little boy standing next to me.

I held my breath, staring at him.

Mum poked her foot at an ancient Frisbee that was lying in the grass. "You need to tidy up a bit out here," she said. Not, "Who's that little boy?"

He looked about. . . I don't know, five? Hair cropped really short, sticky-out ears. He was wearing jeans and a Power Rangers T-shirt, and he was staring up at me, his eyes really big and round, that way little children can. He looked scared, but also. . . familiar. Like I'd met him before or something.

Huuuurrr, he said, like a groan, *tinggg*.

Mum didn't even react, just carried on about how I ought to start looking after the garden.

"After all, you're the one who uses it most, and you're old enough to use a lawnmower."

I lowered the frying pan; I mean, you can't whack a little kid, can you?

"How about you start today?" said Mum. "Since you're feeling better."

She couldn't see the little boy at all. Only I could.

He stretched out his hand. *Huuuuuurrrr*, he groaned, *tinng*.

I took a step back, but the little boy didn't move. He was motionless, like a freeze-frame.

"Mum," I said, trying to sound normal, "can we go back inside?"

She peered at me. "There are no rats out here, so don't think you can just slob in front of the telly. If you're well enough to run around, you can help me with some chores."

"Fine," I said, not taking my eyes off the little boy. "Whatever."

Mum gave me a really suspicious look, but she still walked back inside. I took another slow step away from the little boy, and then I couldn't stay calm any more and I ran straight for the house. As I reached the door I glanced back, and the little boy had vanished.

"You can start by dusting the living room," said Mum, and for once in my life I was happy to, you know? As long as I was in the house, where everything was normal.

Mum's living room is really different to Dad's. The sofa's comfy and there are cushions everywhere. She has loads of little things on the shelves as well, like candles, vases with coloured twigs in, and photos. Ones of Gran and Granddad, my aunt and cousins, Mum and Brian on the beach, a dog Mum had when she was little, all that. There are photos of me too, about ten of them, starting when I was a baby. I've seen them so often I don't even notice them any more, they're just part of the background of the room. But as I wiped the shelf, my mind still on what had just happened, one of the photos made me stop completely still. It was in a silver frame, of me standing proudly in my school uniform, the day I started primary school.

Everything went a bit dark around me and all I could hear was my own breathing.

The little boy in the back garden, he looked exactly like me. Me when I was five. Even down to the haircut, even down to the sticky-out ears.

I picked up the photo and stared at it.

Exactly. Definitely.

Just like me.

Chapter Eight

Isis

Isis felt like her mum and Gil set out to ruin her weekend.
Gil turned up at the flat on Saturday morning, and he and
Cally were obviously making up for not seeing each other:
they filled up the sofa, filled up the living room. Isis didn't
have anything against Gil, but this felt like an invasion. She
retreated into her bedroom and tried reading, but it was
hard with all the giggling and kissing going on.

Her parents had never been like that when they were
still together, it had mostly been shouting. After her dad
left, Isis used to ask Cally where he was, and mark all his
trips onto a world map pinned to her bedroom wall. A
way of being with him, and kind of exciting too, to think
of her dad in all those exotic places so far away.

Then one day she'd done an online search and found half a dozen companies running cruises around Europe, some of them even taking tours around the coast of Great Britain. Why hadn't her dad found a job on one of those?

Isis knew other children whose parents were divorced, but their mums and dads still talked and got on. Perhaps her parents had been too in love to be friends afterwards? She'd heard that could happen.

Isis imagined her dad walking into the flat now and stopping in horror at the sight of Cally and Gil snogging away. He'd ask what they thought they were *doing*, with his daughter only in the next room? Then he and Isis would leave, and he'd take her for an ice cream.

She sighed and reached for her mp3 player, pushing the earphones firmly into her ears. Dad wasn't coming to take her for ice cream; he'd never even been to this flat. He was thousands of miles away, sailing around the holiday resorts and entertaining the tourists, like always.

"I want to play with dollies," Angel announced, her voice piercing straight through the headphones. She was pointing up at Isis's old dolls, lined up on a high shelf.

Isis looked up from her book, unplugging one earphone. She shook her head. "Not now."

Angel put little fists on transparent hips. "But I can't by my *own*."

Which was true – Angel couldn't lift or move any of the dolls. So Isis had to do the actual playing, with Angel directing.

Isis shook her head again and went back to reading, but Angel clambered up onto the bed, then onto Isis's back. She started jumping, each jump accompanied by the word "Dollies!" Angel had no weight, and Isis tried to ignore her for a minute or two, but it was hard to carry on reading throughout Angel's jumping – every time she landed, her feet sent two cold shocks through Isis's back.

Isis put her book down. "All right then."

And so she found herself arranging the dolls into a tea party, while Angel shouted orders. "No tea for her. She naughty!"

As the day wore on, Isis waited desperately for the sound of the front door closing to tell her Gil had gone. But instead, at about five in the evening, Cally tapped on her door and poked her head around. She was smiling, her cheeks a little flushed.

"Isis, do you mind if Gil. . . stays the night?" There was a lightness to her voice, as if she'd just finished laughing.

Isis felt herself cringe, even at the thought of it. Plus that would mean he'd be in the flat tomorrow as well, and then who knew when he'd leave?

"Does he have to?" Isis asked, her voice flat.

The smile dropped off Cally's face. "Well, I suppose he doesn't. It's just I haven't seen him for such a long time. . ."

"You didn't *want* to see him," Isis pointed out. "You told me you never wanted to again."

Cally flinched. "Yes, I know. But now we've talked, and I can see that what happened in August wasn't his fault."

"A monster do-ed it," said Angel, from her place by the dolls.

Isis didn't answer Angel, or her mum either. Surely Cally could work out what this was like for Isis?

"Please," said Cally. "I didn't realise how much I've missed him."

"Mummy been sad," Angel said, nodding wisely. "Now Mummy happy."

Isis sighed. "All right then."

And there was always the chance of. . .

"Will Gray come over tomorrow?" she asked, trying to sound casual.

Cally shook her head. "His mum's being careful. She's keeping him at home, so Gil's going to pop over there in the afternoon."

Isis's feelings must have been obvious on her face.

"I'm sorry, darling," said Cally, "but I'd be the same if you'd been ill."

Cally came into the room a little further then, stepping carefully around the dolls. Angel squeaked out of the way.

"Are you sure you feel all right? You've been in here all day." Cally glanced at the floor. "Haven't you grown out of these?"

Isis blushed. "I was just. . . checking them. I'm fine."

Cally peered at her. "Well if you're sure. . . I'm just concerned because of you going on that school trip. The school says it's nothing to worry about, but why did they call the ambulances then? Gray told Gil that the woman from the mining company really flew off the handle when someone asked if they were mining radioactive rocks."

"I don't think they'd have let us go on a school trip there if the quarry was radioactive," said Isis uncertainly.

"Well, Gil says you shouldn't be surprised at anything big business does. He says it's really suspicious that the school and the hospital are down-playing it so much. He says that only proves something's going on."

"It could just be that there really was nothing," said Isis.

Cally shook her head. "Gil says the mining company's probably bought them off, or put pressure on somehow. He's says they'll get round the parents next, offering money or threatening them. His phone is set up to record every call he receives – that way he'll have proof."

Isis didn't say anything.

"I'm sure Gil's right," said Cally defensively. "He knows a lot about this kind of thing."

"Yeah," said Isis. She didn't care what Gil knew.

The school bell was ringing as Isis walked into her form room on Monday morning. She'd been dreading this moment since Friday – it had loomed over her weekend, turning everything into a countdown. She went the long way round the classroom to her desk, past the usual muddle and noise of everyone getting to their seats and settling down. The route meant she could avoid Jess's gang, but Jess still watched her the whole time.

Isis sat down. Now she felt genuinely sick; she wouldn't even be pretending if she said she was ill. She could put up her hand, tell Mrs Craven that she felt unwell. Jess was obviously planning something.

Isis looked down at her desk, studying the patterns of scratches in the grey tabletop and trying to work out if feeling sick would be enough to get out of class. Maybe if she made a fuss, then went to the toilet and put her fingers down her throat? She'd never tried it, but everyone said. . .

Mrs Craven was taking the register, calling names and ticking them off. She broke into a cough, which ended with a sneeze.

Isis snapped her head up. Just behind Mrs Craven, a dirty cloud was dancing in slow spirals. The posters on the nearby wall began to crinkle around the edges as if soaking with damp, and by the time Mrs Craven finished the register they had all fallen onto the floor with papery slithers.

"Oh!" said Mrs Craven, picking up the posters and

coughing again as she passed through Mandeville. He waved long fingers at Isis.

Go away go away go away.

But no amount of thinking would make him leave. He slid across the classroom, his arms and legs blurred at the edges. Softly he blended into the centre of Jess's table, his upper body cut through by the plastic. The group of girls were talking, taking advantage of Mrs Craven's distraction.

Mandeville nodded at Jess and politely lifted his fez. There were only a few wisps of hair on his scalp and his skull gleamed white through his skin.

"Your grandmother sends her best wishes," he said to her.

One of Jess's friends sneezed, and another pulled the sleeves of her jumper down.

Mandeville looked over at Isis, his eyes lit in blue as if closer than the rest of him.

"Poor girl," he said. "She can't see or hear me, so she is left without the comfort she might gain from her grandmother's love."

Isis pulled her bag onto her desk, opening it up and

pretending to search for something inside. He wasn't going to trick her again!

The bell rang for the start of lessons, and Isis pushed to the door, wanting to get out as quickly as possible. She moved along the corridor as fast as she could without breaking into a run. She didn't look back; she was focused on getting to the next classroom before anyone else. They had French, with Mrs Potter. Jess wouldn't try anything on in there – Mrs Potter was known for sending people off to see the head.

Isis was almost at the door of the classroom when she felt a hand tap her back.

"Isis!" It was Jess.

"Go away!" snapped Isis, not even looking round. Jess was probably wearing one of her nasty smiles and flanked by her little gang. But when Isis did turn, she saw Jess was on her own, breathing hard. Her eyes were wide, and she was chewing her lip.

"I'm sorry," Jess said quickly, "about Friday. Will you sit with me today?"

Isis studied Jess's face, trying to see the signs of whatever cruel joke she was working up to.

"You never want to sit with me," said Isis.

Now Jess's gang were coming up behind them, giggling about something as they walked. Isis had no idea what they were talking about, but she felt sure it was her.

She shook her head at Jess. "No thanks."

She went into the classroom, heading for a seat at the back, but Jess followed, and when Isis sat down, Jess sat next to her. Jess's little gang hovered at their usual table, uncertain, and looking their way. Isis was staring at Jess too. When would the joke hit?

"I'm sitting with Isis today," Jess said to the others. Isis would've smiled at their shocked faces if she hadn't felt so anxious. The other girls muttered together as they sat down. Maybe Jess hadn't told them what she was planning?

"On Friday Mrs Craven had to *make* you sit next to me," Isis whispered.

Jess's eyes flicked down and she fiddled with her pen, twizzling it in her fingers. "No one's making me sit here now."

Isis didn't know how to answer that. So she sat silently, tense and untrusting, as the class settled down. Mrs Potter announced they would be learning sporting vocabulary. Voices broke out again and the room filled with the sound of ruffling paper as the teacher handed around photo-copied sheets.

"Practise the first column of words with your partners," said Mrs Potter.

Isis studied the words, trying to pretend everything was normal.

"*Jouer a tennis*," she said.

"*Jouer a tennis*," repeated Jess.

Isis's finger was on the next word, but she couldn't say it.

"What do you *want*?" she hissed.

Jess glanced around, then whispered back. "I want you to tell me more about Gran Marie."

For a moment Isis was too surprised to answer, then she shook her head.

"I don't know what you mean."

This had to be it. Jess was getting her own back somehow. Except she was chewing her lip, and her voice was hesitant.

"Those things you told me on Friday," she said. "I've been thinking about them all weekend."

Now Isis rolled out the words she'd been practising.

"It was just a joke. I shouldn't have said that stuff, but I don't like being called 'dead girl'."

In her mind they'd sounded firm and she'd even imagined that she might be able to erase the nickname, but now her voice quavered as she spoke, and worse, Jess didn't believe her.

"I hardly ever speak to you," Jess said, "and I've never told you about Gran Marie. I've never told *anyone* at school what she said about me being good at art. So how could you know that?"

Isis lifted her paper up in front of her face, desperately staring at the writing. *What now?*

"We have to do the vocab," she said. Maybe Jess would get bored, maybe she'd go away? "*Jouer a football.*"

But a familiar smell of damp was building. A fibrous, sooty dew blackened the spare chair at their table, condensing into Mandeville.

"How are we proceeding?" he asked, nodding at Jess.

Jess pulled Isis's paper down. "*Please*, can't you talk to Gran Marie again?" Her lower lip was sore and red where she'd been biting it.

"I wonder what this spiteful young person could want?"

asked Mandeville, leaning in close to Isis. "To gain access to her grandmother's inheritance? Or find out a nasty secret?"

"Mum and Dad never listen to me," said Jess, "and I used to talk to Gran Marie about everything." Tears gleamed in Jess's eyes, her chin wobbled.

Mandeville clapped his hands, the bones of his long fingers clattering together.

"A miracle is performed! The bully becomes a kinder, better person." He pressed a bony cold hand onto Isis's. "*This* is the power of the medium, my dear. *This* is the good work you are turning your back on. You think being a psychic is about the dead, but it is all for the living."

Isis pulled her hand away, shuddering at the cold. Jess must have felt the chill too, because she rubbed her arms. Then she stopped, her eyes widening.

"I read on the internet – spirits and ghosts are freezing cold, aren't they?"

Isis opened her mouth, then shut it again. Panic sang through her mind.

"Is she here?" asked Jess. "Is she?"

"Please stop talking," Mrs Potter called out. "We'll work

together on how to use these words in everyday sentences."

Almost gasping with relief, Isis turned to face the white-board, looking away from Jess and the elderly ghost. But Mandeville whispered in Isis's ear.

"What will you do? Hide the truth of your power and undo all the good you have stirred – or carry on?"

"I miss her so much," whispered Jess. "Can you talk to her for me?"

Isis stared at Mrs Potter, not hearing a word the teacher was saying. Could Mandeville be right? Might this be her chance to turn something that had always seemed a burden into something good?

She turned around. "At break time," she whispered. "I'll try."

Chapter Nine

Isis

Raindrops pattered and slid down the classroom window. Outside, the playing field was darkened by mud and the line of birch trees at the end of the field were drooping under the rain, their leaves in murky greens and yellows, waiting to fall.

Isis turned away from the drab outdoors. The classroom was warm and bright with artificial light, cosy compared to the beginnings of autumn outside. Normally Isis hated wet break times, but normally she had to sit on her own, or at a table with the other outcasts.

Isis smiled.

"That's so rubbish! Pink and sparkles are for little girls. I saw a purple one that had these black flowers on." Jess was arguing with Hayley about phone covers. Both of them wanted new ones, even though as far as Isis could see there was nothing wrong with what they'd got.

"What do you think, Isis?" asked Jess. "Isn't pink for babies?"

Isis was sitting with Jess and her gang. On their table. She'd been included for nearly two weeks now, and not because a teacher had made them, but because they'd asked her to. Well, Jess had, and the others did what Jess wanted.

"My mum buys me pink stuff," said Isis.

"See!" cried Jess. "*Isis* agrees with me. You definitely should not get a pink one."

"She didn't say that!" said Hayley.

"If your *mum* chooses pink, you definitely shouldn't!" said Jess. She laughed, and after a moment Hayley laughed too.

"Yeah, I suppose you're right."

"You can't let your mum choose anything!" said Jess.

"Or you get jumpers with fluffy bobbles on," agreed Chloe.

"Frilly dresses," said Nafira, rolling her eyes.

"My mum does that too," said Isis, although she'd never really cared what her mum bought. It had always been the least of her worries, and Cally hardly ever had the money to go shopping. But Isis didn't say that; it felt much nicer going along with things.

Last night, she'd asked her mum if she could go round to Jess's at the weekend.

"Jess?" asked Cally. "I haven't met her, have I?"

"She's my new friend." The words had felt luscious. She'd wanted to keep on saying them.

Isis looked at the girls on the table. Jess, Hayley, Chloe, Nafira. They were all popular and Isis was spending lunchtime with them, instead of watching from across the room. It was like a hug, sitting here. Like warmth after years of cold.

The conversation wound away from phone cases on to shoes, then to a song Hayley liked. Isis didn't say much, she mostly listened, learning this new language of girls together. Basking.

An older girl came into the room, looking around. Isis didn't recognise her; she was probably on an errand or searching out a younger brother or sister. Then she spotted Jess, waved, and walked towards them. Jess waved back.

"Hi, Summer."

"Hi," Summer said to Jess. Everyone at their table stopped talking. Summer's eyes glanced across them with narrowed interest. "Which one is her?"

Jess pointed at Isis.

"Hi," Summer said to Isis. Only to Isis.

"Hello," said Isis quietly. What was going on?

"You're the girl who was dead? The one who sees ghosts?"

Isis felt sick, her throat tightening. She stared at Jess, who only smiled.

"Yes, she is!" squealed Hayley, hands flapping. "She is *amazing*! She sees ghosts *all the time*, and she gave Jess a message from her gran, who's been dead for two whole years!"

"*And* she knew loads about my uncle," said Nafira, "and he died *ten* years ago!"

"She knew *everything* about him," agreed Chloe.

Jess nodded, proud of Isis.

Summer ignored all of them, focusing on Isis. "I want you to do the ghost thing for me," she said.

Isis pulled into her chair, hands gripping tight to the

seat. She searched around the room but there was no hint of Mandeville. And even if he'd been here. . .

"I can't," she said, "not in front of everyone."

Jess stood up. "We can go into the toilets." Her hand was on Isis's arm, tugging her to standing.

"But I. . ." *don't want to. Don't even know her.*

"Come on, Isis," said Jess, smiling. "Summer's in Year *Eleven*."

The older girl nodded. "You can hang out with us after, if you want." Although the way she said it was flat, like a lie.

Jess's smile only shifted a little, but Hayley, Chloe and Nafira all jumped up, talking at once.

"Oh *wow*!"

"Can you get us in the Senior Common Room?"

"It might not work," said Isis, pulling back on Jess's grip.

Jess laughed artificially, looking at the older girl. "Isis always says that, but it works every time. She's amazing!"

Isis wanted to shake her head, she wanted to refuse. But over at the back of the classroom was the table where she used to sit, often alone. For a moment she had a double view: herself now, here with Jess and her friends; herself sitting back there, watching from a distance.

She took a breath, and nodded.

"And where are you all going?" asked the teaching assistant as they headed for the door.

"They're trying out for drama club. I came to get them," lied Summer, looking straight at the woman.

"Oh, okay then." She went back to her marking, uninterested.

They hurried Isis down the corridor. Summer was silent, the others were giggling. When they reached the girls' toilet they all crammed through the door. High frosted windows lit the room and the five empty cubicles. White tiles covered the walls from floor to ceiling, sharpening every sound. Isis caught their reflections in the mirrors: some laughing, some serious.

"So what happens now?" asked Summer, scowling. "Are we supposed to sit in a circle or something? Cos I'm not sitting on the floor in *here*."

"Isis doesn't need tricks like that, do you?" Jess smiled.

Isis shook her head. In the mirror, her reflection was pale, her eyes dark with anxiety.

"I've never done this for a stranger before," she whispered to Jess, but her words bounced back from the walls.

Summer studied her. "Is this just a load of rubbish? Are you all playing some stupid game?"

"No!" said Chloe.

"It's not rubbish!" snapped Jess, looking fiercely at the older girl.

Hayley flapped her hands. "Honestly, Isis is *amazing*!"

Isis felt the warmth of them. Her friends, standing up for her. She had to prove she was worth it, she couldn't go back – but there was a problem.

Mandeville.

Where was he? He'd been following her around almost constantly, and now when she needed him. . .

Summer's frown hadn't softened, and the others were all looking at Isis expectantly.

"Don't worry," said Jess encouragingly, "you'll be *great*!"

Isis lifted a little with the praise, but it didn't help. There was no sign of Mandeville, or any other ghost.

"I've. . . seen ghosts in the playground," she said to Summer, "and in the old hall there's the ghost of a teacher. He's always shouting."

Summer folded her arms. "Is that it? Stories? *I* can make stuff up."

Jess shook her head. "No! She can tell you things!" She glared at Isis. "Go *on*."

But without Mandeville she didn't know anything about Summer. He was the one able to call the ghosts of relatives from whatever faraway realm they were in, and even then it didn't always work. Isis had asked why and Mandeville told her that not every spirit heard when he called out to them. Only the ones still interested in the living would come through.

"The others are too far away," he said, refusing to explain further and looking shifty.

They'd struck lucky twice, with Jess and Nafira, but even if Summer had any ghostly relations who were willing to talk, Isis didn't have a clue how to reach them without Mandeville.

She tried to think.

"I just have to. . ." She pushed open one of the toilet doors and flung herself into the cubicle, bolting it quickly behind her.

"What's she doing now?" Summer snapped.

"I don't know," said Jess. She knocked on the door. "Isis?"

Isis leaned against it.

"Mandeville," she whispered silently. "Mandeville!" Nothing.

"Forget it," said Summer, her footsteps heading for the door.

"No, honestly, she really can see ghosts!"

"What are you doing?" Jess hissed through the door.

"I'll be ready in a sec," called Isis.

"She's a bit nervous," Jess said, and Isis heard Summer's footsteps returning, accompanied by a sigh.

"Mandeville," Isis whispered again, "*please*."

"Isis, are you ready?" Jess would never forgive Isis if she mucked things up now.

A drip fell into the toilet bowl from the ceiling. It plinked loudly, clouding the water. Isis glanced up. The drop had fallen from one of the stains in the ceiling; moisture glistened across the dull white paint, bubbling through the plaster. One drop became another, then another. Water plinked into the toilet bowl, quicker and quicker, the stain growing wetter, the plaster bulging and sagging above her head. Something must be overflowing in the room above this one.

Before she could move, a soggy crack ripped across the ceiling, a rush of putrid smelling water pouring through. Instinctively she ducked, hands over her head, eyes screwed shut. Freezing, sewage-stinking water smashed over her, getting into her ears and mouth. Isis shut her mouth, desperately trying not to swallow any.

In moments the rush of water faded to a last few drips. Isis lifted up her head, opening her eyes.

She wasn't wet.

Overhead, the ceiling was whole and unblemished, the floor wasn't even damp. Standing out of the toilet, like a tall bony heron, was Mandeville.

"Not the most salubrious location for a seance," said the ghost. "Yet I am grateful for any progress." He stepped out of the toilet.

"You finished now?" Jess called.

"Our audience awaits," said Mandeville, smiling. "I'd open the door for you, but I am no poltergeist."

Isis unbolted the door. She dropped her shoulders, lengthening her neck, trying to copy the way Cally stood on stage. Then she pulled open the cubicle door, staring directly at Summer as she spoke the strange, familiar words she'd heard Cally say so many times.

"The spirits are listening. Is there anyone you want to speak with?"

Chapter Ten

Isis

Isis was with Jess and the other girls, queuing for lunch in the canteen. They shuffled in the line, in their own little group, self-contained and talking among themselves. Isis knew the eyes of other students were on them, more today than yesterday, more yesterday than the day before, and the week before that.

Interest in their group had been growing ever since her seance for Summer. Jess had organised other seances in the toilets and the more hidden corners of the playground, and Summer had made good on her promise to let them hang out with the older girls. Isis smiled to herself, still not quite able to believe the way Jess had changed things around, so that what been a curse was now a blessing.

The girls sat down and Isis ate quickly, which was the complete opposite of all the lunches she'd had before joining Jess's group. In the past, the food on her plate had given her something to do. The canteen had been safer from bullies than hanging about the edges of the playground, and less lonely than reading a book by herself in the library.

It was so different now, as she hurried to eat. Lunch break was their busiest time.

"Are you finished yet?" Jess asked, when Isis was only halfway through her potato.

Mandeville materialised next to Nafira, starting as a smudge in the air and a smell of damp.

"Ugh," Nafira said, spitting out a mouthful of apple. "This is all rotten inside."

Mandeville waggled his fingers at Isis in greeting. "Are we ready?" he asked.

Isis shoved in a last mouthful of baked beans, then nodded at Jess, who was rubbing her arms without noticing.

"Come on," Jess said. "I told them to meet us in the gap between the old hall and the science building. No one ever goes there."

Chloe pulled a face. "It's always wet down there, even in summer."

Hayley didn't look happy either. "Tommo said he saw a rat run across. . ."

"Your friend has such charming choices of venue," muttered Mandeville.

"It's perfect," said Jess, looking smug. "It'll set the atmosphere." She smiled at Isis. "Won't it?"

"Well. . ." But Jess was already leading the way from the canteen.

Isis picked up her bag and headed after her, with Hayley, Chloe and Nafira following. Heads turned to watch them leave and talk rippled, but not like before, when she'd run the gauntlet of jokes and sniggering. Now they were being *discussed*, like celebrities.

A Year Seven boy asked, "Where are you going?"

"Invite only," said Jess, not even bothering to look at him.

Isis smiled, relieved, as they walked out.

The girls headed away from the newer buildings of the school, towards the old brick ones built a hundred and fifty years ago, when classrooms were intended to be high and imposing. Always cold and echoing, there were half a dozen tales of ghosts in them. None were right, of course; only Isis knew the truth about the ghosts that haunted there.

She glanced at Mandeville, drifting alongside her. His mouth was drawn into a peevish line, and his complaining began as soon as he saw Isis looking.

"Why do we have to lurk in a dingy corner, like petty criminals?" He pointed a bony finger at Jess. "And why does *she* determine where we go?"

Isis didn't answer. The other girls might be impressed by the seances, but she wasn't sure they'd react well if she started talking to ghosts when they were just walking through school.

Mandeville whinged into her silence.

"We need to start building your following, and I fail to comprehend how that can take place in toilets and alleyways. *You* should be taking charge, not allowing yourself to be managed by that girl. Her choices of location are highly unsuitable, and I have little doubt this is all being done in pursuit of her own aggrandisement."

Initially Mandeville had been delighted by Jess's efforts, but he was increasingly dissatisfied, and nothing seemed to be enough. Isis hefted her bag from one shoulder to the other, swinging it by the handle straight through Mandeville. He drifted and reformed, like oil on water.

"Do you mind?" he snapped.

"Sorry," said Isis. Hayley, walking behind her, looked puzzled and Isis smiled. "I thought I hit you with my bag."

"No," said Hayley, shaking her head.

"You did that *deliberately*!" said Mandeville, and Isis turned her smile on him, with a little nod.

"I'm so glad I'm friends with you all," said Isis blandly. She kept her eyes on Mandeville.

The other girls sparked into happy agreement, while Mandeville stayed close to Isis. They turned the corner of the sports hall, and a cool breeze fluttered their hair and coats. Mandeville shimmered with it, his form spreading out and thinning.

"Your loyalty to these girls is touching, my dear, but remember from whom you really gain your popularity. You should ask yourself, how true are these friends of yours? Would they be with you if *I* wasn't? Would they eat lunch with you then?"

At this threat Isis stopped walking.

"Don't," she said, the word too quiet to be heard.

Mandeville was almost transparent now. "Why *should* I stay, when you treat me with so little respect? When you are merely using me to impress your friends!"

Jess and the others walked on a few paces, then Nafira turned around.

"What is it?" she asked.

"I. . ." Isis thought desperately, then bent down. "I've got something in my shoe."

Nafira nodded, and carried on walking.

Isis whispered at the ground. "I'm not using you."

Mandeville's features grew among the cracks and discolouration of the cement. The dark stain from someone's spilled drink became his face, one of his blue fire eyes glowed through a blob of chewing gum.

"You are wasting your talents and mine. We have a great cause – that is why I fought for you against Philip Syndal and the Devourer. You and I together, we could do so much!" The grey cement appeared to shudder. "Yet here we are, bringing forth dead pets. Hamsters and cats don't even understand the meaning of names such as 'Fluffy' and 'Timkins', whatever their owners believe, which means I have the greatest of difficulty in calling them. . ."

Mandeville paused, his crumbly dirt features going still for a moment. "Philip Syndal had only a finger's worth of your talent, yet he spoke to packed theatres."

Isis drew back. "I'm nothing like Philip Syndal."

"No, you're not! You're a thousand times greater! A thousand, thousand times greater." The ground sighed a little puff of dust. "I want you to shine, Isis. I want to bring us to the world's stage and give hope to the frightened masses of humanity."

Isis glanced up, and saw the other girls had stopped. They were watching her, waiting. She took off her shoe and shook it out.

"I don't want to do what Cally did," she whispered, standing up slowly while still keeping her head bent. All the nights she'd travelled with her mum to village halls and community centres, watching Cally perform to fifty, thirty or just a handful of people. When she'd asked her mum if it was really all worth it, Cally had told her that every great stage psychic started this way.

"You won't have to!" cried Mandeville, following Isis by oozing out of the ground. "You can go straight to the grandest theatres, even to your television." He said the last word awkwardly, as if it were a foreign language.

"How? Do you mean going on YouTube?"

Mandeville frowned. "I have no idea what you are talking about. What I *mean*, child, is that you must introduce *me*."

"How will that help?"

Mandeville's body poured upwards into the air, so they were facing each other. Through him she could see her friends waiting. Jess looked impatient.

"Allow *me* to speak," said Mandeville, "rather than passing on pointless messages from the unwashed dead. Then you will see the difference."

Isis turned around to pick up her bag and, while her back was to the others, said, "You want me to tell them what you say?"

But Mandeville, who was still facing her even though she had moved, shook his head.

"We must be great, my dear. For that, Chinese whispers will not do."

Isis felt herself go cold. "No," she whispered.

"Did the woman in the theatre come to any harm?" Mandeville smiled and his teeth seemed longer than ever, hanging from his withered gums. Isis shivered, remembering

Philip Syndal's performance that she'd gone to see with Cally, and how Mandeville had possessed a woman sitting next to Isis, creeping inside and taking control of her body. The woman had slept through the whole performance, while Mandeville muttered comments through her mouth and waved her hands with jerky movements.

She shook her head. "I'm not letting you possess me."

"I will rest inside you as lightly as a feather."

Behind her, Isis could hear footsteps returning.

"Are you all right?" called Jess.

Isis turned around, her smile false and bright.

Mandeville leaned close, a confidential swirl of damp and mould.

"Let us compromise. I can say what I need to with just your mouth. No other part of your body, and certainly not your mind. Let me try, only for a few minutes, and the rest of the time I will play tricks for these children."

Still Isis didn't answer, shuddering inside at the thought of it.

"Do you want me to leave you alone to face your audience?" Mandeville threatened.

Isis kept her eyes on Jess, but her words were for him.

"Okay then."

She didn't want to, but a miserable, calculating part of her mind knew that she didn't have a choice. Mandeville was absolutely right: without him, she'd be sitting alone in the canteen right now.

The group carried on, turning another corner, and now Isis saw the people already waiting for them. A mix of boys and girls, ranging from Year Nine up, hanging around in twos and threes, as if they'd just gathered by coincidence. A passing teacher might wonder why they were all around here, but no one was doing anything against the rules. Not yet, anyway.

There were so many, though! Isis began counting the students. When she got past twenty she put her hand on Jess's arm.

"How many people did you invite?"

"Only six," Jess replied, not even slowing down. "I guess they asked their friends too." She let out a little squeal. "There's Justin Geds!" She pointed at a Year Ten boy.

Hayley huddled in. "And he's got Harry Lyons with him!"

"They are so hot!"

Jess straightened a little, flicking her hair back. "Come on." She walked confidently towards the older students, as if she owned the place, as if she was the star of the show. Isis walked a pace or two behind, her throat tight.

"They don't look hot to me," remarked Mandeville, studying the older boys, "but I find differences in temperature harder to detect than I did when living."

The twos and threes began to gather into a single mass as the girls walked towards them. Isis heard giggles from behind, and looking back she saw a group of Year Sevens following them around the corner of the science block. They looked both furtive and excited.

Chloe turned as well. "What are *they* doing here?"

"I *told* them it was invite only," said Jess.

Hayley shrugged. "We'll just get rid, that's all."

Nafira shook her head slowly. "We can't, there's Jenna Kay – she's just the type to go running to a teacher if she doesn't get her way."

Jess sighed. "All right, we let them join in." She glanced at Isis. "Okay?"

Not that Isis was really part of the discussion.

In the end, Isis's audience was larger than many of those her mum had performed to. All squashed into the narrow gap between the old Victorian building and the far newer science block. The height of the buildings allowed only a little light to reach the ground between them and so moss bloomed across the crumbling tarmac and up the lower parts of the walls. It was dank, dim and definitely creepy, but the main reason for choosing this spot was that it wasn't overlooked. The side of the science block had no windows, only vents and a locked fire exit, and all the windows of the Victorian building were glazed with frosted glass, since their only view was a wall.

The audience was a jumble of tall and short students. Faces peered between shoulders, the younger ones scuffled their way to the front. The kids from upper years had their arms crossed, standing like they weren't bothered. The Year Sevens jiggled and chatted, always moving.

"Your little friend has acquired a reasonable crowd," Mandeville commented.

Isis took a breath, smelling the moss and wet brick. Jess was introducing the seance now. Setting out the rules and herself as ringmaster. Nafira, Chloe and Hayley had taken their places flanking Isis, their attitudes somewhere between the glower of bodyguards and the basking smugness of a pop star's parents.

When it was time, Isis said the words she was already getting used to. "The spirits are listening. . ."

Jess had a queue of questions lined up, with the Year Ten boys right at the front of it. The first questions were obviously tests, clearly devised with the idea of catching Isis out. People asked what the name of a grandparent or distant uncle was. Mandeville tutted and sighed next to her, but he seemed to be getting more and more adept at drawing ghostly relatives from whatever distant realm he called them. She could see them from the corners of her eyes, a spectral crowd mirroring the living one.

These spirits had a different quality to the ones who'd gathered hopelessly at her mother's seances, waiting for chances that never came. Many of the spirits Mandeville summoned now seemed to waver, as if unwilling or only half present, and instead of yearning, they seemed impatient and uncomfortable, desperate only to leave.

Maybe it was the stupid questions people were asking? Only a girl who asked to speak to her recently dead aunt seemed to be here for any reason other than curiosity.

The conversation relayed through Mandeville to Isis was full of new grief, and as the tears dribbled down the girl's face, even the youngest children became silent and respectful. When she was finished, Isis felt the girl's aunt leave in an exhaling sigh. Isis sighed too, feeling exhausted and a little bit shaky. She asked Jess, "Can we stop in a minute?"

Jess nodded, then turned to the crowd with a threatening posture. "We're nearly done, so you better not tell about any of this. If you do, then the ghosts. . ." she glared at a boy in the front who looked too young for secondary school, "will come to GET YOU!"

He jumped, white-faced.

Jess's glare turned back into a smile. "Any last questions?"

"No!" said Mandeville. "No more questions!"

Isis began to shake her head, knowing what was coming next, but he leaned in close and chilly.

"You promised," he hissed, "and I have kept my side of the bargain."

He was right, and she was trapped.

Isis put her hand on Jess's arm, catching her attention and everyone else's.

"Um, I'm going to do something a bit different now," Isis said. She tried to sound as firm as Jess, but it came out thin and trembling.

Jess frowned at her.

"I'm going to let my. . . spirit guide speak. He's. . ." Isis looked at Mandeville, unsure how to describe him. Victorian? Decomposing? "He's very wise."

Mandeville looked pleased, while Jess's frown deepened. Isis felt guilty, not having told her about this, but there hadn't been a chance.

Isis nodded at Mandeville. "Only what you promised," she mouthed silently.

"Of course, my dear."

Mandeville swirl-stepped in front of her, half obscuring the curious faces of the crowd. A few children coughed and someone sneezed. Mandeville lifted his arms, and his body began to dissolve and lift, spreading out into a dusty, invisible cloud above everyone in the dim alleyway. The air became noticeably chillier, and it seemed as if the moss was growing higher up the dank walls, fat drops of dirty moisture oozing out of the bricks.

"A little effect," whispered Mandeville, dipping his disembodied head close to hers. At the edge of her vision she saw Jess shiver, and she could hear people asking what was going on, their voices nervous. In front of Isis, Mandeville's face was getting more solid, even as his body thinned. Denser, more real than she'd ever seen it, his eyes jolts of blue. He pressed closer and Isis wanted to back away, gasping at his rotten-meat stench.

"Don't worry, my dear."

With a snap of his head, his lips moved towards hers in a grotesque mockery of a kiss. Her hands flew up, but there was nothing to push at. She opened her mouth to scream, but nothing came out.

Mandeville backed off, smiling, and she could see the crowd again. Everyone's eyes were on her, their faces caught between laughter and puzzlement.

"What are you doing?" hissed Jess.

Isis began to answer, but what she actually said was, "Ah, yes. Now let me see."

A girl at the front squeaked.

Isis touched disbelieving hands to her mouth, her eyes on Mandeville. He nodded at her, and she said, "As I promised, just your voice, my dear."

An old man's rasping tone, an old man's rattling words. She felt caught, frozen by shock.

"Isis?" whispered Jess.

Mandeville moved his mouth, and Isis spoke.

"I am Isis's spirit guide. I am the one who guides this child, and allows all of you to make contact with the otherworldly realms."

It was Mandeville's voice exactly. Not Isis's vocal chords mimicking an old man. His words were too deep in tone, and echoed strangely as if being spoken in two places at once. Which of course, they were.

"How's she doing that?" an older girl asked.

"It's got to be special effects," said a boy, too loud. "She's got speakers hidden somewhere."

But Jess shook her head, eyes wide. "She hasn't." And there was something about the way she said it: afraid instead of bossy. Everyone was tense now, even the oldest boys.

Mandeville moved his mouth, and again Isis spoke in his old man's rasp.

"I have things to tell, preparing you for what is to come. And the first is this: you are all going to die. . ."

The girl who'd squeaked began to scream, and a moment later everyone was running, scattering out into the daylight beyond the alley.

"Where are they going?" Isis wailed in his dusty, croaky voice. "I've only just got started."

Hayley, Chloe and Nafira squawked and ran at that, joining the panic to get out of the alleyway. Only Jess stayed, white-faced and trembling.

Isis raised her hand, pointing to her mouth.

"No!" Mandeville croaked through her. "You promised!"

Isis jabbed her finger at her mouth, glaring at Mandeville's drifting form.

"All right then, but I don't see why. . ." His grumbling continued as it disappeared from her mouth, leaving her with a feeling that was something like being unzipped.

"Why did you do that?" Isis cried, now she had her own voice back. She turned on Mandeville, furious and not even caring that Jess was staring, her eyes wide with fear.

"Why did *I* do that?" Mandeville asked. "Why did they all run away like *ninnies*?"

"You said they were all going to die!"

"*Everyone* dies," said Mandeville. "It is the one truth of existence, the inevitable finish to every life. I was going to share my experience of passing through the veil, words to assuage their fear of death. Words of comfort. That's my mission!"

"Is he still here?" Jess whispered, her voice little more than a quaver. "Your. . . guide?"

Isis nodded. "He is."

She could see how scared the other girl was, and yet Jess managed a trembling breath before saying, "What is it that's going to kill us all? Is it a bomb?"

Mandeville turned to look at Jess, and Isis watched the realisation dawning on him.

"Ah," he said, "I see how my words could be misinterpreted."

Chapter Eleven
Gray

It was because of Isis that I kept quiet about seeing that little boy. I mean, I knew what people were calling her, all that dead girl stuff. And then she started her seances, and even when everyone was desperately trying to get in on one, at the same time they were still saying things, you know? More and more people were calling her 'dead girl', just not to her face. And they went on about how creepy she was, that she could make you ill by looking at you the wrong way. All that.

If I'd mentioned anything about seeing little boys who weren't there, I'd have been sucked right into the craze, and all of the stuff being said about Isis would've turned on to me as well, especially after what Mrs Dewson had told everyone in assembly.

So you left Isis to be the butt of school gossip? You did nothing to defend her?

I know I should have said something – I mean I'm not proud of how I behaved then. . .

I am not judging you. I admire your sense of self-preservation.

But people didn't know the half of what I did about her, and I kept quiet about all of it, didn't I? And I still wasn't sure she was even really her. Maybe she was still the Devourer? It would explain why she was behaving so differently to before. I mean, when she told me about being able to see ghosts in the summer, she said no one else knew. But there she was, giving seances to all the giggly girls in our year and any boys they fancied. She'd changed, for definite.

I just kept out of it, that's all. And there wasn't anyone else I could talk to about the little boy in my garden. My mum would've flipped out, Dad would've. . . really enjoyed it, probably. Come up with loads of theories, written a blog about it for his UFO-freak friends. I did try to talk to other people who'd been on the school trip, but it was like they didn't know what I was on about.

"Did you see anything. . . odd that day?"

"No. I don't know what you're on about."

Even Jayden, who'd been screaming at the quarry, just said, "I never screamed." Like that, a flat-out lie.

I didn't know if they were playing it down, so they wouldn't seem weird like Isis, or if I was only one who'd seen the ghostly stuff.

I kept thinking about what had happened the night in August – the Devourer surrounding me, seeing all those ghosts. Had it changed my brain, warped it or something? I was really worried, but I kept my mouth shut.

Fear of madness, such a useful characteristic. Despite depictions on film, we hardly ever need to use memory-wipe devices on witnesses to unusual happenings. Most keep quiet, all by themselves. It isn't only children who are afraid of being made fun of, believe me. It makes our clean-up operations so much easier.

I thought you're a therapist.

Look at my eyes, Gray, that's right. Now listen: I am not a doctor or a therapist. I am just a man you'll soon forget about, and you are answering my questions.

Oh, yes. Just a man.

Please carry on.

So I. . . was. . . back at school and after a while the stuff about the school trip quietened down. I started to feel normal again. Every now and then I'd catch something out of the corner of my eye, like a figure of someone, but when I turned around, there was never anything there. I decided I was probably just jumpy. All in my head.

A good thing was that Mum patched things up with Dad, because she had to admit he obviously was concerned about my welfare, seeing as he turned up to the school trip only a few minutes after she did. That was the best thing to happen in weeks, because it'd been horrible not seeing him for so long. They agreed Dad could take me out for the day the next Saturday, and I got focused on that, counting down the days actually, I was looking forward to it so much.

He picked me up after breakfast.

"Look after him, won't you?" Mum said.

"I always do," he answered, which got him one of Mum's sarcastic, folded-arms looks. But she let me go with him.

We got into his camper van, and he took a left out of our road, which isn't the way to his house.

"Where are we going?" I asked.

Dad smiled. "It's an adventure."

I got my hopes up then, even though I should've known better.

"Is it the dry ski slope?" I asked. Dad shook his head. "Go-karting?" Another shake. I tried to think of things we'd never done, special things. I mean, if you tell someone they're going on an adventure, especially after they've nearly been in hospital twice, you'd think it'd be something good. "One of those places where you climb through trees on ropes?"

Dad snorted. "Can you imagine your mum's face?" He looked at me, eyes narrowed a bit. "How are you feeling, by the way?"

I shrugged. "Fine. So what is it then?" By now I was getting my hopes under control. This was Dad, after all.

"How about a walk?"

"That's it? A walk doesn't count as an adventure!"

Dad squinted at the road, or maybe he was frowning. "It could be one. Like a spy story."

"How could a walk be that?"

"Well, I was thinking of heading up near to the mining site, so we can see what they're really up to. . ."

"No!" I couldn't believe it, couldn't believe him! "It made me really ill, Dad. I don't want to go back there."

Dad shook his head. "No, of course, and I don't want to take you anywhere unsafe, but I want to find out what they're hiding. We won't get close, okay? Give ourselves a safe perimeter distance, say half a kilometre. I've got some portable EM field monitors and. . ."

"I don't want to!"

"Look, I posted what happened to your class and the Network went wild about it. They're pestering for more data. Stu's cross-checking into the Database. . ."

I groaned. If Dad had got Stu and the Network involved I had no hope. The Network's like this club for UFO and conspiracy freaks, and Stu is chief-freak.

"Cally thinks it's all about ley lines, of course," said Dad chuckling.

"Cally?" I asked, and there was a look on his face, one I knew from all the times we've 'bumped into' one of his girlfriends on my visiting days. "Is *she* coming?"

He didn't answer. He didn't have to.

I pulled back in my seat, folding my arms tight. "Can you turn the van around? I want to go home."

"I'm not taking you home!" said Dad. "I've hardly seen you for a month."

"You've hardly seen me for two months actually, but you still invited your girlfriend along!" I was so angry I was shouting. "I nearly *died* in the summer, but all you care about is Cally! I want to go home, because if you've invited *her* I might as well not be there."

I expected him to go mental and for us to get into a full-on shouting match, but he didn't, he just pulled the camper van to the side of the road and stopped. There was only the sound of the indicator and the other cars rushing by.

"Is that really what you think of me?" he asked.

"Yes!"

Dad turned to stare at the road. He sat there for a minute, then twisted back to look at me.

"Maybe I haven't always been perfect, Gray." He put his hand out, touched my arm. "But what happened out in that field this summer. . . sitting with you in Accident and Emergency. . ." His voice went all croaky. "You're my son, Gray, that's what I really care about."

"Then why have you been fighting with Mum for *months?*" I said. "Why couldn't you sort it out?"

"It hasn't been months," said Dad. "It's only been six weeks or so."

"Nine weeks." I thought I might cry, like some little kid. "This is the first Saturday we've had together since the beginning of August."

Dad sat still as a stone for a minute, then he leaned across and put his arms around me. Gave me a hug, if you can believe it.

"I'm sorry, Gray," he whispered. "I should have thought."

And Dad never apologises about *anything*.

"I promise I'll make it up to you," he said, letting go of me. "But the thing is. . ."

"I know," I sighed. "Cally's different. Cally's the one."

Dad laughed. "Actually, I was going to say it's already arranged, and they've probably left by now so I can't cancel. But you're right as well, Cally is special."

I thought of asking, why her? I mean, he's had millions of girlfriends. Maybe because I was studying him I noticed the way his frown lines really carved into his forehead. And the tiny wrinkles all over his face, and his leathery skin from being outside so much. That's when I got it – he was old. He was going to be forty next year, and Mum says men always go a bit strange when they hit forty. "Especially men like your dad."

A thought popped in my head.

"Are you going to marry Cally?" I asked.

Dad snorted another laugh. "Get *married*?" Then he stopped laughing. "Well, I don't know."

We both thought about that for a minute, listening to the *tick-tick* of the indicator and the *whoosh* of traffic. Until I realised.

"You said, '*they*'ve left'."

Dad gave a bit of a shrug. "Invite Cally, invite Isis. You know the score. I thought it'd be nice for you, to have a friend along."

"You could have asked me," I muttered.

Dad narrowed his eyes at me. "Have you two fallen out? You were as thick as thieves in the summer."

I shook my head. I didn't want to go into it.

Dad checked the rear-view mirror.

He flicked the indicator the other way, and we wove back into the lanes of traffic.

"We'll do something else, I promise. Just us," he said. "But be nice to Cally today, and Isis." He flicked a grin at me. "Think of it this way: she could end up being your sister."

We clattered along the road. I thought we'd go the way the coaches had, but Dad took a completely different route out of town.

"We aren't going to the quarry entrance, are we?" I asked.

Dad shook his head. "We can't just walk up to their front door and ask to see their dirty secrets, can we? Anyway, there's a lot of security up there since your school trip. They're obviously hiding something, and we'll get to the bottom of whatever it is, don't worry."

I sighed. Sometimes with Dad you just have to let him get on with it. As long as we didn't get too close.

Beyond the camper van the sky was super-blue, the day was bright and every turning leaf on the trees stood out, oranges and golds dotting the green. Dad turned up a steep lane, revving the camper van to keep us going, then pulled into a small car park.

There was a car already there. Cally's.

They were standing by it. Isis was wearing leggings and this babyish T-shirt with a sparkly pink cat on it; Cally was in one of her floaty-witch dresses. It was warm and the ground was bone dry, but both of them had wellies on. Cally's were black with skulls.

Cally had started waving as soon as we pulled up. Her face was lit by a smile and her eyes were on Dad. He was the same, and it was like there was a piece of elastic pulling them together.

Me and Isis were the opposite. I had to force myself to go near her, trying to tell from her eyes or by the way she was standing if it was really her or not. She looked a bit shocked to see me, arms crossed tight to her chest.

"Hi," I said to her.

"Mum made me come on this walk," she said. "I didn't know you would be here too."

And that was it, for the whole time Cally and Dad were holding hands and being in love with each other. Which was quite a while.

Eventually, Dad remembered us.

"Come on, you two. Let's get investigating." Like we were in *Scooby Doo* or something. He headed for a stile, with a footpath leading away on the other side. There was a council sign telling us to keep dogs under control. Beneath it someone had scrawled

NO OPENCAST! UK-EARTHS OUT!

Me and Isis got ourselves over the stile, but Dad made a show of helping Cally because her stupid dress was getting in the way.

"Why thank you, kind sir," she said.

Isis made this sound, really quietly, like someone being sick.

The path headed off across the fields and we let Dad and Cally take the lead. It was narrow, and Isis was in front of me. I guess I was watching her, the way I'd done every day since school started: keeping my distance, trying to work out if it was really her. There'd been no way of telling at school, and the way she'd changed, getting in with those girls and doing seances and stuff, it had made me really suspicious. But on that track, with her walking right in front of me, and so close, I noticed that her right arm was swinging normally, but her left stayed steady like she was holding someone's hand.

Someone you couldn't see.

And I just knew. The monster inside Philip Syndal had only been interested in eating ghosts, swallowing them down and growing bigger with every meal. If it had still been inside Isis, there was no way any ghosts would be near her. But one was.

I walked in silence for a bit. I mean, I was really happy she wasn't possessed, but that meant all the time I'd been avoiding her at school and stuff. . . it seemed, well, pretty rubbish really.

It took me a while to get my nerve up to saying something.

"Is Angel with you?" I asked her quietly.

Isis spun around, her face turning red as a beetroot.

"Shut up!" she hissed. "Mum's here!"

Actually, Dad and Cally had gone way ahead, and they were clearly too lost in each other to care anything about us.

"Can I see her?" Suddenly I wanted to see Angel more than anything. But Isis glared at me, arms folded.

"You know," I said, "Angel brought me to you in the hospital."

"You've hardly spoken to me since school started. And *now* you want to see Angel?"

I probably blushed a bit. "I just thought. . ."

"Yes. I know," Isis said coldly.

Sometimes you just have to come out with it: "I'm sorry."

Isis looked surprised.

"I shouldn't have avoided you," I said, and her face closed up again. "It's just I didn't know if you were still. . . you."

Isis frowned. "What? Why wouldn't I be me?"

"Because you died," I whispered. "Properly died. Didn't you?"

She nodded slowly.

"I didn't know if it was you who came back," I said, "or the Devourer." I remembered the dark ooze, pulsing around us. Isis didn't say anything, but I could see the memories on her face too.

Then she startled and smiled. Not at me.

"Yeah, we should. That would prove it." And she reached out, taking hold of something from the air, placing it into my hand. The second my fingers touched hers, I could see.

See what? Tell me!

The ghost of a little girl. I know you won't believe me but it's true. Just like when I'd seen her last, wearing a frilly dress and sandals, with a moptop of curly hair. The grass was showing through her. She grinned at me, making dimples in her round cheeks.

I can see what Isis can, as long as we're linked by a ghost. I don't know how it works; it's part of her being psychic, I think. And now she'd put my hand onto Angel's. Me, Isis and a ghost, all holding hands.

"I do'd it," Angel said. "I bringed Isis back."

Of course, I should have known my girls would look after each other.

Your girls?

Forget that! Tell me more about the little ghost. What did she look like, what did she say?

Well I wasn't really looking at Angel, because something else had appeared behind her. Tall and thin, glowing in a greenish sort of way. Half-rotten. A skeleton wearing tatters of clothing, with eyes that were like. . . I don't know, tunnels maybe? Or if you'd been dropped down the bottom of a well and you were looking up into a faraway circle of sky that you could never reach.

The skeleton hovered behind Isis, like it owned her.

"Allow me to introduce myself," it said, in this whispery voice. "My name is Mandeville." Its mouth made a shape, which was probably meant to be a smile.

What it looked like was death.

Chapter Twelve
Isis

Angel whipped her hand from Gray's, skipping behind Isis and scowling at Mandeville. Gray wouldn't be able to see either ghost now, Isis knew.

"What was that?" he gasped, startling back a step.

"Mandeville," sighed Isis. "Angel doesn't like him."

"A dislike which is entirely unjustified," said Mandeville. "I cannot think of anything I've done to deserve her ire."

"Apart from bringing the Devourer to eat her!" Isis snapped. He flicked the comment away with his hand, although she thought that perhaps he looked a little ashamed. Gray turned his head from side to side, peering at the air.

"Is that the ghost from the theatre?" he asked her. "Your friend?"

"We're not *friends*!" said Isis.

"Too cruel," murmured Mandeville.

"He's my. . ." she was embarrassed to say it, "spirit guide."

Gray smiled. "You sound like your mum!"

"I do not!" But she could feel herself blushing, and wished her cheeks would stay the same icy pale as Cally's.

Gray continued peering at the air, trying to spot Mandeville. "I thought Angel was your. . . main ghost."

"I ARE!" shouted Angel.

Isis smiled down at Angel. "Mandeville's just helping me."

"Helping?" said Mandeville, raising one dusty eyebrow. "I hope my contribution is seen as greater than that."

Gray looked at Isis thoughtfully. "So is Mandeville how you're doing all the seances at school?"

"How do you know about them?"

"Everyone knows."

"We're not hurting anyone," Isis said hotly.

Gray didn't answer, which she couldn't help taking as an accusation.

"So what if I'm making friends? At least they haven't

been ignoring me for weeks!" The words hit home, and she felt pleased for about a second.

"I did already say sorry," he said. "But, you know, everything that happened in the summer holidays. . . it might be normal for you, but it wasn't for me."

"It wasn't normal for me either!"

"Normaller, then."

She could feel an argument hovering. Why couldn't their friendship go back to the way it had been?

Mandeville drifted closer, bringing with him a strong stench of mouldy fabric. "Why don't we do a seance for the boy," he whispered. "Isn't that how you win your friendships?"

"I can't do one *here*," said Isis.

"And I already do'd it!" Angel said to Mandeville. "He seen *me*!"

"How edifying for him. A little urchin who would benefit from a good thrashing if she weren't already dead!"

Angel put her fists on her hips. "An' you. . . you. . . STINK!" she shouted, before vanishing.

Mandeville stalked away as well, fading as he did so. "Well don't say I never try to help you!"

"What's going on?" asked Gray.

"They had a fight," said Isis. "Mandeville and Angel don't like each other much."

Further ahead, Cally and Gil had stopped on the path and were waiting for them.

"Come on!" shouted Gil. "What are you two *doing*?"

"Listening to ghosts argue," replied Isis, too quietly for their parents to hear.

"Do you want to tell them?" Gray asked, with a smile. "Or shall I?"

Isis laughed, and he joined in. She wondered if maybe the tension between them and the weeks of not talking didn't matter, after all. Gray was the one who understood Isis, more than anyone else, more than Jess even. Jess and the others had been terrified just by hearing Mandeville's voice, whereas Gray took seeing the ghost in his stride. He knew all about Angel too, while Isis hadn't yet dared to mention having a ghost-sister to her new friends. In the end, she had no other friend like Gray.

"I think we should go that way," said Gil, pointing. They'd been walking for an hour or so, having left the footpath at Gil's insistence and followed a little trail that had now dwindled into nothing at the top of a slope.

Isis looked, but she couldn't see any sign of the quarry. Just the hills rolling in waves, dipping into hidden, wooded valleys. The sun was so bright she had to squint. It was warm enough to be summer again.

Gil peered at a map, turning it around in his hands.

"I don't know," he said at last. "The main path should be around here somewhere."

Cally stood motionless, hands outstretched and her eyes half-closed. "We'll just have to feel our way," she said dreamily. "Constance said the ley lines have been disrupted, but I'm sure I can find my way through them."

"The quarry's probably here," said Gil, his finger on the map. "So if we take this path. . ."

"Not the quarry!" said Gray. "You promised."

"We'll keep a safe distance," said Gil, "but we need to get a *bit* closer, enough to see inside it."

Gray shook his head. "No way."

The grassy slope stretched down from where they'd stopped. Isis could see the snaking line of a path disappearing into the trees that covered the valley floor.

"We could try down there," she said, pointing.

Gil shook his head. "We'll never get to it if we take any old path that we see. I doubt that goes anywhere near the quarry."

"Right then," said Gray, and he ran off, hurtling down the slope towards the path Isis had pointed at.

"Come back!" shouted Gil. But Gray carried on running. "Oh for. . . Why is he being so awkward?" Gil started to stamp down the slope, but Cally caught his arm.

"Maybe he's scared?"

Gil grunted. "I'm scared of things, but I still do them."

"And when you were his age?"

Gil grunted again, and stared after Gray, who was nearly at the bottom of the hill. "Maybe he is worried; he has been going on a bit about the quarry." He cupped his hands around his mouth and shouted, "Gray! Come back, we can sort it out!"

But Gray couldn't hear him, or was choosing not to.

"I'll go and get him," said Isis.

"Would you, love?" Cally said. "That's so thoughtful of you." Isis didn't tell her it wasn't thoughtful, she just didn't want to be left alone with the two adults in case they started kissing again.

She took a step down the hill, then another. The steep slope quickly caught her feet, lumps and bumps of grass dancing her down the hill, pulling her legs into widening steps and then to a run that lasted until the slope flattened off. She slowed to a windswept stop a few paces from Gray.

"Your dad said sorry," she panted, "and that you should come back up."

"To *that*?" said Gray, pointing. Isis turned and saw the small figures of Cally and Gil at the top of the slope, arms around each other, heads pressed together.

"Not again."

"They don't waste time, do they?"

She shook her head, letting out a groan.

"I'm not going near the quarry," said Gray, "whatever Dad thinks."

"I think he's pretty set on it."

"Yeah, but if we go this way, then they'll have to follow, won't they?" He turned, and started walking away. Gray was as stubborn as his dad when he wanted to be.

The track was narrow, worn deep into the earth, and they followed it towards the trees. As the grass turned to woodland, the path crossed a dry stream bed, a line of chalky gravel and rocks that would be filled with water in the winter. As they stepped down into the ditch and Isis's feet hit the rubble of stones, she felt a sudden stab of anxiety.

For a heartbeat she was seeing something other than trees and the curve of the valley. It was as if the landscape had another layer made of silver, which it exhaled in a single breath.

She blinked, and the sensation vanished.

Beside her in the stream bed, Gray was standing stock-still. He had a blanched, frightened expression on his face.

"Are you all right?" she asked him.

He shut his eyes, opened them again. "Do you think being psychic could be infectious?"

"It's not a *disease*," said Isis.

"I know, I just wondered if I could catch it. I mean, after seeing Angel, and the Devourer and stuff. Could it. . . spread?"

"Like a verruca?" said Isis, feeling herself prickle.

Gray looked at her for a moment, his jaw tight.

"Fine," he said. "Forget it." And he carried on walking, his footsteps quick and angry.

"Wait!" she followed, almost having to jog to keep up. Why was this happening? How could a fight bubble out of nothing? But Gray walked silently for a long while, his face blank to her questions, leading them further from their parents. And as she worried about him and their fight, Isis let go of what she'd seen when they were standing in the ditch. Perhaps it had only been her eyes, or a trick of the light?

The path wasn't much wider than a rabbit track. It threaded between the tall spires of the beech trees, the air cooler than it had been out in the sunshine. As they weren't talking, the only sounds were their own footsteps and the occasional chirrups of birds. And now the anxiety she'd felt before was building again. It made her want to move quicker, to get away, or. . . do something, even if she wasn't sure what.

She found herself glancing back as she followed Gray, hoping for the reassuring thump of Gil's and Cally's feet. She worried whether they'd even noticed them walk off, or if they'd been too busy kissing. Thick, autumn light slanted through the branches, and the bright leaves above them flickered shadows across the ground. It was beautiful, but. . .

"Maybe we should go back?" she said.

Gray came to a stop. "I'm not going near the quarry."

"I know."

"I guess we could wait here for them."

Except she didn't want to wait either. She couldn't stay here, with this feeling. "Maybe we should carry on?"

Gray frowned at her. "You wanted to go back a second ago."

"I know, but now I don't know."

"Is something up with you?"

She shook her head. She was fine. Except she was feeling more and more anxious, feeling more and more like she needed to get somewhere, and wherever it was, she had to do it quickly.

"Things always turn out badly when I go on woodland walks," she said.

Gray laughed.

"It's not funny!"

The jumbled patterns of gold-lit trees stretched above them. Up. Up and away. That was where she wanted to go!

"I'm going back to the car," she said, choosing a direction at a rough right angle to the path, and clambering up the slope.

"But the car's not that way!" said Gray, left on the path.

She carried on, weaving her way between smooth and knotted trunks, grabbing branches to pull herself up the raggedy ladder of the hillside.

"You'll get lost!"

"No I won't!"

Somehow she knew this was exactly the right direction.

Chapter Thirteen

Isis

She'd been scrabbling up the hillside for ages but didn't seem to be getting anywhere. It hadn't taken long to run down into the valley, so why was she still clambering, hanging onto tree roots and clumps of grass to stop herself from slipping? Maybe she wasn't going as straight as she thought she was? Except this *felt* like the right way, even with Angel protesting, and even with her legs aching more and more with each step.

"Where are you going *now*?" Gray called from below her.

She gripped onto a low branch, glancing back, and had a spinning moment of vertigo at the steepness of the wooded bank falling away from her. It forced out the strange sense of urgency, which had stranded her here, halfway up the hillside.

What am I doing?

"Are you heading for that path?" Gray called. He was pointing diagonally away from where she was headed, to a footpath following the contours of the slope, little more than a line between the trees.

Isis nodded, too out of breath to answer him and not wanting to admit she didn't even know where she was going. She changed her angle of scramble, heading for the path, hearing the crunch and crack of Gray behind her. Her fear of falling kept her focused on handholds and where to put her feet, so she didn't see the man standing on the footpath until she was nearly there. A tall young man, wearing a rainbow-striped jumper, grey camo trousers and army boots. He peered down at her from under thick ropes of brown dreadlocks, his expression half hidden by a short, wispy beard.

He seemed to have appeared from nowhere, and for a moment she thought he was a ghost. But he had a shadow and he looked a little too solid. She stopped climbing, and they stared at each other for a moment.

"What's going on then?" he asked in a deep, almost sleepy voice.

Isis didn't answer. Her foot was wedged against the base of a small tree, but she felt unsteady all the same. She wanted to get to the path, but now this man was on it.

The man's gaze flicked to Gray as he caught up.

"You two lost?"

"No!" said Isis.

"Yes!" said Gray.

The young man leaned down, putting a hand out to Isis. "Well if you are or you aren't, I know these woods so I can set you in the right direction."

She didn't take his hand so he offered it to Gray instead, who took it and was quickly hauled onto the path.

Isis struggled the last few metres on pride, but when she reached the path her leg muscles sparked little trembles, recovering from the climb.

"You out here on your own?" asked the man, frowning at them both.

"Our parents are just down there," lied Gray quickly, pointing to the valley floor. If only they were, then they'd have been within earshot.

"Do they know you're wandering by yourselves? There's all sorts in these woods."

"You mean, like you?" Gray said.

The young man smiled. "I'm no risk to anyone, man. It's the security guards from the quarry you should worry about. Some of them are really rough."

"Is the quarry near here then?" asked Gray, a note of fear in his voice.

"About fifteen minutes' walk that way'll get you to the fence," said the man, pointing down the footpath they were now on. "But come back in a couple of years and you won't have to walk anywhere to reach it. We'll be standing in the quarry right here. They want the whole valley."

Up close, Isis could see that his trousers were stained with mud, and the cuffs of his jumper more brown than rainbow. Above his beard his face was smooth and unlined, but deeply tanned and ingrained with dirt. His hands were equally grubby, each fingernail lined with black.

"Are you one of the protestors?" asked Gray. "Dad said there's a camp."

The young man shrugged. "I am and I aren't. Same as you are and aren't lost."

"What does that mean?"

"It means I'm Merlin." They both stared at him. "You know? Druid and wanderer. Healer and bard."

Gray snorted. "I know who Merlin is."

"Glad you've heard of me then."

"But you're not actually him!"

"Who else would I be?"

Isis shook her head. The way he'd appeared from nowhere, here among the trees, he did seem kind of supernatural. Except the unwashed smell coming off him – a pungent mix of sweat and woodsmoke – didn't seem very mystical.

"Merlin's just made-up," she said. "And if he wasn't he died a thousand years ago, so you can't be him."

"The king is dead, long live the king," said the young man. "*Merlin* is dead, long live Merlin."

Gray look puzzled, then said, "You mean it's a title? Like the way being king passes onto the next person?"

Merlin made a gun out of his thumb and forefinger. "*Peeeow*," he said, shooting at Gray.

"But the original Merlin was in the eighth century or whenever, so you'd have to be. . ." Isis paused, counting in her head, ". . . about the fiftieth Merlin. At least! How did you get even chosen?"

Merlin shrugged. "I just knew it was me."

Isis and Gray exchanged a look, but Gray said, "My dad knows this man who says he's an alien-human hybrid. I suppose being Merlin isn't any weirder."

Merlin smiled through his beard. "I'll take that as a compliment." He paused, seeming to examine them both. "Look, you should be careful. An ambulance would take a long time getting in here if you broke a leg or whatever. Take the path instead of climbing, all right?"

"It was Isis's idea," muttered Gray. "She wants to get back to the car park."

"Well you're going the wrong way for that." Merlin pointed up the path they were standing on. "Go up here, then double back at the fork, then the path dips down for a bit, and when it starts to head back uphill you take a left. . ."

"No." The word was out of Isis's mouth before she even knew it, her heart thrumming into anxiety just at the thought of going the way Merlin was pointing. "Not that way."

"What is up with you?" Gray said. By the gathering of his eyebrows she could tell he was annoyed, but it didn't matter – right now she didn't care about anything except. . .

"This way," she said, pointing. She was set on a direction into the trees, and up the slope. She had no idea what was there, or why she was so certain it was the right path. "That's where we're going."

Merlin regarded her thoughtfully. "You can feel it, can't you?"

"Feel what?" asked Gray.

"The energy," said Merlin. "The ley lines, man. Seven of them intersect up that way."

Gray groaned. "You as well? Look, Isis, let's just go back. Find Dad and Cally?"

Isis knew that was the sensible thing to do, so why was she shaking her head? She couldn't set aside this desperation to reach. . . whatever was that way.

"Cally will be worrying," said Gray. "She's probably phoned the police by now!"

He was right again, and still she didn't care. "I want to go there, where the ley lines cross."

Merlin inspected her. "You've got a calling, haven't you? I can always tell."

Gray grabbed Isis's arm. "You can't just go off!"

"I need to go there," she answered.

"Why?"

She could only pull a face; she couldn't translate the need to him, it was as if it were in another language. "I just do."

"There's something weird about this valley," said Gray. "What happened at the quarry and now this. Something isn't right, and you've gone all. . . Cally!"

"Don't make fun of me!"

"I'm not. . ."

But Isis pulled out of his grip. Anger was the easiest, because it covered her own confusion. She ran towards Merlin, and then stopped. Through her anger, she knew Gray was right and she was being stupid, dangerous even. And yet the idea of not going. . . it was like giving up everything she'd ever wanted.

She turned around. "I can't explain," she said to Gray. "Will you come with me though?"

His feelings were clear in his face: annoyed enough to leave her, worried enough to tag along.

"All *right*," he said. "But something's wrong, and you know it."

Chapter Fourteen

Gray

The woods were full of little paths. Animal tracks wiggling through the trees, crossing and crossing again. Isis just seemed to be taking one turn then another, randomly, but we kept going uphill. And Merlin was with us, even though we'd never asked him to come along. He walked slowly, like he wasn't in any hurry, but his legs were so long he was going fast anyway. I kept thinking that this was just like one of the stories the police tell when they come into school for those 'stranger danger' talks.

I made plans in my mind for what I'd do if Merlin tried anything. Drop-kick him, grab Isis and run. He only kept walking though, and after a while we were so high I could see the whole valley below us, all the leaves rustling in waves. A line of smoke drifted out of the trees, up into the blue. It must've been from the protest camp, but for a moment it was like going back thousands of years, to when there weren't cars or towns or motorways, to when the whole country must've been wild woods and sparkling rivers. A robin sang its little up and down song, and everything was moving and stirring so you could almost feel the planet turning under your feet. Then, just on the edge of my sight, I thought I saw a little boy staring at me from between the trees.

Huuuurrr. . .

I ran to catch up with the others, not looking back.

Merlin was talking to Isis about ley lines, and she had this studied look on her face, so I couldn't tell if she was interested or just focused on walking.

I followed them, keeping my eyes on Merlin and trying not to see any little boys appearing in between the trees. I wished more than ever that I had a phone, so I could ring Mum, or the police, or someone. I decided on this thing I'd seen on TV, how if you're kidnapped you should try to make friends with your captor, so they'll see you as a person, not someone they can skin or whatever.

"How long have you been at the protest camp?" I asked him.

"I'm not in the protest camp," he said. "I don't see eye to eye with them."

I wondered who he would see eye to eye with. Some of Dad's conspiracy-freak friends probably.

"Okay – how long have you been in the woods then?"

"A year. Year and a half," said Merlin.

"A *year*?" said Isis. "But what about in the winter? Aren't you cold?"

Merlin shrugged. "My teepee's got a wood burner, and this is a wood." He picked up a stick from the ground. "I'm not short of fuel and I don't need much."

"But you don't have electricity or anything."

Merlin shrugged. "I'm not here to write a blog, I'm here to answer the earth's cries." He looked at Isis and me, weighing us up. "Same as you."

"Actually my dad *made* me come."

We walked in silence for a bit after that, then Isis said, "I know where we are." There was something weird to her voice.

"You can feel the energy?" asked Merlin.

Isis shook her head. "I recognise this place. From when I came here before, with my mum in the summer." She turned to Merlin. "Where the ley lines cross, is there a standing stone?"

"Yeah," said Merlin. "An awesome one."

Isis stood still, looking shocked, or scared, I don't know. I wished we weren't here, with Merlin and standing stones and invisible little boys. I also wished I hadn't left a Mars Bar back in the camper van, because I was really hungry. A little further on the trees opened up and we were at the edge of a neat grassy clearing. The standing stone was in the middle, and another footpath led off from the other side of the clearing. The standing stone was small, more like a standing lump. It was the same kind of grey as the rocks at the quarry, but softer-looking, like it was being slowly washed away. Not impressive at all, and there wasn't any sign of any ley lines, not that they even exist. I wandered over and read the notice attached to a little fence around the stone. I can't remember exactly what it said. . .

No, you can remember. You will remember exactly, word for word.

Um, oh. It said: THE DEVIL'S SPEARHEAD. THIS NEOLITHIC MONU-MENT IS MADE FROM AN UNUSUAL LOCAL STONE TYPE, THOUGHT TO BE IGNEOUS IN ORIGIN. ARCHAEOLOGICAL EVIDENCE SUGGESTS THE STONE WAS ERECTED AROUND 3500 BC, BUT ITS ORIGINAL PURPOSE IS UNKNOWN. THE NAME DATES FROM THE LATE MEDIEVAL PERIOD, WHEN IT WAS BELIEVED THAT THE STONE HAD DROPPED TO EARTH DURING A BATTLE BETWEEN HEAVEN AND HELL.

"Come on," said Merlin, next to me. "Let's hug."

I jumped back, ready with my karate kick, but he didn't mean me. He climbed over the fence and hugged the standing stone, face pressed against it, his eyes shut. When he spoke, it was like he was talking in his sleep.

"You should try it. It's tingly."

The day just kept getting weirder. Plus Dad and Cally were probably having fifty fits wondering where we were.

I turned to Isis. "So we're here. Can we go back now?" She was at the edge of the trees, staring with this blank kind of expression.

Merlin opened his eyes. "I haven't even done my chant yet."

"Knock yourself out," I said. "We'll go back, I know the way." Not that I really did.

Merlin looked like a kid who's been told he has to leave the zoo. "At least hug the stone, or there's no point even coming."

I shook my head. "No thanks." I glanced at Isis, but she hadn't moved. She was staring like she was seeing something no one else could. What worried me was that this was probably true.

"You okay?" I asked her.

"Yeah," she said vaguely, like she was concentrating on something else.

"You'll feel the energy," Merlin wheedled at me. "Don't be scared."

"I'm not *scared*. This is just rubbish."

"The stone's an energy channel, that's probably why you're feeling jittery and snappish."

"I'm not either of those," I snapped. "Because there's no energy, and no ley lines! It's just a rock." I really wanted that Mars Bar.

"A rock carved by ancient hands and put in this place, thousands of years ago," said Merlin, settling back into his hug, "soaking up the vibrations like a sponge."

My life is full of freaks, all of them banging on about

their own stupid stuff. Like my dad, like Merlin. Even Isis was being a bit of one then.

"So what if it's been here thousands of years?" I shouted. "The rock it's made out of must be *millions* of years old! Millions of years of being just an ordinary bit of our planet. A few thousand years as a standing stone is nothing compared to that – if I spend a minute in the shower, it doesn't make me a dolphin!"

I reached over the fence to slap the stone, make my point.

"There's nothing special. . ." But even as my fingers brushed its surface, I saw them.

Pale colourless figures, surrounding me in a circle. All different heights and none with a proper face. As I stared, hardly able to breathe, one of the shapes began to shimmer and solidify, turning from a wraith into a human. A black man, with wide eyes and a worn-in kind of frown. He put a hand out towards me and it looked real, even to the bitten fingernails, but his clothes were just smears of colour. A bit of red, a bit of blue.

Meeeeeee, he said.

Another of the figures shimmered into human. An older black guy, his hair going grey, his face wrinkled.

Meeeeeee, he said.

One of the shorter figures shook itself into being a boy. About ten years old, with hair cropped short and sticky-out ears. I took in a shaky-sharp breath. It was me, when I was younger.

Pleeeeeeeezzzzz, he said.

I stared at them, heart battering inside me. More of the shapes shivered and shuddered faces onto themselves and *all* of the smaller ones had mine.

They began closing in, their hands reaching, all moaning the same words.

Meeeeeeee.   Pleeeeezzzz.   Meeeeeeee.   Meeeeeeee. Pleeeeeezzz.

One of them ruffled into nothing as Merlin moved straight through it. He was frowning at me.

"You okay, man?"

Meeeeeeee.   Pleeeeezzzz.   Meeeeeeee.   Meeeeeeee. Pleeeeeezzz.

"Are you feeling ill or anything?"

What I really noticed was their eyes. Not the colour, but the emptiness. The only thing in them was the deepness of space, and I thought, *This is it. This is where the ghosts kill me, or suck out my brains or whatever.*

"Isis." I tried to shout, and it came out a squeak.

I could hear Isis's feet on the grass, heading into the clearing, and I knew I had to make a run for it. Dodge between the zombie-ghost things before they closed in completely.

My heart was beating so hard I thought I was going to be sick. I counted down to make myself do it.

Three. . .

Meeeeee. . .

Isis walked straight past me, up to the standing stone.

Two. . .

Pleeeeeezzzzzz.

She touched it with her hand.

One. . .

The circle of ghosts vanished.

Chapter Fifteen

Isis

It felt inevitable somehow, being here with the standing stone. A piece of rock, and yet it had already twisted the direction of her life before now. When she'd been here with Cally and Philip Syndal, the Devourer had been stalking her through the clouds. The time before, when she'd been only seven, they'd been making their way towards here when Angel was hit by a car and killed. She didn't listen to what Gray and Merlin were saying, her only interest was in the stone itself. And when Gray froze, wide-eyed and staring, she barely noticed.

Her memories fluttered, but couldn't give her an answer to the desperate feelings, which had brought her here. Only the standing stone could tell her.

Gray called her name but only the stone mattered, her fingertips reaching out to touch it. Cold and gritty, slicked with damp. . .

Everything flipped.

Isis was looking at herself. Her own face, her slightly widened eyes, the stretch of her arm. She could also see Gray and Merlin, the grass and the encircling trees. She had a goldfish-bowl view of things, and when she attempted to pull her hand back from the rock she couldn't work out how to. She was immobile, pinned in place.

What's happening?

She tried to cry out, but couldn't find her mouth or lungs. Arms, legs, body, head – those all belonged to the girl she could see standing in front of her. Isis herself didn't seem to have them any more. Instead she had the hills dreaming beneath her, and if she dipped her mind downwards. . .

I have to get out!

She fought to reach her body but even as she struggled Isis saw herself back away from the stone. And now it was Gray who had his hands on the rock, mouth open and eyes blank. Then Merlin, his arms stretched around the standing stone – around her. Merlin vanished, and a small boy slapped his palm on the standing stone, on her, turning back to shout at someone Isis couldn't see.

A succession of people materialised: men, women and children, on their own and in groups. Fingers tapped her, hands brushed casually past. Some clambered to sit on top of her, others leaned against her, posing for photos. Ones and twos soon added up to hundreds. The days peeled backwards into weeks, then years. Hundreds of people became thousands. All the people who'd ever visited here.

Isis was caught inside the standing stone, and she was able to distinguish accompanying phrases for every touch, people's thoughts jumping from skin to stone.

I won the race with Daddy!

Thought this would be bigger.

Look at me, I'm on the top!

Well that was a long walk for not much.

What a beautiful place.

Better hold my stomach in when they take the picture.

She wanted to screw her eyes shut against the torrent,

but she didn't have eyes any more. Instead the thoughts continued pouring in, while the clothes of her visitors changed from ones she recognised to ones she'd seen in photographs, to garments she only knew from history books. Victorian ladies in long skirts; a shepherd in his smock; children wrapped in rough cloth without any shoes.

The years blurred into centuries, time moving differently, backwards and forwards at the same time, as if she was living in a far wider stretch of time than the tiny moment of present that she'd had when human. If Isis concentrated, she could still see Merlin and Gray in the clearing, even see herself, but it was hard to fight the babble of thoughts coming at her from everyone visiting the standing stone in her thousands of years of now. She tried to remember the feeling of her own body but it was lost hundreds of years ago, or maybe hundreds of years in the future.

For long periods she was alone with the weather and the passing seasons. The only touch of human hands came on moonless nights, when people placed bunches of wild flowers at her feet or tied lengths of cord around her, twisted with wishes.

Let him love me.

Make my child well again.

Bring them home safe.

Stop her cow giving milk, the stupid old hag.

People's language changed, but she understood their meanings from the pictures in their minds, the forms that come before words. A Roman legionary put a coin at her base and asked for warmer weather.

On and on, backwards and forwards, until the hands on her were the ones that had carved her out of the ground and set her in place.

Special, came the thoughts as she was put in position. *Now there is a place for you.*

And the thoughts of these people were vivid and bright. Memories filled their minds with a sound like the roaring of a storm, and a perfect circle punched through a cloudy sky. They remembered looking up from their crops and animals, and crying out in fear and wonder.

Their hands stayed on her after they put her in place. *Talk to us.*

"I don't understand. What do you want me to say?"

Isis gasped at the sudden sound of her own voice. She was back in her own body again, arm outstretched, her fingertips touching the cold, grainy surface of the standing stone.

She put a hand to her chest, feeling its rise and fall. Put her other hand to her cheek and the curves of her face.

"What did you just do?" asked Gray, his voice trembling and scared.

"I. . ." She shook her head. "How long was I standing here?"

"No time at all," said Gray. "You haven't even been there a second."

Their walk back was quick, both of them keen to get away.

Gray was ahead of Isis, his shoulders hunched and pulled in on himself. Isis was relieved he wasn't speaking. She didn't want to talk, because she had no words to fit what had just happened to her. Merlin led the way, his few attempts at conversation trailing off in the face of their silence. After a short distance, he glanced back at them, then took out his mobile phone and began to chat with someone. "No, I've been up at the stone. I've got a couple of kids, found them in the woods, just wondered if. . . Oh, you have, okay. . . No! I'm bringing them straight back! Haven't taken them anywhere!"

In front of Isis, Gray slowed down, letting Merlin go ahead of them. Then he turned around.

"Are you contagious?" he hissed.

Isis looked at him, astonished. "What are you talking about?"

"Being psychic," said Gray. "Are you like a carrier or something? Is that what all the stuff with me holding Angel's hand, and seeing the Devourer and. . . everything! Is that what it was all for, so you could make me like *you*?" The last word was grated out. "Because I don't want it! I don't want any of that stuff!"

Isis stared at him, pulled out of her own strange experience by his anger.

"Have you. . . seen a ghost?"

Gray nodded.

"When?"

He nodded his head, back towards the clearing. "And in my garden."

"What did they look like?" she asked, not caring about what he'd seen in his garden. But at the standing stone, had he seen them too, the succession of people going backwards and forwards in time?

But Gray only frowned, and muttered, "Me."

"What?"

"They looked like me."

Isis found herself smiling in answer, trying to puzzle what he meant.

"Ghosts of yourself?"

"Don't laugh!" snapped Gray.

"I'm not. I'm sorry. But I don't think I've ever seen a ghost that looked like me. And if you'd caught being psychic from me, wouldn't you be able to. . . I don't know, see Angel for yourself?"

"I must be going mad then," he said miserably. "I thought I was getting better, but then up there. . ." He looked at Isis. "Maybe it's post-traumatic stress from what happened in the summer? Maybe my brain can't cope with what yours can."

"No!" She wasn't going to believe that! She couldn't bear to think she might be hurting him, by pulling him into her strange world. "It's got to be something else." She tried to think. "What *exactly* have you seen?"

"These fuzzy shapes at the standing stone. Some of them looked like me."

Isis held onto a small tree, steadying herself on the steep little track they were heading down. The trees and the slope of the land all looked so ordinary, yet completely alien, as if she'd never seen such things before. And it didn't feel right to be walking either, one foot after another, only going forwards, when she knew that wasn't how it worked at all.

"Maybe we're both crazy," she said to Gray. "Something really strange happened to me up there too."

His mouth opened with a question, but before she could tell him more, Merlin was stamping back up the path to find them.

"Your parents are at the protest camp, having hysterics about you," he said. "You never told me you'd gone off without telling them. Sounds like they were about to call out Search and Rescue."

He looked at the two of them, and whistled. "You two got a real faceful of energy at the standing stone, didn't you? Told you that place was powerful. You gotta be careful around that many ley lines."

Chapter Sixteen
Gray

When Dad and Cally reached us – led by a couple of pretty grimy-looking protestor types wearing camo gear – Dad started shouting about how irresponsible and reckless I was, even though the whole thing had been Isis's idea.

"Do you know what your mum would've done if we'd had to call the police?"

"And going off with a man you don't know!" Cally shrieked at Isis. "He could be a murderer or *anything*!"

"Nice to meet you too," said Merlin calmly.

Cally didn't even hear, she just carried on shrieking. Then they frogmarched us back to the car park, changing gear between outraged silence and lectures the entire way. Dad and Cally didn't even do any lovey-dovey stuff, which shows how badly they took it, and as soon as we were in Dad's camper, he started up again. As he drove he kept going on about how disappointed he was in my behaviour, you know?

But I only wanted to think about what had happened. Why had Isis wanted so desperately to go to the standing stone, so much so that she went off with someone we'd just met? And what did I see up there? Ghosts, or something else? I wanted to talk to Isis, find out what she had seen. But of course I couldn't.

Eventually Dad wore himself out from telling me off, and just drove in silence, his jaw clenching and unclenching. When we got back into Wycombe, he didn't head to his house, or to Mum's.

"Where are we going?" I asked.

"I'm picking Stu up," he said, like that was somehow my fault.

"More UFO stuff?" I hoped that maybe I could distract him by getting him onto his favourite topic. It didn't work though.

"He's coming over for your benefit, not that you deserve

it. He's been investigating UFO sightings and other activity at the quarry, trying to dig up any correlations with what happened to your class."

"That's what we're doing after this?" I mean, my dad's the only person who thinks good parenting is to sit huddled around a laptop for hours, Stu puffing away on his cigarettes and both of them getting all overexcited about aliens and conspiracies.

"*You're* not doing anything!" snapped Dad. "I've got a mind to take you straight back to your mum's!"

I knew he wouldn't though, because then Mum would ask why we were back early, and he'd have to tell her what had happened. He wouldn't want her knowing I'd escaped on his watch.

"Stu's car is at the garage," said Dad, after a minute or two, "so I told him we'd swing by and pick him up on the way home. You'd better be on your best behaviour."

I nodded. "Sorry, Dad," I said for the fortieth time. And I was. Sorry, and frightened, and wondering if I was going mad.

We headed west, through the bits of town where all the houses are split into flats and the gardens are just bin-holders. I expected Stu to live somewhere like that, but Dad took a turning into a cul-de-sac lined with bungalows, which was all frilly curtains and neat gardens.

"Stu lives here?"

Dad nodded.

"Does he live with his mum?"

I mean, Stu was at least fifty, but he definitely seemed the type.

Dad shook his head. "He lives with his wife."

"He's *married*?"

Dad pulled the van to the side of the road. "Getting on for thirty years. They've got a couple of grown-up kids, I think."

I tried to imagine having Stu for a dad, but I couldn't.

Someone stepped out of a gap between two garden hedges. He had an anorak hood pulled around his face, the way celebs do to try to avoid getting snapped by the paparazzi, and he was carrying a massive holdall. He made a run for the camper, nearly falling over because he was in such a hurry. It was Stu, of course. Anyone else would just wait inside their house, but not him.

Stu pulled open my door. "Let me in quick," he said. "I can't be in plain sight long."

Dad nodded at me and I sighed, climbing over the passenger seat and into the back.

"Don't want them making the connection between you and me," Stu said to Dad. As if anyone would care!

I sat down on the floor in the back of the camper, put my back to a cupboard, and braced my feet against the side of the van. There aren't seats in the back; Dad took them out so he could fit more UFO hunting gear in. It's not too uncomfortable, unless Dad goes over a lot of bumps.

"Anyone follow you?" Stu asked Dad.

Dad shook his head. "I'm always careful." I wasn't sure if he was joking or not, they take it all so seriously.

Dad set off, and I didn't say anything for a bit; I was still getting over the idea of Stu being married. Instead I stared at the sky through the windscreen. The clouds were all piled high and golden with shadows, like when you see old-fashioned pictures of God.

"Full blasting hasn't started," Dad said to Stu. They were chatting about the quarry, of course. "One of the protestors told me they've been holding things up for weeks now."

Stu snorted. "I doubt it's anything to do with the protestors. Probably money or the weather. I went to that protest camp last week, to ask if anyone had seen any UFOs around there, and they didn't even know what I was talking about!"

I spoke up from down on the floor. "Why were you asking them about UFOs?"

Stu turned around in his seat. "There's a lot of activity in this whole area. Unexplained lights, people losing time, mysterious beings. And all the witchcraft traditions associated with the standing stone."

I felt a bit sick when he said that. By then I was starting to think the shapes I'd seen could've been anything, even witches.

"And then this *quarry*, right in the middle of it," said Stu. He turned back to Dad. "I bet a million pounds we'll find out the military is involved in that." He sounded really pleased with the idea.

"There could be some undercover police hiding among the protestors. . ." said Dad.

"Not only the police. MI5 at least. This is just the kind of thing they'll be watching."

"Why would MI5 care about a quarry?" I asked.

Stu still had his hood up, straggles of grey hair poking out of the sides. He gave me this look he has: poor-stupid-you-for-not-understanding, lucky-I'm-here-to-sort-you-out.

"This is a rare earth quarry, Gray," he said.

"I know," I answered. He'd probably forgotten I was one of the people who'd been inside the quarry, now he was Mr Expert.

"So then, where are the main deposits of rare earths?" he asked me.

I thought back to our geography lessons. "China? The coast of Japan?"

"Exactly. Yet right here in our county is one of the richest and rarest deposits in the world, apparently. Don't you think that's odd?"

"No. It has to be somewhere."

Stu leaned over his seat at me. "I know geologists who say that a rare earth deposit shouldn't even *be* here."

I wondered what kind of geologists Stu would know.

Ones who think volcanoes are really a secret plot by an underground lizard civilisation, probably.

"Combine that with it being a hotspot for UFO sightings. . ." said Stu, meaningfully.

"So. . . what? It's an alien base?"

Stu laughed, shaking his head. "Of course not! Everyone knows those are in the Welsh mountains. But it doesn't mean aliens aren't mixed up in this. Think what rare earth metals are used for – tablets and smartphones and so on. Haven't you ever wondered how a technology could be so addictive that people queue all night to buy it, and once they've got it they can't do anything else? All swiping away on their touchscreens. What if it's not just chance?" He turned to Dad. "You still don't let him have a mobile phone?"

"I don't," said Dad.

"Which isn't fair," I said, "because everyone else has one! They said on TV that in three years from now, all kids over ten will have a smartphone. All of them except me."

Stu frowned at me from inside his anorak hood. "You think it's just playing games and tweeting your friends? What are smartphones *really* doing?"

I shrugged.

"Tracking you! Every call, every text, everywhere you go, everything you say and do. It's all recorded and sent off, so they know exactly what you're up to, every minute of every day."

"Why would anyone do that?" I said.

"Control!" hissed Stu, leaning right over the seat. "They talk about monitoring terrorists, when really they mean all of us. And you go along with it because they make it fun. Clever, aren't they?"

Stu's always going on about 'they'. It's why he keeps his hood up, so 'they' can't take his photo. Sometimes 'they' are the government, sometimes 'they' are a secret organisation, sometimes 'they' are aliens. But I bet whoever 'they' are, 'they' aren't even interested in Stu.

"Why would they want to control all of us?" I asked.

"There's a hundred people in the world," hissed Stu, "who between them have as much wealth as the three billion people on the bottom half of the world's heap. Did you know that?" He didn't wait for me to answer. "With that kind of money being piled up, of course they need something to keep people nice and distracted! Stop them asking if it's fair. That's where your smartphones and funny cat websites and phone games come in. You think they aren't loaded with tricks? You're getting mind-warped, and you don't even know it."

"That's not even possible," I said. " You can't mind-control people without them even knowing. . ."

"What about hypnotism?" Stu said. "That's mind control."

Dad shook his head. "Hypnotism's no good on a large scale, because anyone who's got a bit of willpower can break out of the control once they know it's happening. Like me, I could never be hypnotised, because of my strong mind."

Me and Stu shared a look.

"Games and cat websites are just for fun," I said.

"Are they?" asked Stu.

"What else are they for?"

He shook his head slowly, like I was being thick.

"Rates of youth crime are going down, did you know that? Not just in this country, but all over the world. And why? Because you're all being brainwashed, all getting tracked. You're all soft and docile, the way they want you, so you won't fight back when it starts. . ."

"That's enough, Stu," said Dad.

Stu looked at Dad, so all I could see was the blue of his anorak with his nose poking out.

"Don't you want your own son to know the truth?" he asked, like he couldn't believe it.

"Let him be," said Dad.

"Know what?" I asked. "What are you talking about?"

It had to be another of his conspiracies. The freaks in the Network are always cooking them up. Like when Stu told me the scandal about horsemeat in food was really a cover-up for aliens. He said the aliens were kidnapping the horses, doing weird experiments on them, then selling the dead ones to supermarkets in order to infect us with alien DNA. He said the horse DNA was really just a tracer, so the aliens could work out who'd been alien-infected.

I mean, if Stu believed the moon was made of cheese, he'd claim that every astronomer in the world was secretly controlling Stilton supplies.

Now Dad shook his head at Stu. "Gray's heard enough, okay?"

Stu didn't move for about ten seconds, then he quickly scrunched round to face me, before Dad could stop him.

"Think about it," he whispered. "Seven billion humans in the world, and half the wealth owned by just a hundred of them. How can such a tiny group of people keep hold of all that money? With the Organisation, which they set up to. . ."

"Stu!" snapped Dad.

"What's the Organisation?" I asked.

"You've said yourself the lengths they'll go to," Dad growled at Stu. "I don't want Gray involved!"

"You think he isn't involved already? You think you aren't on their radar? He needs to *know*."

"Know what?" I asked. "What are you going on about?"

Neither of them said anything for a minute, just Stu glaring at Dad, and Dad glaring at the road.

"All right," snapped Dad. "But no details, okay?"

Stu turned back to me, and he looked happier than I've ever seen him. It must be like getting a present for him, being able to fill someone in on one of his conspiracies.

"You know about Roswell, yeah?"

I nodded. It's this place in the United States where a UFO supposedly crashed in the 1950s, and the American military found bodies of alien pilots.

"Well that's total rubbish," said Stu. "Just a weather balloon and Cold War hysteria. I mean, aliens don't go crashing flying saucers; they don't even use flying saucers."

Dad nodded. "Think about what we saw this summer, the footage we got."

I wanted to tell him that those balls of light weren't UFOs either; they were ghosts. But I didn't; it would've taken way too much explaining, even if they'd believed me.

"Those of us who've delved deeper," continued Stu, "we know that Roswell is just a red herring. A distraction so people won't even go searching for the real truth."

I didn't ask what the real truth was, he was going to tell me anyway.

"Aliens contacted this planet decades ago," said Stu darkly. "They want to help us; they've got technology we can hardly even imagine. But those people, the ones who own everything, they don't want us having free energy, an end to disease and poverty, the knowledge of advanced civilisations. If everyone had everything they needed, how would the rich be able to control things? How would they make more money? So they set up the Organisation, to stop us finding out about the aliens and all they could give us, and to stop the aliens from contacting us. It's why they do their mind-wiping on anyone who gets close to the truth. It's why I have to be so careful. The trouble is, once you let something like that loose, a secret group with more money behind them than any government, then the genie's out of the bottle, if you get my meaning, and now they've. . ."

"That's enough," said Dad, cutting him off. "I don't want him knowing anything from the top-secret part of the Database."

I stared at the back of Dad's head, wondering how much of all this he believed. Stu's eyes bulged, waiting for my reaction.

I sighed. "So the quarry *is* to do with aliens, is that what you're saying?"

"No," said Stu. "What I'm saying is this quarry isn't about what they tell you. It's about what they *aren't* telling."

And then Dad and Stu started arguing about whether or not the world's super-rich are secretly using alien technologies themselves, and Stu got very het up about film stars who look really young but are actually in their sixties. I stopped listening, because I don't really care if facelifts were invented by aliens.

I mean, it's not true, is it? There isn't some secret organisation paid for by the world's super-rich, with agents creeping about and trying to mind-control people. . .

Gray. Look at the watch. Focus on it. Now, you will continue to believe Stu's story is ridiculous. You will forget ever having heard of the Organisation.

You're hypnotising me, aren't you?

Look at the watch.

Dad said you can break it if you. . .

See the way the watch glitters.

If you. . . If you. . . What was I talking about?

Chapter Seventeen

Isis

"What's going on?" Isis asked. It was Monday morning and they were trying to get to geography, but were blocked by a crowd ahead of them in the corridor. Pupils seemed to fill every bit of space, stopping anyone from getting by, talking over each other. The crowd centred around the entrance to the girls' toilets.

Isis sighed, feeling irritable. She'd felt this way ever since they visited the standing stone: ready to snap, her temper on edge. As if something had shifted with the world, and nothing quite fitted any more. She felt anxious too. She'd managed to explain away Mandeville's words at the seance, but her new friends were more wary of her than they had been, as if she was a bomb and they couldn't trust her not to go off. Only Jess seemed un-affected.

"Out of the way!" shouted Jess, trying to push her way through the mob. She got pushed back and gave up, shaking her head.

Isis could hear a girl sobbing. She stood on tiptoe, but still couldn't see what was causing this crowd.

"None of them will budge, must be a fight or something," said Nafira.

A Year Seven boy turned around. "It's not fighting, is it? Something's *in* there!"

"What's in there?" asked Isis.

The boy pulled his eyebrows into a puzzled frown. "*You* know. You're the one who said it."

"Said what?"

"That it's haunted!" The boy's voice was thick with astonishment. "*You* saw the ghost! You said the ghosts want to kill us all. Johno says your eyes went all weird, like this. . ." he rolled his eyes back, leaving mostly the whites showing, "and then you said—"

"I didn't!" said Isis. "I mean, I did, but it was a mis-understanding."

The boy looked disbelieving, and a little disappointed. "What about the ghost in the toilet that sucks your life out?"

"I never said there was a ghost in. . ." Isis stopped. Because she *had*. Those toilets were where she'd held the seance for Summer, introducing her to her ancestors, with Mandeville's help.

"I never said the ghosts were bad," she said, sounding lame even to herself.

The boy gave her a look, obviously thinking she was just trying to backtrack.

The sobs of the girl in the middle of the crowd continued.

Another boy, further into the scrum, called over his shoulder to report what was going on.

"It's someone from 2F," he said. "She's completely lost it! Says she saw something inside one of the cubicles." He paused to listen. "She's totally freaking out!" he cried gleefully.

A horrified hot feeling ran through Isis. Whoever the girl was, this would follow her all through the rest of school!

"I should do something," Isis said, holding tight to her

school bag. "Tell them there's nothing to be scared of, or tell them it was only a joke."

"No!" snapped Jess. "If you say it was a joke, no one will believe any of the rest! What'll happen if people think we've been messing with them?" She shook her head. "Let's go another way."

"But that means right around the school!" said Nafira. "We'll be really late!"

Jess shrugged. "So? It's not like this is our fault, *is it*?"

As they left, Isis glanced back to see a teacher wading into the middle of the crowd, shouting for everyone to calm down. She tried to convince herself that Jess was right and this hysteria wasn't her fault, but her thoughts kept fixing on the girl, crying in the middle of it all.

There was a strange atmosphere as they hurried through school. Everywhere students huddled in groups or went too fast along corridors, their voices louder than usual, every conversation full of exclamations. She noticed how many eyes turned to look at her as she passed, and while she'd got used to feeling like a kind of celebrity over the last few weeks, the incident with Mandeville had changed things. The looks she got today weren't admiring or curious: there were frowns, and even hints of hostility.

As they made their way past the library, a girl from their year was coming the other way. She started when she saw Isis, then made to intercept them, her face lit with excitement.

"I saw a ghost!" she said. "I must be like you!"

"You didn't!" said Nafira, eyes wide.

The girl nodded.

Isis stared at her. "Where?"

"At the school gates, after Mum dropped me off. A woman with dark hair. She was all blurry, so she *had* to be a ghost. She came right up to me and said, 'Please stop!'"

"A woman?" asked Isis, trying to think of all the ghosts she'd ever seen in the school. "Was she wearing a long green dress, really old-fashioned?" The green lady was the only ghost of a woman Isis could think of, but she was usually outside the back of the canteen, walking the same route before disappearing through a now bricked-up doorway.

The girl shook her head. "Not old-fashioned – she was wearing jeans and this bright orange blouse."

"I've never seen a ghost like that in school," said Isis.

"If she was wearing jeans," said Jess, "then you saw a substitute teacher or a parent, not a ghost!"

The girl pulled back, her cheeks blushing in spots as if Jess had slapped her.

"I didn't, I know what I saw! The ghost said, 'Please, please!' Why would a teacher say that?"

"I don't know, they probably didn't!" Jess pulled at Isis's arm. "Come on, we're going to be late." She led the way, taking them through the library. As they walked quickly past the stands of books, Isis tasted a waft of dust, and Nafira went into a paroxysm of coughing.

They stopped, Jess patting Nafira's back while she coughed into her hands.

Mandeville slid out of the air next to Isis.

"So, what appointments have we today?" he asked. "Cats, dogs and departed rabbits, no doubt."

Isis widened her eyes, shaking her head a little. Jess had decided they shouldn't hold any seances for a while, after what had happened in the alleyway. She still hadn't decided when to start again, which Isis was relieved about.

"No seance," Isis mouthed silently, facing away from the others.

Mandeville shook his head, the disappointment plain on his dried-out features. "How long will this hiatus last? It's no way to go forward with our endeavours."

Isis gave the tiniest shrug of her shoulders. Not today anyway, with the fuss at the toilets and the weird atmosphere in school. Not with the way she was feeling either.

"Not a good day," she mouthed.

Mandeville's patchy eyebrows gathered in a frown. "Well today is more unusual than some I have known. But I don't see why we can't carry on. . ."

Nafira had recovered now and the others started walking again. Isis held back for a moment.

"Why is today unusual?" she whispered. What could Mandeville see that she could only sense as atmosphere and oddness?

He smiled. "So I've caught your attention?" He tapped her shoulder with a bony finger. "Allow me to clarify the difference between the psychic and untalented mind. The psychic sees what is truly there. The untalented mind sees projections of its own imaginings, and believes them to be real."

She glared at him. Why couldn't he tell her, instead of giving little lectures?

He tilted his head. "It surprises me that you are unable to make this distinction today, given the reach of your powers."

"What's going on?" she hissed. "Tell me!"

Mandeville put a finger to his lower lip. "Well perhaps I shall, if you allow me to continue my work."

Isis shook her head, but Mandeville looked smug, in the way of someone who knows they're in control.

"Then we have nothing more to discuss," he said. "Maybe we will, if you change your mind?"

Isis spun around and hurried after the others. He was so infuriating, and completely selfish! She didn't need him to tell her then, she'd work it out. . .

A large window was on her right, looking out over the playground. Through it she could see a boy, Gray's friend from UFO club. He was running, flapping his arms as if fighting off a swarm of bees, and his shouts could be heard even inside.

"Go away! Go away! Go away!"

People outside had stopped what they were doing, staring or laughing uncertainly, as if maybe this was a joke.

"What's going *on* today?" she asked, catching up with

the others, who'd stopped facing the door leading from the library. Mr Gerard, the deputy head, had just pushed it open and was heading straight towards them.

He was wearing the expression of someone who'd found what they were looking for.

Chapter Eighteen
Gray

Jayden was freaking out. Shouting, running a couple of steps one way, spinning around and running the other way. People were laughing and making jokes, but none of them were helping him.

I shoved past a couple of Year Eight boys, grabbed hold of Jayden's arms and tried to pull him to a stop. "Jayden!" He was looking past me, his eyes not quite focused. "Jayden, what are you doing?" He noticed me at last.

"They won't leave me alone," he said.

"Who?"

"The boys."

"Get lost!" I shouted at the crowd gathered around. "Leave him alone!"

But Jayden shook his head, his eyes too wide. "Not them." He pointed, his arm swinging in a wide arc. "*Them!*"

"Come on," I said, pulling him out past the gathering. The Year Eights tried to follow, but I swore at them until they went away.

"What are you talking about?" I asked Jayden. "What are you doing?"

"There's loads of them. . ." He was looking behind us, counting quietly. "Fifteen!" He dropped his voice to a whisper. "They're all different ages, from babies to old men." He gripped onto my arm.

"Who are?"

"Them," whispered Jayden. "The ones no one else can see."

I got this shivery shock.

"You don't believe me!" he said.

"I do." I was so relieved it wasn't just me, but terrified at the same time.

"They're following me around," said Jayden, staring at nothing. "They won't leave me alone."

"Are they still here?" I asked, and Jayden nodded silently.

"I wish they'd shut up. They keep going on, but I'm not *doing* anything. I haven't even touched them!"

Another cold shiver. "What are they saying?"

Stop, stop, stop! Except it wasn't Jayden who said that; the voice was much deeper. I turned around, and my heart nearly stopped in fright. Standing next to me was this tall man. His hair was clipped in angles, and he was wearing a blue hoody, these stupid, ultra-wide trousers and mirrored sunglasses. On his wrist was a massive watch, with a touchscreen display. He looked like someone, but I couldn't think who.

"Stop what?" I said. "What are you talking about?"

Jayden squeaked. "Are they talking to you as well?"

I shook my head, not taking my eyes off the man who'd just appeared.

"How do you know what they're saying then?"

"Because there's a man next to me who's saying the same thing."

Jayden looked either side of me, his face more scared than ever. "I can't see any man."

"And I can't see any babies, Jayden."

Stop! Stop! Stop! Stop! Stop!

It was hard to think through the shouts of the ghost-man.

Jayden was shaking now. "Someone told me Isis has cursed the school, so it's full of ghosts."

"Do you actually *believe* that?"

"I don't know!" he shouted. "I don't even believe in ghosts, and now there's a whole gang of them following me around!"

For a moment even I wondered if Isis had done it, somehow. I mean, she's done a lot of stuff you'd never believe. I've seen a monster go inside her, and light pour out of her like the sun.

Stop! Stop! Stop! Stop! said the man, like a broken record.

Angel and that creepy Mandeville were ghosts, I knew that, but urban-future man didn't look the way they did. He was more solid, and more. . . blank. Like, if you see a photograph on a computer and then you see it printed out, the picture's the same, but they're different too. The man in front of me, he wasn't ghostly, you know? He was something else. He was like the figures at the standing stone, but more. . . finished-looking.

He took a step towards me. *Stop! Stop! Stop! Stop!*

"They're getting *closer*," said Jayden, panicking.

"Merlin walked straight through one," I said to myself.

"What?" squawked Jayden.

I took hold of Jayden's wrist. "Run for the door into school."

"*What?*"

"Just do it. Come on!" This time I didn't count; I set off at a flat-out run with Jayden shrieking and pulling behind me.

"You're crazy! Don't!"

But I didn't let go of him, just kept my eyes on that door and forced my legs to go as fast as I could manage. Across the playground, a girl from our year started screaming like she was getting murdered, even though there was no one near her.

Stop! Stop! The voice was right by my ear, making me stumble, sending my heartbeat so fast I thought it might explode.

"Argh!" cried Jayden, suddenly speeding up, getting ahead of me. He's not a brilliant runner – he must've been half killing himself.

"They're keeping up with me!" he panted.

"We're nearly there!"

And then Gav came running out of nowhere and crashed straight into us.

"They're after me!" he shouted, eyes wide and staring. "They won't leave me alone!"

That was more than Jayden could cope with. He twisted in my grip and started yelling at nothing.

"Get away from me!"

"Leave me alone!" shouted Gav, also at nothing.

"Go away!"

"Get back!"

They were shouting and hitting at thin air, while my own invisible man was closing in, hands reaching out towards me.

Stopstopstopstopstopstopstop.

I lost it too, starting to shout myself. It was the way he just kept coming, and wouldn't give up. . .

"WHAT'S GOING ON HERE?" Mr Watkins came out of the door. It shocked us all still for a second. "GET INSIDE, right now!"

He hauled us through the doorway.

"What do you think you're doing? There's enough trouble today without you three mucking about!"

Normally I would have hated getting told off in front of everyone, people stopping to watch. But I was glad, if you can believe it, because it was only us. No ghost, zombie or whatever he was. Just me, Gav and Jayden, getting shouted at by an ordinary, human teacher.

As Mr Watkins went on about us setting a good example for the younger pupils, Gav and Jayden both kept glancing at the door.

"Break's nearly over," finished Mr Watkins, "so get to your lessons." He gave us a last glare and walked away.

"You all right?" I asked Gav.

He nodded. Slowly, and sort of surprised.

"I was fine until I went outside," he said, "then they all. . ." He frowned, as if trying to puzzle out a dream, then shook his head, looking at his feet.

"Was it someone no one else could see?" I asked.

"Did they look like you?" said Jayden.

Gav flicked his gaze up and nodded. "There were about ten of them," he mumbled. "Four of them in school uniform. They looked like me, even the older ones."

"Mine too," whispered Jayden.

"I only saw this one guy, but he—" I stopped, this

horrible thought in my head. When I'm older, I'll easily be as tall as the man I saw.

"And now they're gone!" said Gav, staring out through the door.

Outside a teacher ran past, chasing the girl who'd been screaming. We all backed away, like we were safer further from the door, but I could still see Imran, this boy from our geography class, standing stock-still in the middle of the playground, crying.

"What's going *on?*" asked Jayden, shaky-sounding, like he was only just holding it together.

"Everyone's on about ghosts," said Gav.

I shook my head, trying to untangle it all. "How can you have a ghost of yourself?"

"Maybe it's a ghost's trick?" said Gav. "Like a disguise?"

Jayden frowned. "Ghosts float, but this lot walk, like zombies."

"They aren't zombies!" said Gav. "Zombies are other people. These are *us.*"

"Clones?" said Jayden.

"Then why did they vanish when we came inside?"

"I don't know!" said Jayden, peering anxiously through

the door. "Do you think they're out there waiting for us?"

Gav backed further away from the door. "I'm not going to find out."

"What about walking home after school?" said Jayden.

We were all silent, thinking the same horrible thoughts, then Gav said, "I'll ring my mum, ask her to pick us up. She would if it's an emergency."

Jayden held an imaginary phone to his ear. "Hi, Mum, can you give me a lift home, because I'm seeing loads of ghosts that look like me, or maybe they're zombies. I'm not sure cos no one else can see them. Oh no, it's fine, we don't need to stop at the psychiatric hospital on the way." He looked at Gav.

Gav scowled back. "All right, what do *you* think?"

"Maybe terrorists have sprayed weird drugs into the school and we're hallucinating?"

"Oh God," groaned Gav. "It's a genetically engineered virus, and this is the first symptom. Next we're all going to bleed out through our eyes and die."

"It's not that!" I said. "Come on, let's think. We only see them outside, right?"

They nodded.

"So they aren't zombies or clones, but they could still be some kind of ghost?"

"An outdoors-only ghost?"

I sighed. That didn't sound very likely either.

"When did you first see them?" Jayden asked. There was something about the way he said it. That's when I started to realise.

"Three weeks ago," answered Gav quietly. "I saw a boy who looked like me. Only a glimpse, and I thought maybe I'd imagined it."

"I saw this thing on the school trip," said Jayden. "Just a shape, but it had my face."

"I saw shapes too," I said.

"Why didn't you say anything?" asked Gav.

"Why didn't *you*?" I took a breath. "And I saw this kid in our back garden, the day after. He looked just like a photo Mum's got of me when I was five." I didn't tell them about the standing stone though. I was still worrying about the wrong things then, like them thinking I was the craziest of all.

The same thing clicked in our heads, all at once.

"The school trip," said Jayden.

"Something at the quarry?" I said.

"This is because of that?" asked Gav. "But that was ages ago!"

"Oh!" yelped Jayden. "Remember in physics, we did all that stuff about radioactivity? How when they first discovered it they didn't know it could make you ill and they used radioactive paint in watches, and made necklaces out of uranium and stuff?"

Me and Gav both nodded, even though Gav probably didn't have a clue.

"So what if that rare earth stuff they're mining is like that? Except instead of radioactivity, it gives you hallucinations?"

It made sense, and even if hallucination-inducing rock wasn't the best, it was way better than seeing stuff with no explanation. . .

Gav shook his head though. "They quarry for rare earth metals in China and America and places. Wouldn't it be all over the internet if it made people go loopy?"

We were quiet for a minute, then Jayden piped up. "Mr Watkins went on loads about it being a really unusual deposit or seam or whatever. Maybe what they're mining there is so special that. . ."

"It makes you hallucinate?" Gav pulled a face. "It won't be much good for touchscreens then, will it? Anyway, why would that Dr Harcourt take us into the quarry if she knew it would make us like this?"

"An experiment!" said Jayden. "Like Frankenstein?"

"Then why is this all happening today?" asked Gav. "Why not when we actually went to the quarry?"

"Perhaps it's slow-acting?" said Jayden. "Like when that Russian man got poisoned using radioactive polonium? He didn't die for ages."

We all went quiet.

"Are we going to die?" asked Gav.

Chapter Nineteen

Isis

"So, are any of you going to explain?"

Isis's cheeks were burning hot, and her stomach and heart seemed to have swapped places. She was standing in front of Mr Gerard's desk with Jess, Chloe, Hayley and Nafira.

"I hope you understand how serious this is," Mr Gerard said into the silence. "You may have thought you were engaged in some kind of game, or a bit of fun, but you've brought serious disruption to the whole school." He leaned forwards in his chair. "I have children claiming to see ghosts and hysteria in the corridors. I have teachers who can't *teach*, because they are so busy calming everyone down. The welfare officers are already overwhelmed with students: thirteen pupils had to be sent home because they'd made themselves ill with distress. You can imagine how pleased I was to have to phone so many parents, and how pleased *they* were to take time off work to pick up their children."

Isis's brow ached from frowning. Why was everything going crazy today? Mandeville's disastrous seance had been over a week ago, so it couldn't be that. It was hard to understand what was happening, especially as her thoughts kept drifting back to the standing stone, and the detached, otherworldly feelings it had left her with. She blinked, trying to concentrate.

Mr Gerard glared along the row. "I would appreciate it if you didn't try to pretend this is nothing to do with you, because a number of Year Seven pupils have identified you as the group at the centre of it all."

"But it can't be us!" said Nafira, saying out loud what Isis had been thinking. "We haven't done anything today!"

Mr Gerard leaned forwards. "So you haven't been holding seances and pretending you can see ghosts?"

"No!" said Jess. "The Year Sevens must be telling each other stories." Mr Gerard scrutinised her, then read aloud from his notes.

"'They summoned this ghost to haunt up the girls' toilets.'" He looked at Jess. "'Jessica Manning invites people to seances, mostly from the upper years.'" His glare turned to Isis. "'Isis Dunbar said everyone in school is going to die.'"

"I didn't. . . I mean, that isn't what he meant to say," Isis blurted. "It came out wrong."

Mr Gerard raised an eyebrow. "He?"

She had no saliva, it had all evaporated.

"Isis is the one who started it!" said Chloe suddenly. "She says she can see ghosts and she does this old man voice to make it sound creepy." She stepped away from the others. "No one likes her cos she's so weird. She must be doing this to get her own back or something."

"No, I. . ."

Mr Gerard turned to look at Isis. He waited, and she tried to think how to explain, but her mind couldn't piece together anything sensible.

I just wanted people to like me.

It wasn't my fault – a hundred-year-old ghost made me do it.

"Does anyone else want to speak?" asked Mr Gerard.

"I only went along with stuff," said Nafira, "because Jess was so into it."

"That's a lie!" said Jess, turning on her. "No one made you!"

Mr Gerard returned to Jess. "Did you invite people to take part in seances?"

Jess shrugged.

He looked at Isis. "Did you pretend to see ghosts, and put on voices to scare the younger students?"

"I. . ." *didn't pretend.* For the first time in her life, Isis had actually told the truth about her ability. She had opened herself up and stopped hiding.

"You do realise how serious this is?" said Mr Gerard. "But you can reduce the severity of your punishment by accepting your responsibility and admitting to your role in this business. If you explain that you made up these stories, it may help calm the situation."

"But everyone will hate us!" squeaked Hayley.

Isis tried to think through the thudding of her heart. The other girls were all popular, they'd probably survive, but her reputation would be destroyed, especially with the way the others were already blaming it on her. She'd be the butt of every joke again, worse probably. *No one would be friends with her after this.*

"You can't make us," said Jess, defiantly tipping her head back.

Mr Gerard tapped his pen on the notebook. "Let me spell this out. You can admit that this was all a game, a joke, or whatever it was, accept your punishment and face the other pupils. Or I will be forced to exclude you."

All the girls gasped.

I've never been in any trouble before, Isis wanted to say. *How can I go from nothing to exclusion?*

The group broke into pieces.

"*Isis* started it!"

"Jess was sucking up to the Year Elevens, that's why it happened!"

"It's not fair punishing me, *I* didn't pretend I can see ghosts!"

Illusions of friendship swiftly dropped away. Jess didn't join in the accusations, but she didn't stick up for Isis either, and she took a small step to the side so that Isis was by herself. The others were back in their original group, with Isis outside it, her heart beating fast in her throat.

They'd *made* her admit she was psychic, and now they were calling her a liar!

She lifted her head up, and spoke into the hubbub. "I didn't make anything up. I *can* see ghosts."

"I told you!" cried Nafira.

"That's what she's like all the time!" said Chloe.

Mr Gerard held up his hand, bringing silence. He looked at Isis. "So, you *have* been telling other students you can communicate with ghosts?"

Isis nodded. *No more lying.* "Because I can."

"And you did tell a large group of students they were all going to die?"

Isis opened her mouth to deny it, but what was the point? He'd obviously rounded up and interrogated the younger children from the alleyway.

She nodded. "Mandeville didn't mean it as a threat. He only meant that everyone gets old and dies in the end."

Mr Gerard was tapping his pen again. "Do you genuinely believe this, or are you just an extremely good liar?"

"It's true, that's all."

She smiled, even though it was probably the worst thing to do, because it felt so good telling the truth. As if she were standing straighter, her head closer to the sky. She'd been carrying silence so long, she'd forgotten how heavy it was.

"There's quite a few ghosts in school, actually." She watched Mr Gerard's eyebrows get higher. "There's two Victorian girls in the playground who play a skipping game, and this shouty teacher with a moustache who's always in the main hall. The ghost in the girls' loos was Summer Bailey's great aunt, but she went back to the other realm and anyway she wouldn't hurt a fly, mostly she talked about knitting."

"See?" cried Chloe. "She's the one, not us!"

Isis didn't even look at Chloe.

"I'm sorry if people got scared, Mr Gerard. But if anyone else says they're seeing ghosts, they're just. . ." Making it up? She couldn't bring herself to say it, not facing the same accusation. She focused on the deputy head, hoping he'd somehow understand. "Psychics are really rare, there *can't* be loads in school."

Mr Gerard was silent, then he said "Are you admitting to holding a seance in the girls' toilet?"

Isis opened her mouth, about to answer with a bold

yes, when she saw the other girls' faces. They were desperate, frightened of what she'd say next, that she'd drag them all down with her. Well, they'd wanted her to be psychic.

"I'm not lying," she said, hearing the shake in her own voice. "But none of them are able to see ghosts." She nodded towards the other girls.

Mr Gerard tightened his jaw, the muscles of his face shifting.

"All right." He pointed at Jess, Chloe, Hayley and Nafira. "You will each have lunchtime detention for five days and be on report for two weeks. If I hear one word from any of your teachers, then the consequences will be far more severe." He turned his gaze to Isis. "As ringleader, and for showing no remorse at all for what you've done, I have no choice but to remove you from school until this can be sorted out. You will leave immediately."

Chapter Twenty

Isis

Cally crunched through the gears, muttering under her breath as she stopped and started through the traffic. Isis sat silently next to her, listening to the rise and fall of the engine, the sounds of other cars. And the singing.

Isis had been marched by Cally from the school to their car, and Angel had been waiting inside it, her head poking out through the shut window, waving happily. Now she was dancing on the back seat, singing the little song she seemed hooked on at the moment.

"The little fish, the little fish, he swimming round and round. He swimming up and down and up with Mummy."

"I'm sorry," Isis said, at last.

Cally didn't answer.

She's too angry to speak to me. That was Cally's way.

"I don't know why I did it," Isis said, although she did, she knew exactly why.

Still Cally didn't answer.

Isis fiddled with the thick fabric of her seat belt. "I just wanted Jess to be friends with me," she said.

It sounded so pathetic. And Jess hadn't even been her friend, that was clear now.

Cally didn't speak; her mouth was set in a line. Only when they'd reached their street and Cally had parked the car in front of the flats did she finally say anything. Not looking at Isis, staring through the front windscreen.

"I just don't understand why you'd do this," she said. "It's like you wanted to make fun of me in front of everyone at your school."

Isis turned in her seat. It had never even occurred to her Cally might view things that way. "No. That wasn't it."

"Then why hold seances?" asked Cally.

Isis started to think of an explanation, but she stopped herself. She'd decided to tell the truth in school. She had to keep to it.

"Do you remember out in the field, with Gil and Gray? The time we saw the UFO?"

Cally shuddered. "How can I forget?"

Isis shook her head. "No, not when I. . ." Died. "I mean before. When I said I saw something, and you said I must be psychic like you." Isis looked at her mum. "Do you remember?"

Cally nodded, slow and reluctant. "But I was very. . . enthusiastic about the spirits then. I've thought a lot about it since, what with everything that happened, and you getting so badly hurt, and Philip Syndal turning out to be. . . not quite normal. I think perhaps I went too far."

"I can see ghosts," said Isis.

Cally held still, before suddenly turning around and taking hold of Isis's hands, gripping too tightly.

"This isn't something to play with, Isis." Cally leaned forwards a little. "I know it must have seemed glamorous, seeing Philip at the theatre with all his fans. I'm sure it looked like fun, but look at what's already happened in your school. It's so easy to make terrible mistakes, even if you're only pretending to contact the other realm. And you don't have to pretend to be psychic, Isis, you're special in so many ways."

Isis pulled her hands out of Cally's.

"Why don't you ever listen to me?" she said, louder than she meant to. "I'm not *pretending*. I can see ghosts!" She found herself shouting, needing Cally to hear. "I can see the old teacher in the main hall at school, and the woman who plants potatoes in the shopping centre, and I could see Philip Syndal's spirit guide. . ." Her mum's astonished face only made her angrier. "I can see Angel!"

Angel stopped singing, stopped dancing. Poked her head between the seats.

"You saw her too," Isis continued, unable to stop herself now. "Down in the mortuary, after they revived me. I know you did, because *I* showed her to you!"

The car was silent but for the sound of Cally's breathing.

"Mummy seed me," said Angel.

"Oh. . . God," gasped Cally, and she began to cry. Choking, gulping sobs that drew up from inside, shaking her shoulders and bending her double, hands over her face.

Isis's heart pounded on, her fury congealing into something less fiery as Cally sagged against her seat, leaning her head back as her sobs subsided into small gasps. She took a deep breath, and turned her head, looking sideways at Isis.

"You used to sit on my lap together when you were little," Cally said quietly. "Do you remember?"

Isis nodded.

"I 'member!" cried Angel delightedly.

"I can still feel the both of you," Cally continued, "even now. The way you held yourself so neatly, while Angel kicked and wriggled. My two arms around my two girls, both so beautiful and so different." She sighed. "Angel wasn't much past being a baby. She hadn't even learned to talk properly."

Cally turned her head back to straight, and Isis watched a tear dawdle its way down her cheek.

"She was so solid," Cally whispered. "She stomped around. She shouted and had tantrums. She was proud when she used the toilet by herself."

Something turned over inside Isis and she looked at her now ghost-sister.

"I did poos," said Angel, nodding wisely.

"I loved her with every particle of myself," said Cally,

"just the way I love you." She sat up and wiped her hand across her cheek. "But that wasn't enough."

Isis clicked and unclicked her seat belt. She couldn't go back, now that she'd started. "You did see her though, didn't you? In the mortuary?"

Cally took in another deep breath, then said, "Yes."

"I tol' you!" cried Angel.

Isis smiled. At her mum, at her ghost-sister.

"Don't you see? Angel's still with us! I'm sorry I never told you before, but I. . ." *was frightened of how you'd react, when being psychic was all you had.* No, she couldn't say that. "I didn't think you'd believe me. But now you do, because you've seen her yourself! And that means we're still a family, all together. You, me, Angel. I know Dad's not here, but we're all right, aren't we?"

Cally didn't answer Isis's smile.

"I wasn't surprised Angel was there in the mortuary," she said quietly, "after all that had just happened to you. I expect she came back, to watch over you and make sure you were all right. But seeing her. . ." Cally fell silent again.

"Weren't you happy?" Isis asked, trying to puzzle her mum's strange reaction.

Cally laughed, and it was almost another sob.

"Angel was going to follow you into primary school," Cally said, but it was hard to tell if she was talking to Isis, or reciting something she'd said to herself many times before. "That's what I was expecting. And I was going to buy her a pink scooter for her next birthday." Angel clapped her hands, while Cally continued without hearing her. "I told people she'd be a handful as a teenager, but I knew in my heart she'd calm down after and get a nice boyfriend. I wanted her to go to college and get a good job." She looked directly at Isis. "That's what I was expecting for her, but she'll never have any of it."

"So it was a comfort then?" asked Isis hopefully. "Seeing her ghost, knowing she isn't gone forever?"

"The ghost of my dead baby girl," said Cally quietly. "Looking just how I remembered. Exactly the same." She put a hand out to Isis's cheek, as if trying to trace something in her face. "Not grown, or lost her baby teeth, or gone to school. Right there beside me, but with no life in front of her. All her wonderful potential ended in a full stop." Cally drew back her hand, and paused for another long moment. "I'm glad she was there in the mortuary, looking after you. Because seeing her that way, it hurt so much, and yet I finally. . . understood. I'd been marking every milestone she'd missed – vaccinations, birthdays, the day she should have started school. But she's not doing any of those things, not anywhere, and I realised that. . ." A tear wound its way from her eye. "I have to let her go. I have to accept that three precious years was all I got."

Isis sat motionless, fast heartbeats whirling blood and thoughts around her head. All this time she'd thought that Cally seeing Angel would heal their family, bring them back together again, but in a few sentences Cally had set that on its head. And her mum was right, in a way Isis couldn't quite face, because Angel was stuck, a perpetual three-year-old. Isis had a sudden vision of herself as an old woman, with a ghost-baby Angel still drifting around.

Angel herself seemed unconcerned however. She climbed in between the front seats, and placed a small, invisible hand on her mother's face. Cally shivered, but didn't move, and Angel leaned to whisper into Cally's ear, something Isis couldn't hear. Then Angel clambered back again, the gear stick passing straight through her body.

Isis stared questioningly at her, but Angel only looked smug. "Mummy got a little fish," she said, sitting in the back seat.

Cally smiled to herself, lost in thoughts Isis couldn't reach. Then she shook her head a little, and turned to Isis.

"Promise me, no more trying to impress people with seances?"

"I wasn't—" She stopped. What had any of them been doing, if not trying to impress? Isis, Jess, Mandeville; all of them, for their own different reasons.

"Promise?" asked Cally. Isis could see the pain etched on her mum's face, and yet she still couldn't bring herself to nod. Cally folded her arms, and set her face to the front. "We'll wait then. We aren't leaving the car until you do."

Isis glanced at Angel while they sat in their stand-off. Cally was right. Angel was exactly as she had been the day she died. She'd never get older or grow up, never do any of the things Cally had wanted for her.

So why was she still here? Mandeville had hinted once that Angel had stayed to protect Isis. . .

Angel grinned. "Look, I can do a roly-poly!" She curled herself into a crab shape and tumbled along the back seat.

A strange protector.

"Mummy got a little fish," repeated Angel, sitting up in her crab position. "He see me any time I want. He do roly-polies too." Angel rolled back along the seat.

What was she talking about? Isis frowned, but Angel only put her finger to her lips. "It Mummy's secret," and she began her song about fishes again. "Little fishy swimming round. . ."

"I'm waiting," said Cally, arms folded, not looking at Isis. "Do you promise?"

Isis pressed her hands against her eyes. There wasn't a way out. When she told the truth, people wouldn't or couldn't believe. But if she said she'd made everything up, she seemed like the worst kind of attention-seeker. Why had she let Jess drag her further and further into doing seances? Why had she listened to Mandeville's threats and wheedling?

"I know seeing Angel in the hospital must have been a shock for you," said Cally.

"It wasn't a shock."

"But I don't want you getting involved with things you don't understand Isis. Even just pretending. And we have other things to focus on now." She twisted in her seat. "Do you remember I was very tired in the summer?"

Isis shook her head. Behind them Angel carried on with her song. "Mummy's little fishy, swimming up and down. . ."

"I thought at first it was just stress," said Cally, "but then I realised that I'd. . . And, well, then that night happened before I got a chance to say, and afterwards I wasn't even speaking to Gil so I didn't know how to—"

"Just *tell* me!"

Cally looked at her. "I'm pregnant."

". . . and down and up, inside Mummy's tummy."

Chapter Twenty-one

Gray

At least thirty kids were crammed into the welfare office, using every chair and sitting all over the floor.

Jayden and Gav had insisted on going there; they were both freaking out that they were going to die. Gav had his sleeve rolled up and was pointing at what he claimed was a rash, although it looked like normal skin to me.

It seemed like half our geography class was there already, plus a load of Year Sevens who were busy crying. The staff were looking really hassled, and one of them was doing nothing but ringing parents.

I'd gone with Jayden and Gav, not because I thought we'd been covered in slow-acting poison, but because there was no way I could find out what was going on if I stayed in school. I needed to access Dad's Network of super-freaks by hacking into his email account, like I had before. But he's so paranoid about security, I could only do that from his computer. If anyone had information about this kind of weird stuff, it was the Network.

The trouble was, the staff weren't actually sending that many people home, not compared to how many there were. It was only the really bad ones. Everyone else was given, "Why don't you sit quietly until you feel better?" or, "Have a glass of water."

I needed something better than Gav's rash to get out of school. I needed the old standby. I walked over to Mrs Bhatnagar.

"Yes?"

"I feel sick."

"Well go and sit over. . ."

"No, really—" And I clapped my hands over my mouth, bent over a bit and made this retching noise, then I looked up all panicky, like the only thing I cared about was not spewing down myself.

"Get to the toilet!"

I ran there, making loads of sick noises, and dabbed a bit of water on my forehead so I'd look clammy. When I got back, Mrs Bhatnagar was too busy to check me over properly.

"I'm going to ring your mother," she said crossly. "The last thing we need is a sickness outbreak as well."

"No!" I said panicking, "Mum's. . . interviewing people for a job all day, her phone'll be switched off. Call my dad."

It had to be Dad; Mum doesn't have any of Dad's geeky-freak mates in her email address book, plus she'd know straight off that I was pulling one.

So Mrs Bhatnagar rang Dad, and told me to wait at reception.

I should've known of course. We're talking about my dad here.

"I *told* you, Gil asked me to come here and pick up his son because he's working." Stu had his anorak pulled right up around his face, even when he was talking to the school secretary.

"Could you lower your hood please, so I can get a clear look at you," she said suspiciously.

"You've got CCTV," he said, pointing at the camera above reception. "So no, I couldn't, because I can't afford to get on the system."

The secretary muttered something I couldn't hear and carried on double and triple checking everything about Stu. I'm not surprised, because he looked like the last person you'd want to send a kid off with. While she was checking him out, Gav arrived in reception and sat down next to me.

"You going home too?" I asked him.

He nodded. "With the rash, and feeling sick, and. . . the rest." He watched Stu for a minute. "Who's that nutter?"

I didn't answer, pretending Stu was nothing to do with me.

"Hey," said Gav. "Have you heard about Isis and her seance mates?"

I shook my head.

"They're all in massive trouble, and Isis has been chucked out of school! The head said this is all their fault." He inspected the invisible rash on his arm.

I tried to get more out of him, but that was all he knew. And by then the secretary had finished checking Stu.

"All right," she said, "Gray's father *did* ring to confirm you could collect his son."

Stu nodded inside his coat, making this crinkly noise. "I'll look after him, don't you worry. Had kids of my own."

The secretary looked like she didn't quite believe him.

"Come on," Stu called at me.

I got up from my chair, wishing Gav wasn't there.

"Why couldn't Dad come?" I asked Stu as we headed for the doors.

"He's halfway through chopping a dead tree down. Said he couldn't leave until it was safe." Stu glanced at me. "You should have rung your mum."

"She's busy too," I lied.

Stu pushed open the door and I stood in the doorway, my heartbeat suddenly drumming in my ears.

"Come on," said Stu. "I haven't got all day."

"Where's your car?" I asked, trying to spot his manky old Volvo in the car park.

"Up on the road – I couldn't get any nearer," said Stu. "Do you know how many cars there are at this school, and half of them are double-parked! How can one school need so many teachers?"

Up on the road. That meant all the way along the drive, through the gates, up the steps, and then however far Stu was parked after that.

I took a breath, and made myself step outside. Made myself start walking.

"Can we go a bit quicker?" I asked Stu, who was walking down the pavement at a snail's pace.

I scanned around as we walked. I got about fifteen metres from the school entrance, then: *Listen, listen.*

I spun about. Behind me was a boy looking exactly like I had when I was in Year Seven, even down to the too-big blazer Mum had bought so it would last longer.

It hurts, said the boy.

I picked up my pace. *Don't let them know you're scared,* I told myself. *Walk fast but calm. There's only one so far, and he's keeping his distance.*

"I thought you were ill," said Stu, shuffling a little bit faster. "You don't seem very ill to me."

"I am though, that's why I need to get to Dad's."

"You're not going there," said Stu.

"What do you mean?"

"I'm not just dropping you off and leaving you by yourself."

Another, older, voice from behind me. *HELP.*

Help. The voice of a tiny child.

My legs overruled my brain. I sprinted down the school drive, yanking open the gate. Voices called out behind me, jumbling together into the same repeated word: *He. . . Hel. . . Helppp. . . Helpppp. . . Help. . . elllppp!* And from the corner of my eye I could see they were keeping up with me.

I ran along the pavement, faster than ever, and threw myself at the door of Stu's car.

It was locked, of course. He was still dawdling his way up the steps, like he had all the time in the world, but *they* were right behind me. All different ages, from babies to old men. At least twenty of them, matching each other step by step. Their mouths opened in unison. *Heeellllpppp meeeeeeeeeeeeeee.*

I pressed against the car, rattling the door handle. *Clickclickclickclickclick.* It stayed locked.

They took another step closer, all those figures wearing different faces of me. Plump-cheeked little me as a toddler, lanky adult me, old man me with my wrinkled face half-covered by a grey beard. But my eyes are nothing like theirs were. *No one* has eyes like that.

"*Stu!*" I screamed.

Old-man me raised his hand, reaching, and all the others did the same.

"STU! Unlock the CAR!"

The figure's hand was centimetres from my face, its eyes empty and filled with nothing. I wanted to look away, but it was like being pulled in. I was going to fall into the darkness in its eyes and carry on falling forever.

Blebeep.

The lights on the Volvo winked, the locks all clicked up. I yanked the door open and flung myself inside.

Clunk. Door shut. Solid Volvo between me and the. . .

Only Stu, walking up the street. Nothing else.

I sat in the car, trying not to choke on my own heartbeats, until Stu opened the driver's door and peered in, frowning.

"What was all that about?"

I told Stu. I had to.

There are things you can keep secret, but running screaming down the street from people only you can see, well that's one of the harder ones. Isis would've thought up a convincing lie, but she's used to making up excuses for behaving weirdly.

Luckily, Stu was more likely to believe me than anyone else I know. Than anyone in the world, probably. Stu thinks about more crazy stuff by breakfast than most people do in their whole lives. So he sat in the car and listened. Didn't roll his eyes, or tell me to stop making stuff up. And as we drove away he started on his theories.

"Sounds like narcissistic projected imagery."

"A what?"

"A hallucination of yourself. Sometimes people see them naturally, as a result of serious mental illness, but there are reports of them having been induced. Military experiments and stuff, you know? And some people say the images can be projected into your brain as a disguise by some of the less ethical alien species."

"Aliens, again?"

"Less ethical ones, obviously. But it can't be that, because I didn't see anything at all in the street. . ." He scratched his stubbly chin, so the car wandered around the road a bit. "Where have you experienced these NPIs?"

He always shortens things to their initials. I suppose it makes them sound more science and less nuts.

I took a breath to calm myself. "At the quarry. In my back garden. At the standing stone. In school earlier. Just then."

"Can you see them now?"

I shook my head. "As soon as I got in the car, they went. And vanish if I go inside a building."

"Interesting. Any other patterns you've noticed?"

"They're getting worse. I mean, the first time was just this one little boy, but today. . ."

I hadn't been able to outrun them, no matter how fast I ran.

Stu nodded at the rear-view mirror. "And you say your friends have had similar experiences?"

"Yeah. And Jayden and Gav both saw something weeks ago, like me, but they didn't say."

"So this started some time ago, and has been slowly getting worse?"

"No, actually it was getting better until this weekend, when me and Isis went to the standing stone. Since then it's gone crazy."

"Everyone's seeing images of themselves?" asked Stu.

"Yeah. No. I mean, Gav and Jayden did, but Isis didn't and the Year Sevens in the welfare office were all crying about ghosts, but they didn't say anything about them looking like themselves."

Stu grunted. "Forget them. Ghosts don't exist. But these friends seeing the same as you, were they on the school trip to the quarry?"

I nodded.

"Ha!" Stu slapped the steering wheel with his hand, and the car wobbled again. "I knew there was something going on up there. Now we're getting closer!"

After that, Stu drove so fast and dangerously I thought he'd kill us both. He couldn't wait to get home and start investigating. But at the same time, being a freak himself, he took it seriously. When we arrived he got out of the car first, opening his garden gate and front door so I could make a run for it from the safety of his car to the safety of his bungalow.

And then we were in the hallway, and I was meeting his wife.

How can Stu have a wife? I still don't get it. She had a

soft, smiley sort of face and short, curly grey hair. She looked like anyone you'd see in a shop, like someone's nice granny. I mean, she was wearing a fluffy yellow jumper.

". . . and now he's getting hyper-real mobile hallucinatory experiences!" Stu was talking really fast at her. "I'm theorising it's the result of low-dose exposure to psychoactive compounds with a delayed onset, possibly triggered by some environmental factor. . ."

The hallway was painted magnolia, with a pale blue carpet. Every bit of furniture and every ornament was dusted and sparkly, and it smelled of furniture polish and lavender, instead of the fags and BO that Stu emitted.

Stu's wife didn't seem to be listening to him. "They sent you home?" she asked me. "You don't look so well – do you want some cake? I made lemon drizzle yesterday, and there's a good chunk of it left."

Stu stopped ranting to tut. "The school said he was feeling sick. You can't give him cake!"

"I don't feel so bad now," I said. "I'm sure I could eat some, thank you."

"And so polite." She smiled at me.

"We're going into the study," said Stu.

His wife rolled her eyes. "He doesn't want to do that, surely? It's very stuffy in there. Why doesn't Gray just watch telly and wait for his dad. . ."

"Because this is an emergency!" shouted Stu. "We can't just sit around. . ."

"Stu," his wife said sternly.

He lowered his voice and muttered, "Sorry."

"He gets excited, that's all," she said to me. "Now, do you want cake and telly?"

"No thank you," I said, even though it sounded good, because Stu was right, it did feel like an emergency. If I didn't sort out what was happening to me, my head was going to explode.

"Well cake at least," she said, going to get some.

Stu's study was more what I'd expected of him, and totally different to the rest of the bungalow. The curtains were drawn, the walls were covered in shelves, and the shelves were filled with books and stacked-up paper. Broken-looking electronics equipment, old magazines and newspapers were lying about everywhere. Dead computers sat in various corners, including this prehistoric one that must have been made in the 90s. There was a narrow gap through to Stu's desk, and on that was a really flash-looking laptop, a printer, a monitor, the tower of a desktop, a shredder and more papers stacked in a leaning pile.

Stu noticed me looking at the broken computers. "I can't throw the old ones away, not once they've had the Database on them. Even wiped, there's ways of getting the info out again. Can't risk it falling into the wrong hands." He switched on the laptop and sat down. "Right, let's start with UK-Earths. What was the name of the woman you mentioned, who showed you round the quarry?"

"Dr Harcourt," I said, through a mouthful of cake.

Stu tapped into the computer.

"Aren't you going to look in the Database?" I asked.

He shook his head. "Google, then darknet, then Database." He glanced at me. "Hasn't your dad taught you the basics?"

I shrugged. He probably had, but I don't much listen to his how-to-conspiracy lessons. I ate the cake while Stu scanned and clicked through page after page after page.

We stayed like that, just the sound of Stu huffing and tapping on his keyboard, and the buzzing of a fly, this really fat one, which was droning around the room in circles. It started to get on my nerves, the way it buzzed a circuit from the ceiling to the lamp, then for the computer screen. The next time it came near, I made a grab for it, but it dodged me easily, so I picked up a piece of paper and crept towards it. It was sitting on Stu's desk, cleaning its legs. I lifted up the paper, swiped as hard and fast as I could. *Whack!*

Stu jumped nearly out of his chair, but the fly buzzed up to the ceiling and started circling again.

"What are you *doing*? Now I've lost my train of thought!"

"That fly's really annoying me."

"Well you won't catch it that way! It's a matter of time perception."

He waited for me to ask what he meant, and when I didn't he leaned back in his chair and told me anyway. "You think time is something fixed and steady. Seconds, minutes, hours. But that's just *your* perception: Gray time. Eighty-odd years of it, a hundred thousand heartbeats, and then you die. Now that fly, he only lives a few weeks, so you probably think he feels his life is short."

"How do you know it's male?" I asked.

Stu shrugged. "All right, *she* feels *her* life is short. But she doesn't!" He smiled, proud of himself. "Because her perception of time is different to yours, so she thinks her life lasts as long as yours does. She *perceives* a second as an hour, an hour as a month. Her weeks of life are like eighty years to her."

"I don't see what that has to do with me being able to swat the fly." I couldn't help arguing back. Stu makes you like that.

"A second for you is like an hour for a fly. So she's got plenty of time to see your big slow hand coming and get out of the way. A fly doesn't even have to rush; for them it's like avoiding a tortoise."

He went back to his typing, and I let the fly buzz. But I've thought about it since, especially after what happened. How we're all travelling along our own piece of time, every living thing on earth, each at our own speed.

An interesting observation, but organisms from this planet perceive time in a similar manner, even if they do so at different speeds.

And what if they're not from this planet?

That is another matter entirely.

Chapter Twenty-two

Gray

I watched Stu clicking on a couple of the web pages for ages.

"Have you found anything?" I asked eventually.

Stu clicked another page, then stopped. "No. Time to go into the darknet."

That was kind of exciting, because Dad talks about the darknet a lot, how it's this underworld of the internet, where everything's secret and nothing's traceable. How you can't get in unless you know the special routes and passwords.

"What's your access point?" I asked Stu, trying to sound like I knew what I was talking about.

"Well, there's a website—" He stopped, and looked at

me with narrowed eyes. "Nice try, but I know your dad wouldn't want me telling you that." He waved his hand, shooing me back.

"Oh come on!"

Stu folded his arms, refusing to do anything until I was right across the other side of the room. "I'm sorry, Gray, but the darknet isn't for mucking about in. It's not funny cats in there. In the darknet, everything's for sale, even humans." He looked at me. "And the people aren't nice; they won't care that you're a kid." He paused. "Or they might care too much."

"So why are you going in then?" I muttered. "If it's so bad and full of psychos?"

Stu grinned. "Because the main thing on sale in the darknet is information. Stolen credit card details, stuff hacked from mobile phones or scavenged out of people's bins. Identities, bank accounts, government secrets. You name it, you can buy it, if you've got enough cash. Not that I would, of course, since I'm not a criminal." He sighed. "Most stuff is out of my price range anyway, but I should be able to afford an identity check on this Dr Harcourt."

I had to spend ten slow minutes in the corner, before Stu whistled to himself.

"Interesting."

"What?" I took a step nearer, trying to see, but Stu closed off the web page, leaving nothing but his screensaver. Which was a picture of himself Photoshopped into *Doctor Who*.

"The prices on her are astronomical – you'd need to be a millionaire to afford them."

I sagged, feeling a bit hopeless. "So that's a dead end?"

Stu shook his head. "Actually, it tells me a lot. If the prices are that high, it means someone is paying to stop the information being sold." He smiled. "And I've got other ways of finding things out."

He shooed me away and carried on tapping. After a while he leaned back, put all his fingertips into his hair and scratched thoughtfully. Little flecks of white appeared on his shoulders.

"Nothing, nothing, nothing." Scratch, scratch. "Makes me think maybe she isn't a real person."

"What? Like a robot, or a zombie takeover?"

Stu glanced at me. "Fake persona. A cover story. Good

enough to fool your average web search, but here in the darknet. . ." He hummed the *Star Wars* theme tune to himself. "Let's try another way. Tell me the names of your classmates, the ones who went into the quarry site with you."

I went through everyone I could remember and he tapped away, but it was obviously getting nowhere because he got grumpy.

"Useless. Nothing and nothing." He glared at me. "Is that all of them? What about that girl? Daughter of Gil's girlfriend. Isis something."

"Dunbar," I said. "But she wasn't even in our group, she didn't go into. . ." Stu was tapping as I talked, and then he burst out laughing.

"What?"

Stu shook his head, like it was a really good joke. "If I put her name in, I just get stuff on Mr Dunbar."

"Her *dad's* in the darknet?"

"No! It's a coincidence. She's just some girl you know, and Mr Dunbar is, well, he's a Mr Big. Supposed to be high up in the Organisation – there's stories about him you wouldn't believe, but never any evidence of anything.

He's very good at covering his tracks. My own theory is it's a code name, not a person. A cover for lots of different agents." He sucked through his teeth. "Nothing to do with this though. . ." He stopped, clicked back through a few pages. "Or. . . oh! Why didn't I think of it before?"

"Think of what?"

"Who has the money to keep information about Dr Harcourt out of the darknet?"

I shook my head, I mean, how would I know?

"The Organisation!" He got up and hurried into the hallway, grabbing my coat. "Let's go!"

"Go where?" I followed him. "I thought we were waiting for Dad?"

Stu shook his head. "We need to be at the quarry, gathering evidence! If this is to do with the Organisation, I might be able to find something out, get a lead on them!" He was practically hopping with excitement, probably imagining himself getting some kind of super-freak medal for being the one to unmask the Organisation, or whatever.

But going to the quarry; I thought my heart would stop. "No, no way! That's where all this started, and you want me to go back there?"

Stu shoved my coat at me. "Don't you want to find out what's wrong with you? How can you unless you're willing to take a few risks?"

"You don't even know it *is* the Organisation!"

Stu made a noise. "Pfft! I know their fingerprints when I see them!"

"I don't want to!"

Stu shook his head. "You're my canary, literally in the mine. I need to see if you drop inside your cage."

"Oh, great."

He was practically dragging me out of the door. "Please?" he wheedled. "They're only hallucinations. They can't actually hurt you, can they?"

I stared out at Stu's garden, and the street beyond. It looked so ordinary, but I knew that as soon as I took a step out there they'd know, somehow. The ghosts, or zombies, or whatever they were. And I didn't believe Stu about them not being able to hurt me, or that they were only hallucinations. But if I didn't face them, would my life be like this forever? Too scared to go outside?

I knew I couldn't do it by myself. Stu was no use, he was already off on his own thing, chasing secret societies and conspiracies and Mr Dunbar. . . Oh.

That's you, isn't it?

I have gone by that name.

But Isis said her dad works on cruise ships and that's why he's never around. . . That's a cover story, isn't it?

Your suggestion, not mine.

How could you just leave her? Don't you care about your own daughter? Or, were you sent off on a mission? Is Isis being psychic something to do with you? Is that why you married Cally?

I have revealed some things to you because you'll forget them anyway. But certain information, like the answers to these questions, I will not give.

You're only a boy, Gray, not an agent.

Chapter Twenty-three

Isis

Cally had to work at Crystal Healing in the afternoon, and Isis was alone in the flat.

"You wanted me to get a job, so this is what happens," Cally said as she went out.

"You can't just leave," said Isis, taken aback by this new, hard Cally. "You always tell Gil you can't leave me alone."

"Well I can't get a babysitter without any notice, can I?" answered Cally. "And I can't afford not to work, not now." The door clunked heavily behind her.

Cally was punishing Isis for what had happened in school, but in her own odd way: by leaving Isis alone. Isis went to the sofa and sat staring at nothing. After a minute or so, she slapped one of the cushions.

"Why didn't you tell me?" she shouted at it.

Angel's head poked out from the arm of the sofa, her neck melting into the fabric. "You dint ask."

Isis glared at her, trying to sort out her tumble of thoughts.

"We going to have a baby brother," said Angel happily.

Cally and Gil's baby. Meaning she and Gray would be. . . what? Stepbrother and sister?

"And Gil will be my stepdad," she said gloomily.

"Brothers and sisters and a whole new daddy," said Angel.

"I don't want a new dad!" said Isis.

There was a sound from behind the sofa, a rasping cough tinged with embarrassment and scented with mildew.

"Ahem. I apologise for interrupting during such a delicate conversation but. . ."

Isis twisted around to see Mandeville, who was hovering in the kitchen doorway, his feet not quite on the carpet.

"Things are afoot. At your school and throughout the area. Underfoot, to be more precise, so as your spirit guide I thought I should tell you that—"

"This is all your FAULT!" Isis shouted, kneeling up on the sofa. "Why couldn't you leave me *alone*?"

Mandeville floated back, a frown crinkling the peeling skin of his forehead. "I fail to see. . ."

"Wasn't it bad enough that I nearly *died* in the summer? Now you're trying to ruin my *life*!" Being excluded, her argument with Cally, the shock of the news of the baby; it poured out of her at the nearest target, crashing straight for Mandeville. "All this time going on and on about the wisdom you've got, but as soon as you get the chance you say the most horrible, stupid thing ever! You frightened the whole school, and now I've been suspended and everyone *hates* me!"

"Well I'm sorry, my dear, but I really didn't intend. . ."

"Don't call me 'my dear'! I'm not your dear, I'm not anything to do with you!"

Mandeville floated further back, seeming to decay a little as she watched, crumbling and fraying around his edges.

"But you are my medium, the channel through which. . ."

"No." Isis stood up, her hands clenched. "I'm not doing it any more. You said I'd help people – well what about *me*? How does it help me?"

"You'll be rich, famous and doing all manner of good," pleaded Mandeville. "You can't turn your back on your powers. I've been waiting all my life and all my death to find a true psychic, such as yourself."

She picked up a cushion, wanting to throw it at him. "Is that really all it is to you? When you were alive, was your ambition to be a *ghost*?"

"Well, I. . ." Mandeville shook his head, a cloud of dust swirling out into the air. "I'm not sure. I can't remember. . ."

"You're a dropped sock!" she said.

"Pardon?"

"You said it yourself, don't you remember? How you felt like the main part of you is already gone, and you're just a leftover of hopes and dreams, the bits your soul didn't really need." She glared at him, hating him in that moment. Glad to have someone to take this day out on. "*Remember?*"

"I'm not just a leftover. . ."

"Yes you are!" she cried. "You said a psychic sees what's really there – well that's what I see looking at you! A stupid bit of nothing, who's never done anything but bring bad things and make my life worse!"

Mandeville was almost translucent. "Is that really how you see me?" His voice was hardly more than a whisper in the air.

She nodded fiercely, adrenalin and fury fizzing in her blood.

"I shall go then. I will not burden you with my presence again."

"Go on!" But she was shouting at nothing, because Mandeville had already faded, not even leaving a damp smell in the air.

"Good!" said Angel, her face embedded in the sofa arm. "He horrid!"

"Oh. . ." Isis slammed her hands on the fabric. "You're as bad as each other!"

Angel vanished, leaving Isis alone. For a few minutes anger pumped through her, justifying what she'd said and done. But as it faded, she began to see her actions in a less flattering light.

"Mandeville?" she whispered. "Angel?"

But there was no reply. She was alone, sitting on the sofa, her legs pulled up and her arms around her knees.

*

She was lying on the sofa, half worn-out from crying, when the downstairs buzzer rang.

Maybe it was Cally?

Isis got up slowly and went to the front door. Cally had probably forgotten something for work, and her keys too.

She pressed on the intercom button.

"What?"

"Let me in! You've got to let me in!" Gray's voice shouted through the little speaker.

"What are you doing here?" Isis said in surprise. "Shouldn't you be in school?"

"Just open the door, please!"

She pressed the second button, releasing the lock for the main entrance downstairs.

After a brief pause, the intercom buzzed again. Gray was almost screaming now. "Open it, please!"

"I'll come down," she said. "It doesn't always work."

She opened the door and ran out into the hallway, skittering down the stairs to the foyer. Through the wire-reinforced glass of the front door she could see Gray pressed against it, punching with balled fists.

She turned the latch and Gray fell through the door,

his face pale and slick with sweat, breathing heavily.

"You took your time!" he gasped.

"What's the matter? What's going on?"

He looked ill, frightened.

"Things have got worse. Way worse," he said. "It was bad when I left school, but now they're everywhere. Following me, shouting stuff. Loads of them, seems like hundreds."

"Who's following you?" asked Isis, confused. "Is it a gang or something?"

"Not a *gang*!" He gave her a look, like she was being an idiot. "And it's not just me. Jayden and Gav too, people in our year. School's gone crazy. People are losing it all over, running around screaming."

A cold slick feeling spread over her. "Because of what I did, because of the seances?"

Gray shook his head. "No! I mean, actually, I don't know about Year Sevens seeing ghosts in the loos – maybe that *is* you? But I'm seeing me. Hundreds of me. Old, young, and the worst are the ones. . . I mean, they look like mirrors. I don't know what they want, but they don't give up, they just keep coming."

She looked out of the door. "I can't see anything."

He stayed back. "You can only see them when you go outside."

She looked at the road and the houses lined up along it. There was nothing out of place. "But ghosts aren't like that," she said. "Half of them haunt buildings."

"I didn't say they were ghosts!" snapped Gray.

"Then what are they?"

"Go and see for yourself," His words were sharp, but his face was desperate and pleading. "Gav and Jayden think it's poison; Stu has a load of crazy theories. I thought you might be able to see something we can't?"

She put her foot over the threshold, anxiety trembling up her leg. Mobs of ghosts had sometimes chased her after Cally's seances, frantic to be heard.

"Please," Gray said. "I'll hold the door so you can get back in quick."

A man with his hood pulled up was walking along the road, but there was no one else.

She took another step, and now she was out on the pavement. A flash of colour on the ground caught her eye: a flicker, like a rainbow sparkling away from her foot. Then it was gone.

The man gave her a short wave, as if he knew her, but his face was shadowed by the hood of his anorak.

Was he one of them? One of the things Gray was talking about?

He was coming straight for her, his gait furtive, as if he didn't want to be noticed. As he got closer, she saw there was nothing about him that looked like Gray, and then there was the strand of long grey hair curling out from inside his hood.

"You were at Gil's house that time," she said. "You're. . ."

"Shhh!" He flapped his hands at her. "Don't say my name!"

"Why not?"

Stu pointed up at the windows of her building, then vaguely at the air. "You don't know when they're watching. Listening."

"Who?" Were they in the air, these ghosts?

She noticed another flash of colour from the corner of her eye: like seeing through tears, except she wasn't crying.

"I can't tell you out here!" said Stu, pointing at the flats. "CCTV is everywhere. We live in a surveillance state!"

Isis glanced back but couldn't see any cameras, only Gray peering out of the door of the flats.

"Are they there?" Gray called.

She shook her head, but then another flash of colour flickered, this time along the pavement, like a goldfish in dark water. It curved in a wide arc away from her, or maybe towards her, it was hard to tell. Another colour in the stones, green this time, swirled around her then darted away, and almost at the edge of hearing she heard a wordless sound, like the wind through leaves.

"Can you see anything?" asked Gray. He'd stepped out of the flats, his face anxious and sweat-sheened.

"I don't know. . ." Slivers of colour sliced through the tarmac, like oil on water. Were they just a trick of the light? She looked down at the paving slab beneath her. Was it moving?

Suddenly everything twisted, upside down. For a moment she was looking at herself from underneath: the soles of her shoes, her dangling fingertips, her body foreshortened by the strange perspective.

"Look out!" shouted Gray. His hand was on her arm, pulling her into the flats. She stumbled with him through the doorway, coming out of the ground and back into her body.

"They were all around us!" gasped Gray. "Worse than ever! They reached out, grabbed hold of you." He sounded close to terror. "Didn't you see?"

Stu came through the door, looking pleased. "I told you. Psycho-active contamination. Think of it as brain poisoning. Like when the US government wanted to create super-soldiers and gave them loads of drugs."

"Is that meant to make me feel better?" snapped Gray.

Isis looked back through the doorway. Gray was scared of these. . . whatever they were. Had they really grabbed her? And if it was ghosts, why were they pulling her into the ground? Were they dragging her back to their buried bodies?

A true psychic sees what's really there. She'd thrown that back at Mandeville; now she had to use it.

She took a step outside and tried to concentrate. Her brain was showing her colours and whispers, swirling in patterns around her feet, but that wasn't really what she was seeing.

"What's up with her?" said Stu behind her. "Why's she

squinting that way? Are you sure she isn't contaminated like the rest of you? Just because she didn't go right into the quarry. . ."

"Shhh!" said Gray. "She's. . ." He paused, then muttered, "Psychic."

"What is *wrong* with you, Gray?" said Stu. "Have you swallowed a gullibility pill or something?"

Isis shut him out, focusing on what she could really see. But her mind kept shying away, as she fumbled for the truth.

A boat lost at sea.

An abandoned child, frightened and alone.

A hand reaching for her own, out of the deep water.

She shook her head. None of those were right. She went deeper than words, feeling it in the hairs on the back of her neck and the shiver in the soles of her feet, while Stu ranted about the impossibility of ghosts.

"We need to get there," she said, cutting through.

Gray looked at her. "Where?"

And she was certain, just as she had been in the woods. Here was a part of the message she could understand. "The quarry."

Chapter Twenty-four

Isis

They were about a mile from the quarry entrance when they came to a long queue of almost stationary traffic. Stu slapped the steering wheel and launched into furious muttering.

"It's Thursday afternoon! What are you all doing? Come on, we haven't got all day."

Isis and Gray were squashed in the back between the clutter. Stu had moved all the papers, bags, plastic boxes, shoes, long bits of metal and other assorted junk onto the front seat in an attempt to make room for an extra person in his car, but they were still surrounded. In her seat, Isis could only find the ragged end of a seat belt, the clips cut off it.

"Oh, yeah. I cut the seat belts," said Stu, when she showed him, "to make it easier when the seats are down." He tried to pull a cardboard box from the footwell, but gave up and stamped it flat instead. "You could always brace with your legs. Don't worry, I'm a very careful driver. The quickest way to get onto their system is to be stopped for a traffic offence."

Any other time, any other trip, she would have refused to travel without a seat belt, but Isis could feel the twitch of invisible fingers, pulling at her from the hills outside town.

No, not fingers.

It was like trying to remember a forgotten name; some-where beneath her mind she knew what was really calling to her, but she didn't have the vocabulary to phrase it.

They were inching along in the traffic jam when Angel materialised between Isis and Gray.

"You still a meany," she announced. "I still not playing with you! And you go-ed off without saying!"

Isis realised she hadn't even left a note for Cally. After this, Cally probably wouldn't leave her alone in the flat until she was twenty. But it was Angel she cared about now, and she spoke to her without noise, only moving her lips.

"Sorry."

Angel's face instantly cleared. Sorry always made things better, in her little world.

"It's cold today," said Stu, turning the heating up into a loud, petrol-smelling roar. The car didn't get much warmer though, because of Angel.

Under cover of the heater's noise, Gray spoke quietly. "When you first showed me Angel, I thought it'd be so cool to see stuff no one else can. But I hate it." He looked out of the car window. "I didn't know it would be so. . . frightening."

Isis put her hand onto his, only lightly, barely touching him. "I was scared in the summer," she said. "I thought I was crazy, but you believed me."

Angel bounced up and down on the seat between them.

"He sad!" she said excitedly. "You got to tell him about our baby!"

Isis had forgotten about that for a minute or two, but now it came flooding back in all its life-jolting strangeness.

"Tell him!" Angel said. "Then he'll be happy!"

Isis didn't even shake her head, because there was no way she was going to. Cally might've made a mistake. It was in soaps all the time: a big fuss about a baby until it turns out no one's really pregnant. Isis wasn't going to say anything until it was definite, until there was no turning back.

Angel glared at her. "You *tell*!"

Isis glared back, trying to make Angel understand without actually speaking that this wasn't the right time and Gray had enough on his mind.

Angel looked furious.

"I do it then!" she shouted, putting her hand on top of Isis's, quickly sliding her fingers between Isis and Gray's with a freezing wriggle.

Gray gasped, his eyes jolting wide open.

"Mummy having a BABY!" Angel shouted, right in his face.

Isis snatched her hand away, but she knew it was too late.

Gray stared at Isis, unable to see Angel who was dancing in between them and singing, "We got a baby brother," to the tune of her fishy song.

"Must be an accident on the road," Stu muttered from the front. "There's police up ahead. Oh come on, why do they have to talk to every *single* car driver?"

The car trundled another metre forwards. A policewoman was working her way down the queue, and the cars in front of them were doing three-point turns, going back the way they'd come.

"Is it Dad's?" Gray whispered.

It took Isis a moment to realise what he meant. "Of course it is!"

"Sorry." He put his hands over his face. "It's just, you know, a lot."

She nodded. It was.

"Baby, baby brother," sang Angel.

Gray spoke through his fingers. "Do you think Dad and Cally will move in together?"

Isis stared at the policewoman in her bright reflective jacket. Of course Cally would want to be with Gil, and since Gil's house was bigger. . . But Isis didn't want that!

"How did this even *happen*?" she said.

Gray looked at her, and snorted. "Well, your mum and my dad love each other very much. . ."

"Oh!" She started to giggle. "No! Don't make me even think about it!"

"Cally and Gil, sitting in the tree. . ." said Gray.

"Eugh! Shut up!" They were laughing, hysterical with it.

"What's going on back there?" asked Stu.

Isis managed to stop, her cheeks aching.

"Me and Gray are going to be related," she said, and it didn't seem so bad, put that way.

"Are your parents getting *married*?" Stu's voice squeaked up in amazement, sending Isis and Gray into more helpless laughter.

A knock at the window interrupted them. Stu pulled his anorak hood closer around his face and wound down the window.

"The road's closed," said the policewoman. "You'll have to turn around."

"Is it an accident?" asked Stu.

The policewoman shook her head. "There's a problem ahead."

"Problem?" Stu asked, his voice sharpening. "What's that meant to mean?"

"There's a protest up at the quarry which is causing

some disruption. Representatives from the mine are available if you have questions." She pointed further up the road, to where Isis could just make out three people wearing high-visibility jackets with the UK-Earths logo.

"I do, actually," said Stu.

The policewoman sighed, and raised her hand to wave at the group. One of the people began walking over, a woman. Next to Isis, Gray stiffened.

"That's Dr Harcourt," he hissed.

"Really?" Stu's face lit up.

He turned back to the policewoman. "I know why you're keeping the public out: so no one will find out what's *really* going on."

"I've told you what's really going on," said the policewoman, sounding tired. "Now if you go back about four miles, you'll come to a turning. . ."

"I know my way!" said Stu. "I just don't believe you. You're doing their dirty work, aren't you?"

The policewoman pursed her lips. "I'm directing traffic," she said, just as Dr Harcourt arrived.

"Can I help?" she said brightly, until she got close enough to see inside the car. Her eyes widened a little, as if she was shocked. "Oh. So. Um, do you have a question?" Her eyes were fixed on Gray and Isis.

"I do," said Stu. "I'd like to know how you explain the large number of sightings in the vicinity of your mine."

Dr Harcourt's gaze snapped his way. "Sightings?"

"Of UFOs," said Stu.

Isis expected Dr Harcourt to laugh, but she didn't. Her eyebrows pulled together a little, her mouth stiffening out of its false smile. She was silent a moment, then she said, very pointedly. "These are your children, are they?"

"Yes," said Stu.

"No," said Isis and Gray together.

Now the policewoman frowned.

Stu gave a little laugh. "You know kids. Joking about." He flicked a furious glance back at them. "Why did you say that?" he hissed.

"You're not my dad," said Gray.

"But I'm looking after you!" exploded Stu. "In *loco parentis*!" He glanced at the policewoman. "That's what I meant, not that they're related to me."

Dr Harcourt checked her watch. "Shouldn't they be in school?"

"I'm sick," said Gray quickly.

Isis didn't say anything; she couldn't bear to tell a policewoman she'd been excluded. And it probably wouldn't be a help, given the situation.

"You don't look very sick," the policewoman said to Gray.

"I. . . um. . ."

"He's experiencing a psychotic breakdown," Stu said, scowling at Dr Harcourt.

"*Psychotic breakdown?*" said Gray.

"Yes!" said Stu. "He'll probably have to go on sedatives and see a psychiatrist, and it's all the result of exposure to toxic substances being released from *your* quarry!"

"This boy's mental illness is nothing to do with toxic substances at UK-Earths' quarry," snapped Dr Harcourt, "because there are none! You are misinformed if that's what you believe." She flicked a glance at the policewoman, and let out a short, brittle laugh. "He thinks there are UFOs flying around. Are you going to take him seriously?"

"Please," said Isis, leaning forwards. "Can't we just turn around?" The stack of paper she was perched on top of slid, pitching her forwards, so she fell almost between the seats.

"Are you wearing a seat belt?" asked the policewoman. She leaned her head through the car window. "Where *are* the seatbelts?"

"They, um. . ."

"Right, could you step out please?" The policewoman opened the driver's door.

"I know my rights!" cried Stu, not moving.

The policewoman rolled her eyes, and spoke into the walkie-talkie on her shoulder. "Could I have some assistance, please? I've got a right one here."

"You have no evidence!" Stu said to the policewoman. "I know what you're up to, but they won't get me that easy!"

The policewoman looked down at him. "I do have evidence," she said. "It's right here in your car. You have children sitting in the back, but no seat belts."

"But I never have children in my car normally!" cried Stu. "This is the first time in years!"

"If you don't get out of the car, I will be obliged to additionally charge you with failure to comply with an officer's directions."

"Additionally?" sputtered Stu, flinging himself out. His anorak hood fell backwards, but he didn't seem to notice. "Don't you see you're doing her dirty work?" He pointed dramatically at Dr Harcourt. "This country is in the grip of a takeover by malign forces!"

"I wouldn't know about that," said the policewoman.

Dr Harcourt was ignoring them, her eyes on Gray and Isis. "Shouldn't they get out as well?" she asked, a nasty triumph in her voice. "I could take them up to our offices and give them. . . biscuits. Look after them until you can sort this all out."

The policewoman threw a surprised glance at her. "I don't think that will be necessary." She leaned into the car again, now taking in Isis with her eyes red from all the crying she'd done earlier, and Gray obviously frightened.

"We're here of our own accord," Isis said nervously.

"All the same," said the policewoman. "Perhaps you should get out."

Gray's face was tight with strain, a sheen of sweat gleaming across his brow.

"I don't think I can," he whispered.

"You're going to accuse me of abducting them, aren't

you?" cried Stu. "Silencing truth-seekers with scandal. Well it won't work, not on me!"

"I wonder why the children want to stay in the car?" said Dr Harcourt, her tone insinuating and sly.

"We better get out," Isis said to Gray.

He nodded, opening his door, but he moved as if stepping out to his doom.

As soon as Isis's foot touched the ground, the air seemed to fill with the rushing sounds of the wind, even though she couldn't see a leaf or blade of grass moving. Angel popped out alongside her and let out a little squeak.

"It too big," she said, before vanishing back into the car.

Gray made a noise, and Isis turned. He was pressed against the other side of the car, eyes wide in his terrified face.

"Are you all right?" said Dr Harcourt, a false kindness in her voice. She turned to the policewoman. "I could take them up to the quarry offices, wait for their *real* parents to turn up."

"Don't you go anywhere near them!" shouted Stu. "I know what you're up to!"

Another police car pulled up, and two policemen got out of it.

"Is it *them?*" Isis asked Gray, although she still didn't know what Gray could see, or why she couldn't.

He nodded.

"I think the children are ill," said Dr Harcourt. "We have a medical station, and several trained first-aiders."

Isis walked around the car, her feet seeming to swirl colours out of the tarmac. She shook her head. She knew she wasn't seeing what was really there.

"I'd be happy to take them up to our offices," said Dr Harcourt, walking around the car in the opposite direction to Isis.

"No you don't!" shouted Stu, moving to block her, his hands up in something like a karate pose.

"Stop that!" shouted the policewoman, and now the policemen were running, hurtling in to grapple Stu, pulling him back while he flailed at Dr Harcourt.

"Can't you see? She's one of them! Where's the rest of your *Organisation*, Dr Harcourt? Is that even your name?"

Gray was wide-eyed and pale beside the car, not even watching the scene going on behind him. Isis spotted a small, unfenced spinney of trees, just ahead on the road.

She knew the way now, in the part of her that wasn't using words.

She took another step, leaned close and whispered in Gray's ear.

"Run."

Chapter Twenty-five

Gray

I didn't look, didn't think, I was just running. One foot after another, fast then faster.

"Stop!" shouted Dr Harcourt.

"Don't stop!" yelled Stu. "Don't let her get you! You'll wake up tomorrow and you won't *remember any of this!*"

I don't even know what Stu thought was happening, I only knew I couldn't stay still, not with them everywhere.

They were with me as soon as I got out of Stu's car. Hundreds of them, walking towards me from the road, standing by the hedges, surrounding us. It was like a hall of mirrors, except reflections don't move and call out. They don't reach for you, crying, *Listen! Listen! Listen!*

I thought, *This is a dream, isn't it?* I even squeezed my

eyelids shut, hoping I'd wake up. But all those versions of me were still there when I opened my eyes. So many of them. Like zombies in the films, their words blending into a solid murmur: *Listenlistenlistenistenlistenlistenlistenlisten.*

"Run!" whispered Isis.

I thought, *Are you crazy?* But what else was there? Stu was going mental, that Dr Harcourt was getting creepier and creepier. And also Isis knows this stuff, better than Dad, better than Stu. They're all about the theories, but Isis lives it.

We raced up the verge and into the trees. Air burned in my throat, but I was only thinking about keeping ahead of the mirror-mes. I had to swerve and dodge to keep out of their grasp, my heart slamming every time one of them came reaching for me.

There'd been hundreds on the road, but more were stepping from behind trees, as if they were sprouting out of the ground, and they all had my face. Me a few years ago; me taller than I am now; crawling baby versions of me; toddlers with little grabbing fingers. Me with greying hair; me as an old man, hardly able to walk.

I started panicking that I was going to find myself as a

corpse, its dead hand reaching for me. I ran. Trying not to get caught by one of them, trying not to trip on tree roots or crash into low branches.

"Do you know where you're going?" I gasped at Isis.

"That way!" And we broke from the trees into a wide grassy field, with the sky bright above us and the hills curving. My feet thudded into the rough grass, and it was easier and quicker now, the ground sloping away.

I looked behind and I thought, *We're going to make it – we're leaving them.*

Then I turned my head back. In front of us were hundreds of people scattered across the field. A blink and it was thousands. A me for every day I've been alive, for every day I'm going to be. All with their hands outstretched and eyes as black as space. Calling, shouting, crying, their words blending like storm waves crashing on a beach.

Huuuuurrrrttttinnngpleeeeeeeezzemeeeeeestopppp.

I stumbled. Couldn't swallow, couldn't catch my drumming heart, couldn't think. I looked back, and now there were as many mirror-mes behind us.

There wasn't a space between them, nowhere to escape through.

"Do you see?" I whispered to Isis.

"Yes," she said, at last.

"What do we do? How do we stop them?" I thought she'd know, but she didn't even answer. They closed in, shrinking the circle of grass between them and us, and I realised she wasn't looking at them, she was staring at the ground. She put her hands in front of her eyes, waving her fingers.

"What are you *doing*?"

"I. . ." She flickered her fingers in front of her face. "No!" She stumbled back a step.

"What? What is it?"

Now there was no space left. I was trapped in a wide open field, the crowds closing in. Everywhere I looked, my face. Whichever way I looked, I saw me looking back. So many versions of me, but all with those torn-out, black-hole eyes. And still I thought Isis must be doing something, saving us, like when she broke open the Devourer. Then she spoke again.

"*You're hurting me*," she whispered. "*It hurts.*"

A horrible shaky feeling started in my legs and went up through my stomach, into my heart.

"Isis?"

She looked at me, but she'd gone. Her eyes were black stars, just like them.

"*Isis!*"

A hand, my hand, reached out to grab me. There was no space left. There were fingers on my cheeks, my nose, in my hair, pulling at my arms, my clothes. I punched and twisted and kicked, but even as I tried to beat them back, the creatures only gripped tighter. I couldn't get away, I couldn't fight them off. I couldn't see anything but reaching hands.

They pulled me under.

Chapter Twenty-six

Isis

Colours were travelling through the ground. Except they weren't colours, they were something else.

Nerves in the land, Merlin had said.

Next to her, Gray was gasping for breath, his face a mask of terror. They were in the middle of an empty field, but he was twisting and turning, staring wildly around.

"Do you see them?" he asked, his voice cracking and high.

"Yes," she whispered. Shades of red and orange, green and blue, purple, pink and yellow. Zigging and zagging through the ground towards her, bringing a sigh of words:

I won the race thought it would be bigger I'm on top long walk beautiful place hold in my stomach curse her cows make my baby well let him love me warmer weather.

On and on, the words she'd heard through the standing stone, prayers and pleas made to a piece of rock in the woods.

"What do we do? How do we stop them?" shouted Gray.

She tried to focus on his question, but the colours were hypnotic, like oily rainbows on water. She put her fingers in front of her eyes, trying to shield the sight, cutting the colours into a cross-hatched pattern.

"What are you *doing?*"

"I. . ." She didn't know, but that wordless part of her mind did. She wiggled her fingers, finding a point, a speed of movement matching the flicker of the colours in the ground. They flashed upwards, creating mirror images of herself, an infinite hall of mirrors. . .

A psychic sees what is really there.

"No!" she said.

"What? What is it?" cried Gray, looking terrified at her. But she didn't have time to answer, she had to focus her attention, bend her mind around this corner. She stared through the moving net of her fingers, trying to understand what was hidden.

A pattern. Like the ripples from a stone dropped into still water.

She lifted her head, looking out over the gently rolling hills, the shape beneath them becoming clearer. A hidden layer, the one she'd seen when she'd stood with Gray in the rocky bed of a dried-up stream. She hadn't given it much thought then, but now. . .

She breathed out a sigh.

Ship.

Its curves blended perfectly to the contours of the hills. It was covered by layers of soil and earth, grown over with trees and grass. She peered through her fingers, trying to catch the truth of it. Not just a ship, this was something more alive than that. Merlin was right! There *were* nerves in the land; thoughts made of colours, mapping the shape of a something huge, blended into the hills. It was miles across, this ship-creature, far too big and strange to be anything human. Understanding leaped from the part of her brain that had no words, fixing onto one word that explained it all.

Alien.

Every cell in her body instinctively knew it. This couldn't possibly be from Earth.

And now she understood the standing stone too. A piece of this enormous ship, raised up by prehistoric farmers. Their memories made sense at last – the clouds smashing apart and everyone looking up in open-mouthed wonder – they'd witnessed an alien spaceship landing. No, it had seemed more chaotic than that. The craft had crashed from the sky, falling like a wounded bird, huddling itself into the safety of the earth's crust, safe from harm. . .

And now people were digging it up. . .

The quarry was where this had started for Gray. The shapes he'd seen must have been the alien, trying to send a message through the stones and earth it had slipped underneath. A creature trying to speak in a language learned through thousands of years of listening to the people who came and wished at the standing stone.

"*You're hurting me,*" she whispered. It was a cry for help.

As if in relief at being understood, colours poured in through her fingers. She had a dizzying sense of time stretching and expanding to take all of her life into a single heartbeat. For the alien creature, the crash had happened very recently, and the diggers had arrived there a moment later, scraping and churning, causing a pain the creature couldn't fathom.

"It hurts?" Isis asked.

An answer came in words learned so laboriously. *I scared.*

It feared the roar of explosions, rocks flying up, of being disintegrated in a future it could foresee but couldn't understand.

It's a mining company, she wanted to explain, blasting its way into your body, taking away the valuable metals that make up your skeleton. But she didn't, because the alien couldn't understand these things. She imagined its answers: *What is mining? What is a company? What is valuable?*

Instead it pressed on her, overwhelming in its fear, confusion and desperation.

Helphelphelphelphelphelphelphelp.

"*Isis!*" Gray screamed, but she couldn't answer, couldn't stop either of them from falling.

Chapter Twenty-seven

Gray

Silence and blackness. No sound, no air. On and on. I thought it would never end.

And then. . . the slow-moving shift of stars. A distant gleam ahead of me, getting brighter and brighter. A yellow star, with its circling dance of planets. One of them, so beautiful. Glowing like silver, even from so far away. Except that's wrong. It was. . . like a beautiful tune. No, that's wrong too!

Take your time. Don't rush. You've seen things I need to understand, just try to explain them clearly.

It was. . . like coming back from a long journey and getting somewhere you recognise, knowing that soon you'll be back home. That was what Neptune was like for them, they could smell-touch-taste-hear-see-feel-love it.

Earth was a kind of shortcut, I think. Like, when you have to cross the road, and you can't be bothered to go all up the way to the traffic lights so you risk crossing over where you are.

The risk went wrong for one of them.

Them?

My dad always says the movies haven't done us any favours, because we think we know what aliens and spaceships look like, when in fact that's just Hollywood. He says we think life is only like ourselves. But there are billions of stars, just in our galaxy, and there are billions of galaxies. Anything is possible. A creature made of rare metals, flying between the stars.

You saw it?

I was with him in the silence and blackness. Flinging out from one star, gliding to another. They can feel our sun's gravity like. . . how swallows migrate thousands of miles, and they always get to the exact same spot, you know?

Or maybe it's more like whales, singing their way home.

And the shapes by the standing stone, all those visions of yourself, what were they?

He was just trying to talk to me, the only way he knew how. Scared, trying to show me something I could understand. I mean, he'd only been on Earth a couple of thousand years, which is like. . . I don't know, a few minutes for them? It'd be like you trying to learn a whole new language in a few seconds.

At last you are telling me something interesting. Of course, we knew the dust from the quarry induced hallucinations, but we had not identified the reason. Now I understand. A mineral-based organism would continue to exist in the minerals absorbed from the dust into your body, making you, by some measure, part of its body. Your bones were its bones.

Perhaps Isis had talents unusual enough to allow her to perceive the creature without assistance?

So the value of what you destroyed was greater than I previously thought. Such material could have been used for communications, weapons, perhaps even space travel. It would have brought our sponsors great wealth.

I didn't destroy anything, I keep trying to tell you.

The evidence only a few miles outside of this town makes a liar of you. How do you explain that?

Chapter Twenty-eight

Isis

They were on the ground, sitting in a tangle of legs.

Gray's eyelids lifted open.

"*You're hurting me,*" he said, his eyes wide with wonder. "*Please stop. Listen. Help.*"

"Are you all right?" Isis whispered.

He shook his head, laughing. "All those things that looked like me. Everything they said. It was a message."

"Merlin thinks there are ley lines here," Isis answered with a smile, "but it's thoughts."

The field was full of them, the swirl and circle of colours seeming to drift within the land. She could see far more clearly now, but they were still unreadable, still alien. She turned back to Gray. "You weren't seeing ghosts, you were seeing her trying to talk to you."

Gray was lost in his own thoughts, gazing at the hills and fields around them. "Everything me and Dad have been looking for. All those nights we spent staring up at the sky." He pressed his fingers onto the ground, as if he'd never seen it before. "There was an alien already here."

"Beneath your feet," said Isis.

Gray kept his hand on the grass. "This whole valley is *alive*. That's why no one can explain why the rare earth metals are here. Mr Watkins went on about the geology not matching and all those different theories about how it happened. No one said the obvious, that it's not from Earth."

Isis crinkled her brow. It seemed so evident now, but before – how could anyone even have guessed?

"They're mining her," she said, "because they don't even know she's here." Isis could feel the quarry, like a hot poker against her skin. "And it hurts." The machines were cutting into the alien, a being of metal and stone, killing her bite by bite, turning her body into the ingredients for smartphones and computer screens. "They'll kill her, won't they?"

Gray looked up. "The alien's not female."

"Yes she is! Definitely! Her name is—" Isis stopped. She'd been told, only moments ago through their link, but there wasn't a human sound to match the name. "It means the sparkle of sunshine on the ice crystals in a comet's tail. . . I think."

Gray made a face. "He *just* told me, and his name means the crash of a meteor onto the rocky face of a moon, actually."

"The alien isn't a he. . ."

"It's not a she!"

They paused.

"Maybe she's both?" said Isis.

"Maybe he's neither?" suggested Gray.

"Hey, man, what are you doing?" came a shouted voice from behind them.

Isis and Gray pulled themselves out of their tangle, standing up awkwardly. Instantly embarrassed. A tall, thin man was running across the field towards them, his thick wedge of dreadlocks bouncing at his back.

"Merlin?" said Isis.

He reached them quickly, running to a stop and frowning anxiously.

"Whatever you've done, you'd better not hang around."
He pointed towards the trees and the road behind. Isis
caught a flash of fluorescent yellow. "There's security
guards swarming all over. I saw them from way off. Saw
you too, and put it together. They're headed this way."

"We ran from the roadblock," said Gray.

"Every time I meet you two, you're escaping from
someone." Merlin tilted his head. "I like that, shows you
got sense."

"We're not escaping," said Gray. "We need to get into
the quarry."

Isis looked at Merlin. "Will you help us?"

He folded his arms. "Sorry, man, no can do. I'll take you
out of harm's way. I'll ring for your parents or whoever."

"We don't need to go home!" said Isis.

"The quarry's dangerous," said Merlin, shaking his head.
"Please. . ."

"It's not a playground in there! I'd be crazy taking you in."

Beneath them, colours shifted, and through the patterns
Isis could read the creature's pain and fear. She wanted
to lie flat on the ground and spread her arms, to whisper
words of comfort into the grass.

How could she tell Merlin what lay beneath them, that his 'ley lines' were actually the thoughts of a creature as large as the landscape? A living ship, a life made of stone, a star-beast? None of which really described something she could barely imagine.

Someone in a yellow jacket emerged from the woods behind them, and let out a shout.

"You said the earth was calling us," Isis said desperately to Merlin. "You said we were here for a reason! Well we know what it is – we have to—" She stopped; how could she ever explain?

"I'm glad you've got connected, man, but even though it's shut down, cos of the protest, the quarry's still dangerous."

"If it's shut down, we'll be perfectly safe!" said Gray.

Someone else joined the figure at the edge of the trees. Two yellow-jacketed men were heading out into the field.

"Please?"

Merlin sighed. "Okay. Cos there's something about you two, I can tell. So I'll take you for a look, but that's all. There's a place where foxes dug under the wire, takes you up above the quarry."

A wave of gratitude coloured the field in ripples of hundreds of different shades.

"You! Stop there!" shouted one of the yellow-jacketed men.

"Better hurry," said Merlin.

They set off running, following Merlin, their footsteps landing in pools of rainbows.

Chapter Twenty-nine

Gray

It was muddy getting under the fence, and I got a rip in my school blazer from the wire. I hardly even noticed doing it though, because all these versions of me were calling, *Graaaaaayyyyy, Graaaaaayyyyyyy.*

Now I knew they weren't zombies or ghosts, but only an alien trying to talk, they were almost funny. Especially the babies, toddling about.

We lost the security guards easily enough because Merlin knew his way round the valley way better than they did, and soon we were back in the woods. We scraped our way underneath the fence and Merlin led us between the trees and tangles of bramble.

Almost between one step and the next we passed from

autumn woods into open space. The woodland had been cleared, all the trees cut down in a wide area around the quarry. Most of that side of the valley was nothing but circles of pale, newly cut tree stumps. From where we were standing, among the sawn-off remains, I had a whole new view of the quarry. I could see that where the diggers had been working was only a tiny part of what was planned, judging by how far back they'd cleared the woods.

The alien me-ghosts shuffled their way out of the trees, filling every space around me on that hillside. They looked into the quarry, and all began whispering. *Hurtinghurtinghurting.*

Isis winced, like she'd heard them.

"Will the protestors be able to stop the mining?" she asked Merlin.

"For a bit. Hours, days maybe. After that. . ." He shrugged.

"Why aren't you there then?" I said to him, feeling angry. If he cared, like he said he did, he should've been with the protestors, trying to make a difference.

He tucked his dreadlocks behind his ear.

"I never said I was a protestor. Those guys down there won't stop what's coming, not with big money and the government behind it. But someone's gotta see it happen, man. Someone's gotta walk every footstep of these woods, and remember all the trees and plants, the birds and the insects that live here." He bent down and gently stroked a patch of moss on what was left of a tree trunk. "Even the moss. Someone's gotta remember, so it can be mourned."

"You can't just let things happen and then feel sad!" I said.

"Sometimes that's all there is."

I tried to think what we could do, my brain going forty miles a minute. "What if we told everyone?" I said to Isis. "What if they knew the truth?"

"How would we do that?" she asked.

"Stu could get it out through the Network. Release it to the papers and stuff. Then they'd have to stop the mining, wouldn't they?"

It felt like the answer, for about ten seconds, until Isis said, "No one would believe us."

"Yes they—" I stopped, because I knew she was right. Me and her, how would we get anyone to take us seriously? A girl suspended from school for saying she can see ghosts, a boy whose dad is a well-known UFO nut.

"We better get back," said Merlin. "Now you've seen the quarry up close, I wanna get you out of here."

But every one of those faces, all the different ages of my life, they all turned and looked. Eyes wide, hands reaching.

"We can't leave the alien," whispered Isis. "She's frightened. She's all alone."

I wonder if we could have told Stu and got people to believe us? Maybe it would've been enough. Whoever was behind the quarry, they would've stopped if they knew they were killing a living being.

Do you eat chicken?

What's that got to do with it?

If you eat chicken, you kill a living being to do so. Yet it doesn't stop you.

But. . . the first alien there ever was on our planet! You're not saying they'd carry on, even if they knew?

The problem with aliens is that they are so. . . alien. We cannot do deals with them or interest them in trade. They contribute nothing, financially. In any case, what you've described is hardly better than an animal. No technology, no assets: the properties of its body were its major value. So yes, I'm sure our sponsors would have continued with the extraction.

Extraction? You mean killing!

Call it what you want, but let me assure you that even if you had revealed the presence of this alien it would have made no difference. Do you think anyone would have believed you? Do you think we would have allowed them to, when so much money was at stake?

And you go along with that?

Why not?

But. . . my dad wants to meet aliens so we can talk to them, understand other worlds. . .

Then he is naive.

No he isn't! I'm glad you never see Isis, because she still thinks you're great, and if she knew. . .

BE QUIET!
No more chats, Gray. Just you telling me what I need to know.

Chapter Thirty

Isis

They hurtled downhill, running towards the quarry, Merlin waving and shouting as they left him behind.

"Come back! What are you doing?"

Isis didn't stop, nor did Gray. They left the cut-off remains of the woodland, slip-scrambling down a bank of soil and debris. Gray was ahead of Isis a little as they ran across the flattish stretch of hillside that sat directly above the quarry. All the soil and vegetation cover had been removed, but it was still hard-going because of the regular pattern of mounds, like oversized molehills, which they had to weave around. Yellow wires criss-crossed between the humps, catching at their feet.

And then Isis was standing next to Gray at the top of

a perilously steep slope, where the soft clay-rock had been gouged away by the diggers. At the bottom of it was the quarry floor.

"That's where the alien wants us to go," said Gray, looking down.

Isis knew she and Gray saw the alien very differently, but she could feel its desperate call: *Down, down, down.*

She felt a little dizzy looking at the slope. There was no way to scramble or climb down, all you could do was fall.

Gray cocked his head, listening, then he sat down on the edge, his feet dangling over. He looked at her.

"Come on."

"No. I can't—" Before she'd even finished he'd pushed himself off, slithering down the almost vertical drop, his feet digging in, his arms out wide, hands catching at anything he could. Dust flew up around him, the dirt and pebbles falling in tiny avalanches.

"Ooph!" He stumbled forwards as he hit the bottom, nearly falling over. Then he turned around, staring up at Isis in triumph.

"Come on. It's easy!"

She looked for another way, but there wasn't one. Trembling, she sat on the edge of the bare slope. It looked even steeper now.

"Come *on*!" shouted Gray.

Don't think, just do it, she told herself.

She only needed a small push with her hands, and gravity took her; she slid down through the rocks and pebbles, her feet and hands scrabbling for purchase, dust coating her hair and face, and entering her open mouth as she screamed. Isis was falling properly now, then. . . "Ow!"

A shuddering slam smacked through her body as her feet hit the bottom. She fell forwards, landing hard on her knees and palms.

"You all right?" Gray asked, coming over.

"Ow. . . I think so." She stood up, her legs and hands stinging with pain. She glanced down at her uniform, now streaked with pale clay and mud. Gray's was just as bad, his back smeared almost white, his hair looking as if it had been dipped in flour.

Looking around, Isis could see there was no one else here. The diggers and trucks had been driven away, leaving only their criss-crossing tyre marks on the wide track that led out of the quarry. The Portacabin offices and car park were hidden behind the high mounds of earth and rubble. No one could see them here.

In the distance, Isis could hear chanting and whistles.

"That must be the protest going on," said Gray. It sounded like a wild party, except the voices were angry instead of having fun. "All the workers must be guarding the gates or whatever."

Isis looked around the stony slopes of the quarry. The dust in her eyes was making her sight teary and smeared, but at the same time it made the alien almost fully visible. Flickering in different colours, covered in something between the scales of a fish and the crystals of a snow-flake. But the texture was neither of those.

"It's like my mind tries to find what she looks like," Isis said quietly, "but she isn't a whale, or a spaceship, or ice, or any of those things."

Gray's eyes were darting around, constantly looking about them. "You know, I'm getting kind of used to this. I quite like having a crowd of myself."

Glancing at him, Isis realised what it must've been like for Jess and the others. *When I talk to Mandeville and the spirits, it's just me talking to the air.* No wonder they'd turned on her in Mr Gerard's office. If she didn't know, she'd think Gray was mad right now. And yet here they were, in the rubble and dust of a living being. She shook her head, wanting to run, to get away. This was too big, too impossible; too frightening and inexplicable. . .

"Escape," she whispered, suddenly understanding the alien's message, the one speaking into the back of her mind and giving her those feelings.

Gray was listening to his invisible crowd, reacting to things she couldn't see or hear. "Can't you just. . . fly away or whatever?" he asked the air.

The answer came in patterns, in colours slipping across the rocks. Incomprehensible, and yet Isis understood some of it.

"She was hurt when she fell," she said.

Gray nodded. "But he's almost healed. He can. . . limp?"

Isis smiled. 'Limp' was Gray's word, nothing like the movements of a wounded alien.

"Even limping, you should go!" Gray said to the air.

A shift and spiral of the colours beneath Isis's feet. Deep reds and blues, a flash of fluorescent green.

"There's something she has to do first?" she said, not quite certain. "It takes time."

"Calculations," said Gray, nodding in agreement, but not at Isis. "He can't lift off like a rocket or something; he has to work out a trajectory and his route. . ."

Isis shook her head. It felt more instinctive than the way Gray was describing it. Like judging how to catch a ball, or run through a narrow gap.

"She can't react fast enough," she said, realising. By the time the alien could work out *how* to leave, it would be too late.

Gray stared at nothing. "How long do you need?"

The answer took Isis a couple of seconds to disentangle – thoughts from feelings, words from sensations.

"Years?" she said. She couldn't tell the number exactly, but she had a vision of herself as an old woman. This alien was as large as the landscape, and moved as slowly as the rocks it was part of. It struggled to grasp the speed with which humans passed through time. Gray half leaned against a pile of rubble, his body sagging. "But there'll be nothing left of him by then," he whispered.

A rattle and slide of pebbles came from above them.

They both jumped, getting ready to run, but it wasn't anyone from the quarry, only Merlin on the level above.

"Oh, man," he said, panting and catching his breath. "You gotta get out of there. It isn't safe!"

Gray shook his head.

"We can't just leave," said Isis.

"But there's charges *set*!" cried Merlin. "Didn't you notice all the yellow wires?"

They both looked at him blankly.

"The mounds you ran through like crazy people? It's where they've drilled down and dropped in the explosives – I've been watching them do it these last couple of weeks. They're sealed and ready; all the wires are in place, set for detonation. Anytime now someone's going to press a button and all this rock around you. . ." He mimed an explosion with his hands. "Boom!" He looked frightened and sweaty.

Jagged lines of purple and blue pulsed through the rocks, answering Merlin's fear. In Isis's mind, they sounded like a loud and frightened wail.

Gray was glancing about frantically, his hands up. "It's going to be okay, I promise."

"Oh *man*," said Merlin, and he slide-slipped his way down the rubble slope, landing easily on his long legs and jogging over to them. "Look, I get it that you care, and I'm glad you feel the energy. But it ain't worth *dying* for!" He waved his hands. "It's gonna go off like bombs in here!"

"We're not like *you*!" Gray snapped. "We won't just stand by and watch!"

Merlin frowned, like Gray was being stupid, childish.

"You don't know!" shouted Gray. "It's not ley lines or energy, it's an alien! Its ship crashed here thousands of years ago – actually it *is* the ship – but that's why people see stuff and feel things around here. That's what they're mining, and they'll kill him, because he can't get away in time. So you see, we've got to stop them!"

Merlin pulled his dreadlocks back from his face with both hands. "*What?*"

"We can't just leave her to die," cried Isis. "She's all alone." A pale yellow began to dominate the colours moving in patterns over the quarry. Isis wanted Cally suddenly, and her dad, wherever he was. She desperately needed them to swoop down here and save her, somehow. . .

"She's only a baby. . ." Isis said, realising those weren't her thoughts, but the alien's. "She's waiting for her parents—" She halted, unsure if she was understanding it right. The word 'budded' sprung into her mind, instead of 'born', and she had a sense of many parents or maybe none at all. However the alien had emerged, by its own lifespan it was only an infant. "She's waiting for her. . . family to come back," she said.

Merlin stood still, holding his hair. Then he nodded. "Makes sense."

He let his dreadlocks fall again.

"You. . . believe us?" asked Isis, astonished. She hadn't expected him to, even as she'd explained.

Merlin shrugged. "I've heard a lot of theories about this place, but I never choose one as being the truth. Some people say there's an ancient goddess in the woods, or it's the earth's Energy. . . others say aliens. All I know is there's something in this valley, because I've felt it."

Isis watched the rainbow colours dancing through the stones. "She's all around us here."

"But they've cut him open," said Gray. "We're standing in a wound!"

Merlin's expression was full of pity. He folded his lanky body and knelt, putting his hands flat on the ground.

"You know me, don't you?" he said quietly, talking to the rock beneath his fingers. "I've been here in your valley, walking with you every day." He shook his head. "I wish I could help you, and I know you're scared and this blast is gonna hurt you bad, but. . ." He glanced up at Isis and Gray, "If they stay, they'll die when it happens. Is that what you want?"

A shimmer in Isis's eyes, as if the world blinked. And then. . .

"They've gone!" gasped Gray, spinning around, staring wildly. "All the mes — they've all gone!"

The world had lost its colour, it was back to being grey rocks and dust. Isis's mind felt empty where it had been full. The alien under them, all around them, had disappeared.

"Where are they?" cried Gray. He turned on Merlin. "What have you done?"

"She wants us to leave," said Isis quietly. "She wants to save us."

An alien whose skeleton was made of rare and precious metals. A vast creature born in the belly of some distant planet, that had swum or tumbled or flown across space, only to become trapped here like a fledgling bird caught in a net. Lost and frightened, reaching out to the tiny pinpricks crawling on her surface, whose lives must have seemed to pass in an instant, while her own stretched far into the future. This enormous creature was showing its kindness, and giving them permission to leave.

Isis knelt on the ground, like Merlin had.

"I'm sorry," she whispered. Sorry for the pain to come, and their own helplessness.

Gray took it differently. "Come back," he shouted, spinning at the blank rock faces. "Please, come back!"

But the ground was just the ground again. The colours of the alien's thoughts had vanished.

Chapter Thirty-one

Gray

"Why can't you get the alien back?" I shouted at Isis. I wanted to grab her and shake her!

"Because it's not like a ghost!" she shouted back. "I don't know how to do this – you're supposed to be the expert on this stuff!"

We hadn't left. Merlin was jiggling on the spot, looking anxious. "We need to get outta here."

"But you *saw* the alien!" I said to Isis. "So can't you—"

"I don't *see* her," she snapped. "It's more like she talks in colours, or maybe that's her thoughts? They map out where she is."

"But me, Jayden and Gav, we were all in the quarry on the school trip. We got covered in dust, got bits of the alien in us or whatever. You weren't even there, and you can still sense the alien, so that's got to be your. . ." I waved my hands, "you know, seeing ghosts and stuff."

"She can see ghosts?" said Merlin. "Nice one."

But Isis shook her head. "I don't know how to call it back."

Merlin put his hand out, touching my arm. "Look, man, we need to leave."

I shook his hand off. "You go! I'm not!" It was the first alien humanity had ever come in contact with; I couldn't just let it be killed before anyone even knew.

"Look up there," said Merlin, pointing to above where we were standing. "When the explosive charges go off, we'll be underneath an avalanche of rocks!"

"But the protest. . ."

Merlin yanked his dreads up, like he wanted to pull them off. "Listen, man! There's hundreds of police and security up there, all doing whatever they can to get the protestors rounded up and away. As soon as the protest is over it'll be back to business. Press the button, boom go the rocks!"

"Isis?" I said.

"What can we even do?" she asked, and it sounded like she'd already decided the answer.

"Call your ghosts!"

"How would that help?"

"I don't know, maybe one of them can speak alien? We can't just do *nothing*!"

"Oh this is bad," said Merlin, jittering. "It could go off any second. Look, I'm sorry." And he ran off along the track, his dreads bouncing, his feet sending up puffs of dust.

"Where are you going?" Isis shouted after him, sounding really frightened. She made to follow, but I grabbed her arm.

"Please?" I asked.

"Angel won't come," Isis said, shaking her head. "She wouldn't even get out of Stu's car." I could see that Isis wanted to run after Merlin. "I think we should get out of here. What if—"

"What if they blow the place and the alien is killed?"

A pebble fell away from the quarry face, clinking and clattering down to the ground. We both froze for a moment, but nothing happened; the world didn't explode around us.

Isis glanced back at me, looking caught between guilt and anger. "I can't make Angel do anything she doesn't want to. She's scared. *I'm* scared!"

"The alien just needs a bit more time!" I shouted.

"A hundred *years*!" Isis shouted back.

I punched at the rock face, then sat down, clutching my stinging hand. I wanted to never move again. I'd blow up with the alien, if that was my only option.

"She wants us to go," said Isis, squatting down next to me. "So maybe she's worked out some way to get herself safe?"

"No!" I didn't want to look at Isis. At her fear, at the dust coating her clothes and smeared across her face. Alien dust. "We're like the flies, moving too fast for him to catch. Except we're flies with explosives."

"What?"

"You can't catch a fly because a second for you is like an hour for them. You need to think as fast as a fly to catch one." A tear splashed on my hand, washing off a circle of dirt. "It's like that for the alien, except we're the ones moving too fast."

Isis didn't say anything for a minute, squatting there on

her heels. Then she said, "Mandeville spoke through my mouth. He made my lips move for me."

"What's that got to do with anything?"

"He made a woman in the theatre fall asleep so he could watch Philip Syndal's show from inside her body. He calls it possession, but he must take control of nerves, or a bit of the brain or something." Isis paused, looking at the dirt and rocks. "The alien's thoughts run through the ground. Maybe Mandeville can take control of those and. . ." She trailed off. "I don't know. It's a stupid idea."

But it clicked, you know?

"How long would it take *us* to get out of here?" I asked her.

"A few minutes?"

"Get Mandeville!" I shouted, jumping up.

Isis twisted her fingers together. "I had a fight with him. I don't know if he will."

"Try! Please?"

She stood up. "Mandeville?" She looked around blankly. "Mandeville?"

Her eyes widened a bit and she took a step back, then

another, grabbing hold of my hand and shoving it with hers into a patch of cold, slimy air.

"Ergh!" Isis's warm fingers were with mine, but I was also holding a set of bony fingers, the skin peeling off them in mouldy flaps. They belonged to that ghost I'd seen before, a half-man, half-skeleton.

"And now this!" Mandeville was shouting. "Do you think I have nothing else to fill my time than responding to your every call?"

His damp mouldy smell made me retch.

"My feelings exactly!" Mandeville snapped, glaring at me. "You abuse me, then demand my attendance, just as your whims dictate. I am a nothing, yet now you cannot do without me? Perhaps you wish to impress some friends, is that it?"

Isis held my hand tighter. "You talk to him," she said. "He's really angry with me."

I took a breath and gabbled it all out. "There's this alien from another planet, you know? He's made out of stone and metals, and he's trapped under where they're mining—"

"Yes, yes," said Mandeville, "I know about the star-beast. I've been haunting these environs for many years, did you think I hadn't noticed it?"

Isis stared at him. "You never said!"

"Why would I? It was hardly relevant to our business, nor likely to come up in general conversation." Mandeville shrugged. "In fact, I twice tried to inform you that it had extended its appendages – or whatever its limbs should be called – directly beneath the town of Wycombe and into your school. But on the first occasion you would not even countenance my request of a return to seances, and the next time you were too busy unfairly rebuking me to listen."

"We want you to possess him!" I shouted.

The skeleton turned his scary blue eyes on me. "You want me to *what?*"

"Possess the alien. . ." It didn't sound such a good idea now. "Isis said you can take control of people's brains, make them do things."

"Utterly repulsive, when you describe it that way. And what would be the purpose of my efforts?"

"He needs our help – we have to help him get away."

"*Him?* Well, by all means let us all risk everything for some wretched monster. Except there is one small problem. I notice it is hiding. Subterranean." Mandeville tapped his nose. "Possession requires contact, and I have no intention of poking my head into the ground like an ostrich." The skeleton looked at Isis. "I refuse to degrade myself. Not after the way I have been treated."

"He's going to die if we do nothing!" I said.

"I'm dead," said the skeleton. "It's not so terrible."

I turned to Isis. "What can we do? Can you change its mind?"

"I'm not an *it*, and no she can't!" snapped Mandeville.

"Angel," Isis said. "She's helped me see through solid objects. We did it all the time when I was younger. Maybe together we could search for the alien?" She didn't sound very sure though. "She might not agree. She kept saying it was too big, and I think she meant the alien. I think she's scared of it."

"Please?" I said. "Can you try?"

"Of course," groaned Mandeville, "bring the child into this."

Isis ignored him and closed her eyes. "Angel." And then it was like hearing someone on the phone, half a conversation. "No, it'll be all right. . . me and Gray are right here. . . okay, you can watch *Peppa Pig* whenever you want. . ."

She went on in that way, promising and persuading, until at last a see-through little girl appeared in the quarry with us. I could see her because I was already holding Isis's hand, linked by Mandeville. Angel was grabbing hold of Isis's leg.

"What he doing here?" she asked, pointing at Mandeville. "He horrid. And stinky."

"You place your faith in this brat?" he sneered.

"Well *you* won't help us!" I said.

"And I notice that the child gets every carrot possible, while I receive only the stick."

Isis spoke to Angel. "Will you help us find the alien?" She put my left hand gently on Angel's, and I could let go of Mandeville's creepy fingers, which was a relief. "She's hiding down there." Isis pointed at the ground.

But Angel shook her head, her eyes wide. "It too big!"

"Ha!" said Mandeville. "This is why *I* am your spirit guide."

"Please, Angel?"

The little ghost didn't speak, but held herself really still, the way toddlers do when they're frightened. I knelt down, face to face with Angel, the rubble and rocks visible through her.

"I know it's big," I said, "but you don't need to be scared. He's only a baby. Like a baby. . . elephant."

Angel looked down at the ground, then at me. "It a effelant?"

"*Like* one," said Isis.

Angel stood for a moment, thinking, then she said, "Effelants is nice." She pressed her lips together, then leaned down like she was going to do a handstand, and put her head right into the ground. She did look a bit like an ostrich.

Me and Isis sat on the ground, still holding Angel's hand.

"Shut your eyes," Isis said. "This will be a bit. . . different."

I closed my eyes. At first all I could see were a jumbly whoosh of blurs that instantly made me feel sick. Then Angel's vision settled, focused onto a deep yellowy-grey. I was seeing underground.

"Is she there?" Isis asked Angel.

"Nuffink," came Angel's voice in the ground. "Effelant's hiding."

"It's not an elephant, you stupid child!" That was Mandeville.

"Try looking down," Isis said.

The view tilted through the rock. I know that sounds impossible, but with Angel's eyes it didn't seem so solid. I mean, everything is really made of whizzing electrons and nucleuses and stuff, with loads of space in between. Maybe ghosts can see how things really are, instead of them seeming solid, like they do for us? Anyway, I had this feeling that I could've put my hand right through the gaps if only I knew how to do it.

Somewhere into the murk I saw a flash of green.

"There it is!" cried Isis.

"Effelant!" called Angel. "Come here, baby effelant."

The patch of green got bigger, but I don't know if it grew in size or moved closer to us.

"Please!" called Isis. "We want to help you."

"And how exactly will you do that?"

Angel's vision turned sideways, and I nearly screamed! A skeletal face was staring from inside the rock. It was Mandeville, his eyes glowing blue even through solid matter.

I flicked my own eyes open. Now Mandeville had his head stuck into the ground as well, his bony body bent completely over. I guess he couldn't bear to be left out.

"You goway!" Angel's voice came out of the earth.

I shut my eyes, and could see through Angel's eyes again. Mandeville was scowling.

"Don't stick your tongue out at me!" he snapped.

"You stinky!"

"And you are a precocious little urchin!"

"Please!" That was Isis. "Can you stop arguing?"

Mandeville's underground face took on a superior, patronising expression.

"Of course, Isis my dear. Though I am not the one being difficult."

"I not neither!" Angel's little voice.

"They could blow up this quarry any second!" I shouted, trying to get everyone back to the point.

"Angel, can you reach the alien?" said Isis.

My vision blurred, which must've been Angel nodding. Then her view turned downwards and I saw her small hand reaching, stretching towards the smear of green. It might've been a thousand metres down, or only centimetres, I couldn't tell. Angel's little arm pushed through the rock, her fingers spread out like a starfish.

"I get you!" she cried. "Naughty effelant!"

The green smudge narrowed into a thin line, swaying

and moving in the darkness, trying to get away from Angel's grabbing hand.

"It got a trunk!" she cried happily.

"Oh for goodness' sake," muttered Mandeville.

The green snapped back and forth, while Angel giggled and flapped her hand about. My stomach was tied in knots from the weird perspectives.

"Got you!" Angel cried. Her fingers gripped tight round the alien, and she pulled. Colours flashed into every part of the rock, psychedelic rainbows, everything spinning, as Angel twisted her head about to look at them.

I opened my eyes so I wouldn't be sick, but it didn't make any difference. Every rock, every pebble, every grain of dust in the quarry was suddenly dappled with eye-bending colours, swirling in ripples and jaggedy-crossing patterns.

It was beautiful.

And then the noise began. Starting low, getting louder, echoing through the quarry so everything seemed to vibrate.

Isis snapped her eyes open.

"What's that? What's happening?"

Voices in Stone

A siren, sounding like a foghorn.

"Is it the police?"

A cold prickle swept all over my body, fear setting in as I remembered the safety talk from our school trip. The quarry sides seemed taller, more looming than earlier. All that stone and rock towering above us. "It's the warning siren. Before they start blasting."

Isis's eyes grew huge, her face white.

We'd run through the explosive charges, not even paying attention, and now we were right underneath them.

Chapter Thirty-two

Isis

She was still seeing the world through a ghostly doubling. She was Angel, gripping tight onto an alien, and she was herself, seeing Gray's terrified face and the quarry pressing down on them.

The siren wailed on. What would happen when it stopped?

"We have to get out!"

She searched for an escape route. Not the way they'd come – it was too steep, and they'd be scrambling straight into the formation of charges. The quarry track also wound its way under the rock face, only metres from the blast area. They'd be killed there too.

The siren stopped, its echoes fading away.

"We'll be all right," Gray said.

"How?" She'd died before, but there'd been a chance that time, a frozen heart that could start beating once more. Not this time. "There won't be anything left of us!"

She let go of Angel, of Gray. "We have to run!"

"Don't!" Gray's face was desperate. "There are two more sirens – we've got time. Please!" He looked up at the quarry face, then stood up. "I'll pull out the wires!"

"What?"

"The yellow wires, the ones going to the explosive charges." He was already at the steep bank, pulling up with his hands, scrabbling for footholds. "Stay with the alien! Help him!"

Gray climbed fast, his long limbs powering him up. In a few moments he was on the top, and he disappeared from view.

Isis stared at the empty space where he'd been standing, her heart pounding. Was he really pulling the wires out of the charges? Could you even do that?

Mandeville pulled his head from the ground. "Well I doubt we'll be seeing the boy again. Probably running for his life."

"He isn't!" Isis said.

"I think you should run away as well."

Isis stared at Mandeville.

"You'll be no good to me dead. I can hardly be your spirit guide if you're a corpse."

Of course, the seances. It was what he always wanted. . . Isis smiled, realising that she had a bargaining point.

"I won't leave," she said. "I'll die here."

"Ridiculous! Especially as you know what it means to be dead!"

"You said it isn't too terrible."

"I was *lying*."

She wasn't going to let Mandeville see her fear. "I won't leave until we've helped the alien."

"Oh yes, let us be the valiant heroes," Mandeville sighed. "And how, exactly?"

"You have to possess the alien, and make it leave, because we're the flies and it can't catch us."

"I beg your pardon?"

It had made sense when Gray explained it, but now she wasn't sure what they were meant to do. She looked up at the blank face of the quarry, her body shivering with the urge to run. Would the explosion start with a tremor? How much would it hurt, all that rock blasting into her?

She swallowed. "Can you possess such a big creature?"

"Why should I?" Mandeville brushed his hands on his jacket, creating clouds of cloth fibres.

"I'll start the seances again. And not just in schools, wherever you want." She knew she had him, by the flash in his blue eyes.

"Will you keep to your promise?"

The echoes of the first siren had faded now, and the whistles and distant shouts of the protest had been silenced too. There was only the sound of her own breathing.

"Yes."

"This possession won't be easy. It may even be dangerous."

"I don't care."

"Then we have a bargain." Mandeville's skeletal finger poked onto her forehead.

"Whuh. . ." She couldn't speak; the cold pierced her brain with a biting pain.

"I said this wouldn't be easy," said Mandeville. He leaned

closer. "You will have to give me all of your power, all your strength. You'll need the help of your little sister as well, and even then. . ."

He pushed her to the ground, using only his fingertip. The gravel pressed into her cheek.

"Shut your eyes."

Chapter Thirty-three
Gray

I ran between the mounds, desperately trying not to step on any. I couldn't believe I hadn't realised these were the piles left from drilling holes, that I hadn't paid attention to all the wires. Now, every time my foot came down, I thought the ground was going to blow up.

My school shirt was sticking with cold sweat.

There were mounds of earth everywhere, and hundreds of wires, like a net covering the ground. I had to get started! I knelt down and grabbed the nearest wire, yanking as hard as I could.

Nothing. It didn't even move.

I dug down with my hands to where the wire went into the drilled hole, and heaved with my whole weight.

The wire cut into my palms; I got a few centimetres of it out, but that was all. It didn't break, or pull out completely.

I scrabbled deeper. In films, it's always cut the red wire or cut the blue one. I only needed to pull this one out, but it kept on going. As far as I could dig, there was yellow wire. It didn't seem to have an end to it.

I sat back, gasping with the effort, sweat trickling into my eyebrows. All around me were neat piles of rock powder, lines of them in every direction. Every one had a yellow wire coming out of it.

"I can't." Merlin had said the workers spent weeks putting in the charges. Of course I couldn't dismantle the whole lot in a few minutes.

Weeeeeaaaaaaaaaaaa. A wailing siren, the second blast.

A million thoughts sparked in my head: *Get out of here! Tell Isis! Run! Save the alien! Run! Any second now! Save yourself! Runrunrunrunrun!*

And then the part of my brain that was still thinking straight said, *They only press one button.*

"Of course!" The yellow wires were laid out neatly in a net pattern, but if there was only one button to blow the lot, then somewhere there had to be a single wire joining all these ones together.

I ran, stumbling and tripping, my feet landing anywhere, racing for the furthest line of drill mounds. There there there! I could see a different colour wire, grey and red-striped, leading away from the field. I threw myself on the ground, tracing it along, trying to find where it joined the yellow wires. There! A junction: a connector with a load of yellow wires going in one side, and the grey and red one coming out the other. It would only have taken a second to undo it if I had a screwdriver. But I didn't.

I grabbed the grey and red wire, trying to pull it out of the connector with my hands. I smashed at the little plastic box with my fist, bashed it on the ground, stamped on it, but it wouldn't come apart, I couldn't make a dent on it.

"Why. . . won't. . . you. . . break?" With every stamp, every second that passed, I was expecting a spark of electricity, the surge to rush into all those other wires and blow the ground from under me. I put my mouth around the grey wire and bit it, hard as I could, chewing and grinding the wire, spitting out bits of plastic.

The wire gave! The two chewed ends now lay apart from one other. I sat back panting, nearly crying, and stood up slowly, the relief pouring off me. I'd done it. I'd saved us!

Then I saw another grey and red wire, about twenty metres along the line of mounds. And beyond that, another one. I stared at the field of charges. There was a red and grey wire every twenty metres or so, at least another ten of them.

My heart and mind seemed to stop.

I'd wasted so much time! It was obvious I couldn't ever prevent the charges going off, and worse, I'd left Isis, told her to stay where she was – right underneath the explosion.

I turned and ran, sweat sticking my shirt to me. I practically threw myself down the slope, landing in a tumble at the bottom, my ankle a shot of pain as it twisted under me.

"Isis!" I hobbled towards her. "Isis, come on! We have to go!"

She was kneeling awkwardly on the ground, the side of her face pressed flat in the dirt.

"Isis!" She didn't pay me any attention. "Isis?"

I knelt down next to her. "Isis, I can't break the wire! We need to get out of here!"

Her eyes opened. "I need more," she said, in this raspy voice. "You'll have to do." And one of her hands snapped out, clamping around mine.

I was back underground again.

I could see Angel, her whole body upside down in the dim and rumbling rock, like she'd dived in. It took me a moment to realise I was seeing through Mandeville this time, and it was his skeleton hand holding onto the line that curled and coiled around the darkness, flickering with every colour imaginable. They grew and brightened, as if we were sinking into them, and I realised Mandeville was pressing his face close up to the alien's body.

"What's happening?" I gasped.

"I am doing what you demanded." Mandeville's voice seemed to come from three places at once. Far away and right by my ear.

"We hepping the effelant," Angel squeaked from three different places.

"Mandeville's trying a possession," said Isis, also weirdly tripled.

"Work of this magnitude requires great concentration, great power," said Mandeville. "Are you ready?"

"Yes," said Isis.

". . . yes." I don't know if it was me said that, or Angel or Isis or Mandeville. We were all together. All part of the same thing.

And then Mandeville. . . I don't know how to explain what happened next. How can I tell you what it's like being an alien?

Try. Whatever you can remember.

It was. . . like going down a slide into a whirlpool made of rainbows. Swirls of colours getting nearer, until they were everything, until we were. . . him. The-crash-of-a-meteor-into-a-rocky-planet. That's the alien's name. Or maybe it's more of a description.

He stretched underneath the whole valley, going beyond it and down so deep his belly was sitting on molten rock.

Not that he had a belly.

The alien's body was stone, but also soft and always moving, like water seeping through sand. It flowed and floated inside the bedrock, while all of us tiny humans were scurrying around on top, going to work and school and all that stuff, not even knowing what was underneath. All the houses and roads, they were like insect bites or nettle stings. The diggers, working down to start the quarry, they were knives slicing in. And the blasting, the explosions that were all set up. . . They were, would be, the most incredible pain. Agony. It was happening so fast, like a burning rash, or a killer virus eating the alien alive.

He was panicking. He was trying to reach out to those of us who'd breathed him in that day in the quarry. He was trying to get our help.

So you could you sense its thoughts?

Well. . .

He was alone, and frightened at being alone. He was hoping the others, his family, would turn back for him, but they probably hadn't noticed he was gone yet.

That's the thing. The aliens live at this other speed, so

slow we can't even tell it's happening, like continents moving. To them he'd only just crashed to earth. To us it was thousands of years ago. In hundreds of years from now, when his family returned to find him, he'd have been mined away to nothing. They wouldn't even have known what had happened, only that he'd vanished.

He was terrified. He'd speeded himself up as fast as he could, the way we get an adrenalin kick, but he still wasn't fast enough. It had taken him weeks just to say one sentence to me.

That's what some of his thoughts were.

There were other things too.

Other things?

Things that made sense when I was joined to his mind, but now. . .

Like what?

Like. . . he could taste gravity, and the Earth's was really bland.

He rotated his body with the changing of the seasons, because it made him feel. . . sun-happy?

He saw our life through the standing stone – soil and plants, trees and birds, animals and humans – and he couldn't understand why we'd bother. All of us stuck to the skin of our planet, never going anywhere else – he thought it was funny. Until we started hurting him.

I told you. It sounds crazy.

To aliens, human behaviour seems inexplicable.

Yeah, well. That's for sure.

I was the alien. But I was me too, kneeling in the quarry with the grit digging into my knees. And I was Isis, lying with my face on the ground, and I was Angel, holding colours with my hand, and I was Mandeville telling everyone what a magnificent possession this was. . .

Through Isis I was joined to all of them, their thoughts crowding into mine so it was hard to tell which was whose, and shot through with the slow-moving hopes of the alien, like a river flowing, or currents in the ocean.

And even though I'd come down here to tell Isis the charges could blow any second, I knew we couldn't just leave.

The alien was caught and lonely, trapped and in pain, too slow to get away. He needed to escape before the electricity buzzed down the wires and hit the explosive charges, but only we could do that for him, because to do it he needed to be as fast as a human, running away from it all.

I was Isis, she was me. I didn't need to explain things like I am to you. Isis was me, and we were Mandeville and Angel. We listened to my heart thundering, and felt Isis's legs aching to run. We poured our own quick lives through the ghosts' hands, into the slow pulse and sweep of the stone ship-creature. Moving it faster, dragging its reactions. Giving the alien our kind of time, those minutes left before the final siren.

We pushed up, all of us. Tumbling into the sky, throwing off the Earth and heading into the beautiful darkness of space. . .

"Gray! Isis! Get up! What are you doing?"

It took me a moment to adjust. It was a man's voice.

I opened my eyes. Grey and white, blue above. A dot moving, getting bigger.

The quarry, the sky. Merlin running along the track, shouting at us.

"I told them! I had to! You've only got a few minutes before she'll be here."

I sat up, my hand still in Isis's. She was motionless on the ground.

Merlin slowed to a jog, panting and clutching his side. "Man!" He gasped a breath. "I told them you're in here – I had to so they wouldn't do anything stupid, like pressing buttons. That Dr Harcourt. . ." he gasped a few more breaths, "she's coming for you, man."

I smiled, so big it made my mouth hurt.

"We're nearly done—"

Weeeeeeeeaaaaaaaaaaaa. The final siren.

And then the shivering in the ground. The horrible creaking of massive forces as the earth began breaking apart.

Merlin stared in horror around the quarry. "No! Dr Harcourt said they wouldn't. She said the sirens are just to warn you – she said it was safe!"

The air filled with splinters of flying rock.

Chapter Thirty-four

Isis

She was made of star-born metals, her thoughts running in colour. She was arms and legs, muscles and a beating heart. She was nothing but spirit, the lightest of all.

Human, ghost, alien.

I feel like I'm stretching too far, holding all this together.

Whose thought was that? Hers, the human girl? Or hers, the vast alien? Or hers, the little ghost?

Don't worry about it, my dear. A Mandeville thought.

There's no time! Was that Gray?

No time! Not human time, not alien time. The explosion would be quicker than either. She had to move, fast as a heartbeat, fast as a human thought. Rise up, fly up, right now.

Now?

Now now now NOW!

The shaking rattled her eyelids open.

Blazing, teary light. A blurry shape. Gray was shaking her, trying to get her standing.

"We have to get out of here!" He was shouting, his words almost lost in the loud, relentless pattering, like a hailstorm. He pulled her by her arm. "Come *on!*"

Strange, unfathomable images filled her thoughts, and whatever part of her mind had been stretched when holding the ghosts and alien together, now it had ripped apart. Her legs were stiff, and the ground. . . it wasn't Gray who was shaking her – everything was moving. A downward dance of pebbles was falling from every slope in the quarry; a boulder shook, high in the rock face above them, then tumbled out of place, crashing and cracking as it fell. Gray yanked Isis backwards as the boulder thudded into the dirt where they'd been standing.

Without warning the ground beneath her foot dropped away. She staggered, her ankle twisting sideways, and someone else grabbed her. Dreadlocks and a beard. Merlin.

"What's happening?" Her words were a croak.

"They've set off the blast!" Gray shouted.

Merlin was clutching his dreadlocks. "But they know we're in here, I told Dr Harcourt!"

"She'd do it anyway," screamed Gray. "She's one of them!"

"One of who?"

Another rock crashed out of the quarry face, spinning and splintering as it fell.

"Out!"

Isis ran, following Gray and Merlin, trying to reach the track, as the ground shuddered and shifted with every step, quaking so hard she could barely stay upright. Dust filled the air as an avalanche of rocks and boulders collapsed out of the quarry wall.

She ran faster. *Don't fall don't fall don't fall!* A thunderous, cracking sound roared through the quarry, and Gray stumbled backwards, crying out. A deep gully had opened in front of them, the ground plummeting away.

"Look out!" screamed Merlin as a gaping rent appeared, just to their right. They scrambled sideways, the solid dirt they'd been standing on collapsing into a deep hole. Isis held onto Gray, onto Merlin, as the ground shook and shook beneath them, shuddering in every direction. A deep rumble filled the air, punctuated by loud popping sounds. Thick dust coated their throats and stung their eyes. Through the haze, up on the hillside, Isis saw trees lean and topple sideways.

"This isn't mining!" yelled Merlin, his hair white with dust. "They only put charges over there." He pointed to where rocks were rattling and spinning out of the quarry walls. "This is everywhere!"

With another thunder-crack, the gully in front of them widened, the ground pouring into it. They staggered and Gray's foot slipped off.

"Get down!" cried Merlin, hauling Gray backwards. "It'll be safest sitting!"

Angel caught up with them, drifting up as if all this were normal. "The effelant baby!" she shouted happily.

By her hand, Isis saw a pebble vibrate so fiercely it slowly began rising off the ground. Another vibrated itself upwards, also defying gravity, then another and another.

"Oh man!" cried Merlin. "Look at that!"

Isis tore her gaze from the floating pebbles, and saw a

stream of dirt and rocks pouring straight up into the air from the chasm that had opened in front of them.

"What. . .?" said Gray.

With a deafening crash, a huge boulder tore itself out of the quarry face, but instead of falling it drifted upwards.

"Look what the effelant's doing!" cried Angel, spinning in circles on her bottom.

"What's going on?" yelled Merlin.

"She's leaving," answered Isis, but her voice was lost in the noise. Dust and rock poured up around the group, creating an upward draft that lifted Isis's hair and pulled at her clothes. Everywhere the ground was funnelling into the air, in an impossible avalanche.

She heard words in the roaring wind. *I won the race.*

And every pebble, every rock, every particle of dust was suddenly dancing with rainbows.

Gray let out a yell of delight: "They're back! My mes are back!"

Beautiful place, whispered the brightly coloured dust, flickering and darkening. Tilting her head, Isis saw that the rocks pouring upwards were spinning now. Faster and faster, beginning to glow, first red, then orange, then into white-hot droplets. The heat of it warmed her face, like standing in front of a fire.

Make my baby well, hissed the burning air.

"Bye!" shouted Gray, waving madly with both hands at people only he could see. "Bye!"

Let him love me, said the rising pebbles.

"Bring warmer weather," Isis whispered back.

"Oh man," breathed Merlin. "*Oh man*."

The ground flowed upwards; only the spot they were sitting on stayed solid. Pebbles, dust and boulders spun over their heads, melting into lava droplets. And now the molten drops were forging together into incandescent lines, hardening almost instantly into a softly gleaming metal, thin as wire. Each one joined to another, building a shape in the air above them.

"Is that its body?" asked Gray, eyes huge in his dirt-caked face.

Dust and rock cascaded into the air, melting together and drawing more of the glimmering wires. Fractal patterns began dividing, like the veins in a leaf or the crystals of a snowflake, as the strange metallic lines filled the sky with a vast outline, impossibly big, city-sized, yet so finely wrought it should not have been able to hold its own huge form.

In places the wires welded into extra structures, poking out from the main body.

"Are those. . . fins?" asked Gray, shielding his eyes with his hand.

"Wings?" suggested Isis. It was hard to tell, hard to get the scale or understand what anything might be.

"Antennae?" said Gray, puzzling out the shapes. "A sail?"

Green light flickered along one of the lines. Another flashed into blue; somewhere else it was yellow.

"Oh maaaan," sighed Merlin.

More and more of the lines above them picked up a colour, the alien drawing itself in the sky above. Red, orange, mauves and greens, a dart of silver, the pinks and gold of dawn. The colours drifted and shifted, getting faster until thousands of wires were flashing through multiple shades. They bled together, filling in the huge spreading shape of the star-beast with a hypnotic, spangled pulse. The colours began to cycle, aligning themselves into spirals and waves playing across its flanks.

Isis sat staring; next to her Gray and Merlin were open-mouthed. The wind picked up as the creature drifted higher. The rushing of the ground began to slacken; the upward avalanche faded to a trickle, then stopped. The last molten wires jointed into the alien's body, and with a ripple of never-ending colour it started to move, more like a cloud than any kind of star-ship. They couldn't look away, caught by its beauty, as it floated into the real clouds, tinting them with colours of storm and sunset.

While they watched, the dust slowly cleared from the air and the rest of the world became visible again. Isis glanced down for a moment and froze. She nudged Gray. "Look."

Gray gasped, staring down. So far down.

Merlin tore his gaze from the sky. "Oh *man*!" He grabbed hold of Isis and Gray, gripping tightly to their arms.

They were sitting on top of a sheer column of rock, only just wide enough for the three of them. Everywhere else the ground level had dropped, and was now thirty metres below, leaving them perched high above a wide plain. The trees in this new land were standing drunkenly, leaning at odd angles. The grass and vegetation was ridged into long low mounds, like wrinkled skin. The alien had pulled itself from the ground, leaving only the coverings of soil and vegetation, which it no longer needed.

They stared, speechless, at the altered landscape. Dotted through the plain were other tall columns, and on the closest Isis could see the tiny shapes of people. Where the gates of the mining company had been, there was something like a vertically sided hill. On top of it a crowd of stunned protestors were still holding their banners.

"She kept all the people safe," said Isis.

"And after everything we did to him," said Gray.

Their smiles answered each other, cracking the dirt on their faces.

Chapter Thirty-five

Gray

You're telling me aliens did it?

Not aliens. *An* alien. I know on telly they said it was a massive sinkhole, and all that stuff about underground rivers making hidden caves. But that's rubbish.

We know it wasn't a sinkhole, because we planted that particular explanation, with a few discreet payments to some eminent geologists. At short notice, it was the best we could do.

It won't work! Loads of people *saw* the alien. It was all over the news, and that film of us being airlifted off by helicopter got millions of hits on YouTube. Stu went mental because he was shut inside a police van at the time. He and Dad have spent the last couple of weeks trying to get copies of any footage, but it turns out people were either too freaked out to film the alien, or their camera phones stopped working. I reckon there was some kind of feedback – I mean, if you think his whole body was made of rare earth metals. . .

Your story is most inconvenient. Now I will have to edit significant parts of this recording, and use some quite heavy-handed techniques to induce a more useful statement from you. This case has caused considerable economic losses to our sponsors, and as it was me who involved you in the first place, well, let us say there have been questions. But if I could show that you'd been radicalised, perhaps by exposure to an eco-extremist, such as this Merlin character. . .

'Radicalised'? Merlin's not an eco-extremist – I'm not even sure he's all there!

Even better. Look in my eyes, that's right. Now, I want you to retell your story, but this time you will say that you stole explosives from the quarry stores and set extra charges around the site. You will say that the alien didn't escape, that you destroyed it to make a political point.

What political point? That doesn't even make sense!

Extremists never do, that's why it will be believable.

I can't believe you're related to Isis, I can't believe you're her dad. You're just a. . . user!

Enough! I want to you relax, I want you to focus on my watch, and when I tap your forehead. . .

No! You should stay away from her, and from me.

That's not for you to decide. Look at the watch. Look at it!

Stay away, or I'm going to tell Isis about you, and what you really are.

You won't, because you won't remember.

How do you know? You say I'm being hypnotised, but Dad said that all you need is willpower to break from it.

Yes – you've already tried that and failed.

I won't this time! I'm not looking in your eyes or at your stupid watch. I'm un-hypnotising myself, right now.

Stop it! You can't just get up. I haven't counted you out of the trance.

I'll count myself out. Tennineeightsevensixfivefour-threetwoone!

Stop that!

No. I'm leaving. And if any weird things happen I'll tell Isis everything I know about you.

She won't believe you.

She will! Because you're just her runaway dad and I'm her brother.

Her what?

Brother! Cally and my dad, they're getting married! Didn't you know that, Mr Secret Organisation with all your secret knowledge? Didn't your oh-so-powerful sponsors tell you? Isis has got a proper family now.

Do not try to threaten me.

You said I was here to tell you about Isis, well she's got ghosts protecting her too. If you don't leave us alone, I'll tell them about you. You wouldn't be able to buy them off, or hypnotise them. . .

Sit down! You can't just leave!

I can. Goodbye, Mr Dunbar, or whatever your real name is. I hope I never see you again.

Chapter Thirty-six

Isis

Isis sat on a low wall, staring out through the school gates at the cars passing by on the road. Gray wasn't around this lunchtime – he was probably at his UFO club. It was really popular since the events at the quarry a few weeks ago. Isis had gone a couple of times, but felt uncomfortable with the level of awe directed at her by some of the more enthusiastic members.

And if Gray wasn't around, she'd rather spend time by herself. Being asked about the alien wasn't quite as bad as "What's it like being dead?" but no one wanted to talk about everyday stuff. No one treated her as normal. Along with Gray, she was one of the survivors of what was now being called the Wycombe Event, and not just by people like Stu.

At least Mr Gerard had let her back from suspension. Mainly because the pupils who'd had the worst of the 'ghost hysteria' turned out never to have attended any of Isis's seances. In fact, there was a much clearer link between the riotous behaviour at school and the pupils from Mr Watkins's geography class who'd visited the quarry. They'd even been treated by a therapist brought into school especially. Isis had heard one of the teachers saying that whatever the therapist was doing, it was definitely working. The pupils involved seemed to have forgotten why they'd been upset in the first place.

"You've never been in any trouble before," said Mr Gerard, the first day Isis was allowed back. "So I'm giving you the benefit of the doubt. But you're on report for the next month, and if I hear of a single incident. . ."

He wouldn't, though. Isis couldn't do seances now, even if she wanted to, and she kept away from Jess's gang, just in case. Sometimes she spotted Jess looking in her direction, but Isis always turned her head and walked away.

The air turned cold around her, filling with a damp musty smell as Mandeville appeared on her left. She noticed the twinkle of a sparkly sandal to her right, and Angel appeared, sitting on the wall.

"By yourself again?" asked Mandeville. "You know, it really isn't conducive to a healthy mental state."

"She not alone," said Angel. "She got us."

"Well, I suppose that is true," conceded the older ghost.

Isis waited for an argument to brew between the ghosts, but none did. She still wasn't used to it, the way they were getting on. It was something to do with being mixed together inside the alien's mind. Perhaps it was easier to accept someone else when you'd shared each other's thoughts. Isis and Gray now often finished each other's sentences, much to their parents' bemusement.

Isis looked from Angel to Mandeville. Her last two ghosts.

Whatever it was she'd felt pulling out of her when the alien left, she'd lost most of her ability to see things other people couldn't. Now she couldn't even see regular spirits like the school's ghosts. Even if she'd wanted to continue with the school seances, she couldn't have.

"Do you think it'll come back?" she asked Mandeville.

He turned his bony head towards her. "What are you referring to, my dear?"

"Being psychic. Do you think it'll come back, like recharging a battery?"

"If I knew what a battery was, I might comment. As to your abilities, I doubt they will return. They may even fade further. Possession of a creature as vast as the one we tackled. . . it would tax any psychic's powers, and I was forced to draw strongly on yours, which were already weakened by your encounter with the Devourer." He paused for a moment, then pointed at the pavement outside the school. "For example, can you see him?"

To Isis it seemed an empty stretch of road. She shook her head.

"Ah, that is a pity," said Mandeville. "It really is striking, the way he can remove his head."

"You're making that up!"

"I take offence at the suggestion. Ask your sister!"

"A ghostie *is* there," said Angel, kicking her feet soundlessly against the wall. "Head off, head on. Off, on." She started giggling. "Again! Do it again!"

"Don't you mind?" Isis asked Mandeville. "What about all your plans? Me being your psychic, and your message to the world. . ."

Mandeville was silent. Isis could see gaps in his body now, daylight showing through. He seemed frail and crumbling since their encounter with the alien. The possession had taken it out of him, as well.

Mandeville narrowed his blue-fire eyes. "I had always imagined that speaking to millions through a world-renowned psychic would be the pinnacle of my achievements, but the feat we achieved with the star-beast. . . no other spirit has ever come close to such a deed, nor is ever likely to. It was an experience that I have still to fully fathom. Being so vast, so stretched, so other. . . it has made my earlier hopes seem much less important." He put his skeletal hand on Isis's. "I would like to thank you for persisting, and persuading me to undertake such a magnificent possession." He let go of her hand again. "And I believe diminishing powers will be a blessing for you, saving you from the fate of so many psychics. You will not go mad. But on the other hand. . ." He transferred his gaze to Angel, who was still sitting giggling on the wall.

Isis looked at her too. Would the little ghost-girl become as invisible to Isis as the ghost out on the road? Would their special bond finally end?

"I'd never see her again," she whispered to Mandeville.

Mandeville tutted. "Angel is dead. *Not* seeing her is the normal way of things."

Isis shook her head. "That's not what you said before! What about giving comfort to people by telling them about what happens after they die?"

Mandeville coughed. "Yes, well. Do you know, I think I may have been in. . . error. Did anyone at your seances ask anything meaningful, or make any serious enquiry about the afterlife? During our little spat, you accused me of having only one aspect to my ghosthood."

Isis blushed, remembering how she'd taken everything out on him that day.

"I'm sorry. I shouldn't have said that."

"But you were right. A psychic of your talent was bound to spot it." He sighed out a plume of mould spores. "I do feel rather. . . lacking in depth, one might say. I'm sure there is a better part of my soul, somewhere beyond." He pressed his thumb and finger onto the bridge of his nose, as if he had a headache. "Recently, I've been feeling quite faded. It makes the endless hours of existence something of a chore."

He looked like an old man for a moment, rather than a skeleton. Isis almost wanted to hug him.

"Cally always says lost spirits need to find the light," she said.

She waited for Mandeville to mock Cally, like he usually did. But instead he only sighed again. "You know, I'd like to, if only I knew where the light was."

Angel stopped kicking her feet. "It just up there," she said, pointing at the sky with one of her chubby little arms.

Mandeville peered at the air, then shook his head.

Isis looked as well, but could only see the flat white clouds of a chilly autumn day. "I can't see anything."

Angel laughed. "You not dead, silly! You can't see it 'til then."

She peered past Isis to Mandeville, then took one of Isis's hands with her weightless fingers. "His hand too," she commanded.

"You want me to hold Mandeville's hand?" Isis asked.

Angel nodded. "Do for him what you do for Gray. Hep him to see."

"I find this rather. . . demeaning," said Mandeville. "I am the spirit guide, after all."

Angel shrugged. "Okay, not then."

"No!" he called, and Mandeville quickly clutched Isis's free hand, his grip icy around her own.

"See it now?" Angel asked.

"Aaaahhh," whispered Mandeville. "It's beautiful."

Isis stared at the sky, but saw only the clouds in their blank layer, even with the ghosts' hands in hers. Was it because her powers were weakened, or simply because she was still living? She returned her gaze to the ghosts, and noticed a few dusty crystals tumble from Mandeville's eyes. It took Isis a moment to work out they were tears.

"You going then?" asked Angel him, very matter of fact.

Mandeville gazed at whatever the two ghosts could see. He faded for a moment, the shivering cold in Isis's hand lessening, but then he shook his head, letting go of Isis's hand.

"Not quite yet," he said. "Maybe later." He looked at Angel, and winked one of his ice-blue eyes. "I believe the dollies have a few more parties to attend?"

Isis was about to ask if Mandeville was really going to play dollies with Angel when she heard footsteps behind them. Isis went very still. Angel turned around, and stuck out her tongue. The footsteps got nearer, stopped, and then carried on, hesitantly.

"Isis?" It was Jess.

Isis turned around. "What do you want?"

"I. . ." Jess faltered, a blush creeping up her neck. She took another step, hands clasped together, fingers twisting around each other. "I wanted to say sorry."

Isis could hear her own blood in her ears. After everything that had happened, this wasn't what she was expecting.

"Sorry for what?" she asked suspiciously.

"For making you do the seances," Jess said quietly. "I know you didn't want to, and I pushed you to because I. . ." Her eyes flicked away. "I wanted to be special, like you are."

Isis was blushing too now.

"You didn't say anything," Isis said. She meant in Mr Gerard's office, and Jess knew it, because she nodded, looking even more miserable.

"I'm sorry about that too. I was just. . ." Her blush had reached her ears, which were glowing red. "I've never been in trouble before, not for anything. I was really scared."

"Pooh to you!" said Angel, sticking her tongue out again.

But on the other side of Isis, Mandeville shook his head. "I must say, that is a most thorough and admirable apology. Coming from one so young, it takes a lot of courage. This young lady must truly value your friendship."

Isis looked at him in surprise, and Jess spotted the glance. "Are they here?" she asked quickly. "The ghosts?"

Isis gripped the rough edge of the wall. "You said I was making all that up."

"That's what *Chloe* said," Jess answered. "I'm sorry I didn't stick up for you, but I never doubted it, not for a second. You helped me, letting me talk to Gran Marie." She took a deep breath. "Anyway, I know you won't want to be my friend any more, but I just wanted to say this, that's all."

Jess turned and began to walk away. Isis didn't move; she was still a little stunned.

"Are you just going to sit there?" snapped Mandeville. "Have you never made any mistakes?"

She felt a cold shove on her back, as Angel poked her off the wall. "Now you got to make up," said the little ghost.

Isis took a step, then another. "Wait!"

When Jess turned around, Isis felt a pure happiness swell inside her. Being special, being all alone – having a friend would be better.

"I won't do any more seances," Isis said, walking up to Jess.

"I don't want you to."

Jess shrugged. "I've been doing some paintings at home, and I wondered if you'd like to come and. . ."

But Isis wasn't paying attention – suddenly her gaze was caught by a man walking out of the school entrance and heading to the car park. He was frowning, walking quickly, and didn't notice the girls.

"Who's that?" she asked, and Jess turned to look.

"Oh," she said, "that's the therapist. The one sorting everyone's heads out after the school trip. Haven't you seen him before?" Jess stopped. "Are you okay?"

"He looks like. . ." *an old photograph.* One she'd stared at so often it was imprinted on her mind. Isis and baby Angel, Dad and Cally. If Dad had pale hair, cut differently, if he dressed in a way she'd never seen him dress, if he wore glasses, which he didn't. . . No. Her dad was on a cruise ship somewhere, so far away he hadn't even made it back when Isis was in hospital. He wasn't a therapist, at school every day and never even coming near her.

She shook her head. "He looks a bit like my dad, that's all."

Jess peered at the man. "Your dad? You don't mean Gil, do you?"

Isis laughed. "Gil's my stepdad, or he's going to be when Mum and Dad get married. Did you know Mum's going to have a baby?"

"No!" Jess squealed. "Oh, you are so lucky! I'd love to have a baby brother or sister!"

As Jess was pattering on, Gray came around the side of the school. He seemed to be searching for someone. Then he spotted Isis and Jess, and headed straight for them.

"Gray can tell us about the therapist," said Jess. "He was the one called in today."

Isis shrugged. "I don't care."

She glanced behind her and saw Angel spinning circles on the grass behind the wall, her arms outstretched.

Mandeville had wandered out into the road, and seemed to be having a conversation with the ghost Isis couldn't see. For how much longer would she be able to see Angel and Mandeville? Her heart tightened at the thought of losing them, but at the same time she understood that the day would come when her two ghosts would take a journey they both needed.

And if that would be a hard parting, she had other people to rely on now. Like Cally, who really was trying to be the sort of mum they both wanted her to be. And Gil, who was a new kind of dad to Isis, one who was actually around. She had a brother in Gray, and another one to come when the baby was born.

"Come on," said Jess, shyly putting her hand out to Isis.

She had a best friend too, something she'd never had before.

"Do you want to come over sometime this week?" Jess asked. "We can watch that new film if you like, the one about the dance competition."

"If my mum says it's okay," Isis said, smiling.

"Oh, she will — I'll get my mum to ring and. . ."

Isis walked with Jess, wrapped up in the other girl's

chatter, as they headed across the grass to meet Gray. Isis gave a last glance back to where she'd been.

Angel waved a transparent hand, then carried on spinning.

If you enjoyed VOICES IN STONE,
you might like to discover the spooky goings-on
at St Mark's College for Girls in
THE BLUE LADY by Eleanor Hawken.

Read on to find out more . . .

Headmistress Beaton
St Mark's College for Girls
Oxfordshire
England
4th May 1786

Dear Brigadier Marshall,

It is with deepest regret that I write to inform you of the sudden death of your daughter, Isabelle. Miss Isabelle Marshall's body was discovered on the steps of the school soon after sunrise this morning.

As you know, Sir, Isabelle was expelled from St Mark's College for Girls only two days ago. I must make it clear to you that despite her recent expulsion from our guardianship, the school accepts no responsibility for Isabelle's death. Given her condition in recent months, we cannot help but feel that her tragic fate was unavoidable.

Isabelle's body is currently with the police pending a post-mortem investigation. Her immortal soul is now in His judgement, and all at St Mark's will pray for her.

With deepest regret,

Headmistress Beaton

Chapter 1

I was never the sort of girl who believed in ghosts. I never played with Ouija boards, held séances or felt afraid of the dark. That stuff was for other people, not me. But that all changed when I went to live at St Mark's College.

Unlike the other girls at St Mark's, I hadn't lived away from home since the age of eight. I didn't come from a posh family who had a house in the country and a yacht in France. The only time I'd ever been to France was when Mum and I did a day trip using ferry tokens she'd saved up from a newspaper. Boarding school wasn't for girls like me. I ended up there by mistake.

The mistake happened last December, when Mum's friend Lynn invited her to an army officers' Christmas ball. Lynn's brother is a major in the army and had just got back from a tour of Afghanistan. Apparently his wife used to write to him every week while he was out there, and then one week the letters stopped. Two months later he had another letter from her – only this time all she sent him were divorce papers. Lynn wanted to set Mum up with this guy – although I wasn't keen. Mum's had enough loser boyfriends without adding a jilted army officer to the list.

But that night, at the ball, Mum accidentally sat on the wrong table and chatted to a guy who she thought was Lynn's brother. Turns out the man she was taking to wasn't Lynn's brother, but Lynn's brother's boss. His name was Lieutenant Colonel Phillip Walker. They got married eight months later. And thirteen days after the wedding, Phil was posted to Germany. Instead of taking me to Germany and putting me into a German school, Mum and Phil decided to send me to an English boarding school. So it was all just one big mix-up – if Mum had chatted to the right guy that night, I would never have been sent to St Mark's. If I'd never gone to St Mark's, then I'd still believe there's no such thing as ghosts . . .